Ghost Hunter

This Large Print Book carries the
Seal of Approval of N.A.V.H.

Ghost Hunter

Jayne Castle

Published in 2006 by arrangement with The Berkley Publishing Group, a division of Penguin Group (USA) Inc.

Wheeler Large Print Hardcover.

The text of this Large Print edition is unabridged.
Other aspects of the book may vary from the original edition.

Set in 16 pt. Plantin by Al Chase.

Printed in the United States on permanent paper.

Library of Congress Cataloging-in-Publication Data

Castle, Jayne.
    Ghost hunter / by Jayne Castle. — Large print ed.
      p. cm.
    ISBN 1-59722-293-3 (lg. print : hc : alk. paper)
    1. Large type books.   I. Title.
PS3561.R44G49 2006
 813'.54—dc22   2006015722

*To heroic dust bunnies everywhere
and to those who admire them.*

A Note from Jayne

Welcome back to my other World: Harmony.

Two hundred years ago a vast energy Curtain opened in the vicinity of Earth, making interstellar travel practical for the first time. In typical human fashion, thousands of eager colonists packed up their stuff and lost no time heading out to create new homes and new societies on the unexplored worlds. Harmony was one of those worlds.

The colonists brought with them all the comforts of home — sophisticated technology, centuries of art and literature, and the latest fashions. Trade through the Curtain made it possible to stay in touch with families back on Earth and also to keep the computers and high-tech gadgets working. Things went swell for awhile.

And then one day, without warning, the Curtain closed, disappearing as mysteriously as it had opened. Cut off from Earth, no longer able to obtain the tools and materials needed to keep their machines functioning, and with no hope of rescue, the stranded colonists were abruptly thrown back to a far more primitive existence. Forget the latest Earth fashions, just staying alive suddenly became a major problem.

But on Harmony folks did one of the things humans do best: they survived. It wasn't easy, but the descendents of the first generation of colonists have fought their way back from the brink to a level of civilization roughly equivalent to the early twenty-first century on Earth.

But here on Harmony, things are a little different. You've got those dangerously sexy ghost hunters. Exotic nightclubs that cater to a clientele that likes to get buzzed on the psychic energy left in the weird alien ruins. And a most unusual kind of pet.

Still, some problems never change. Take Elly St. Clair, for example. She thought she'd ended her engagement to a Guild boss named Cooper Boone. But Cooper has other ideas . . .

If, like me, you sometimes relish your romantic-suspense with a paranormal twist, Harmony is the place for you.

Love,
Jayne

Prologue

Harmony
*Two Hundred Years after the
Closing of the Curtain . . .*

"Please, wait, Miss St. Clair." The small, neat man behind the reception desk leaped to his feet. "You simply cannot burst in on Mr. Boone like this."

"Watch me, Melvin." Elly kept moving.

She crossed the vast expanse of the reception area with quick strides, her tailored pumps making no sound on the thick carpet. Her goal was the massive, elaborately inlaid spectrum-wood door that guarded the inner sanctum of the executive offices of the Aurora Springs Guild.

Melvin flapped his manicured hands.

"Mr. Boone is in a meeting," he gasped. He bustled around the desk and hurried toward her. "He gave strict orders that he was not to be disturbed."

"Don't worry, Melvin, Mr. Boone will see me."

Elly reached the imposing door three

steps ahead of Melvin. She grasped the oversized steel-and-amber knob with both hands.

"Mr. Boone is involved in Guild business, Miss St. Clair," Melvin yelped.

"Mr. Boone is always involved in Guild business, Melvin." She gave him an icy smile and shoved the heavy door inward. "But luckily for both of us, I have just discovered that, as far as he is concerned, I *am* Guild business. So you see, there's really no problem here, is there?"

"Miss St. Clair, please —"

She nipped smartly into the inner office, whirled, and slammed the door shut in Melvin's appalled face. There was a sharp snick when she rezzed the lock.

She swung around to face the two people who occupied the executive suite of the Aurora Springs Guild.

The man behind the massive green quartz desk regarded her calmly through a pair of black wire-and-amber-framed glasses. The serious, studious looking spectacles did nothing to veil the impact of his eerily compelling blue eyes. They also failed utterly to soften the implacable, unyielding lines of his fiercely etched features. His hand-tailored black silk dress shirt, trousers, and black amber-trimmed bolo tie underscored the invisible aura of power that he wore like a cloak.

Just in case anyone missed the point, he wore the traditional emblem of his office, a heavy black ring set with a large amber stone engraved with the Guild's seal.

Cooper Boone was the best argument against the quaint, old-fashioned, badly retrograde tradition of arranged Covenant Marriages that she had ever met, Elly thought. And to think she had been on the brink of becoming his wife. A shiver whispered down her spine.

In fairness, there were a couple of valid reasons why she had allowed herself to become engaged to him, she reflected sadly. Reason number one was that she had fallen head over heels in love with Cooper.

Reason number two, the one that had proved to be her biggest mistake, was that she thought he had fallen in love with her.

She knew the truth now.

"Good afternoon, Elly," Cooper said quietly. "I wasn't expecting you."

Translated, that probably meant, *What the hell do you think you're doing barging into my office?* But Cooper was far too controlled to allow his irritation to show.

With the aid of twenty-twenty hindsight she could see that Cooper's seemingly un-

11

limited powers of self-control had been a major warning sign. But in the few weeks that they had actively dated, she had told herself that it was an admirable characteristic.

"I happened to be in the neighborhood," she said, giving him what she hoped was a smile as dazzling as sunlight on snow and just as chilly. "Thought I'd drop in."

He raised his dark brows a quarter of an inch and very gently narrowed his mesmerizing eyes.

Okay, she thought, taking a deep breath to steady her nerves, *he now knows I'm furious. And he's a little surprised. Wow. Fancy that.*

She ought to be experiencing a little glow of vengeful satisfaction, she thought. It wasn't easy to catch Cooper Boone off guard. He was a master strategist, always one step ahead of everyone else around him.

He had certainly been one step ahead of her for the past couple of months.

She had actually convinced herself that his formal, traditional courtship had been a sign of respect for her and her family. Here in Aurora Springs a lot of things in the Guild were still done the old-fashioned way, including high-ranking Guild Covenant Marriages.

Cooper was watching her intently now. She could almost hear him mentally calculating, assessing and strategizing, deciding on the best way to deal with her and control the situation. *Because that's what he does,* she reflected. *He deals with people and takes charge of situations.*

The reason he could do that so well was because he had complete mastery of his own emotions. *That's his real talent,* she thought, *and it has nothing to do with his impressive parapsych profile.*

The second man in the room frowned in paternal disapproval. "Cooper and I are a little busy at the moment, my dear. Did I forget a lunch date?"

"No, Dad, you didn't forget anything," she said quietly. "Don't worry, this won't take long."

Her father was several years older than Cooper and a couple of inches shorter. He wore his mane of silver hair in the traditional Guild style, tied back at the nape of his neck with a black leather cord. Her three brothers wore their hair in the same manner.

One of the things that she had liked about Cooper Boone right from the start was that he cut his hair in a short, decidedly non-Guild style.

Every male in her family also wore a lot of khaki and leather, another Guild tradition. Today her father was dressed in a khaki shirt and multipocketed khaki pants tucked into chroma-snakeskin boots. A leather belt set with a large amber buckle wrapped a waistline that had softened only a little in recent years.

John St. Clair was one of the most powerful men in the Aurora Springs Guild, second only to Cooper. He had, in fact, helped engineer the selection of Cooper as the new head of the organization. That transition had occurred after the former Guild boss, Douglas Haggerty, had been found dead of a heart attack in the catacombs.

No one had been more stunned by the Council's choice of Cooper Boone than Elly. As the daughter of a high-ranking Guild family whose forebears included a couple of the founders of the Aurora Springs Guild, she was well aware that it wasn't the strength of a ghost hunter's psi power alone that propelled him onto the Council or into the executive offices of the Guild. Savvy intelligence and a will as indestructible as green quartz were the primary characteristics of all of the men who had held that position since the founding of the organization.

The paranormal ability to resonate psychically with amber and use it to focus the brain's natural energy waves had begun to appear among the human colonists on Harmony shortly after they came through the Curtain to settle the new world. At first the talent had seemed to be little more than a curiosity. But gradually the true potential of the phenomenon became apparent.

Today, two hundred years after the discovery of Harmonic amber, the stuff was routinely used as a power source for everything from automobiles to dishwashers. Any kindergartner could generate enough psychic energy to switch on a rez-screen to watch cartoons.

Some people, however, working with specially tuned amber, could generate more than the usual amount of psi power and use it in some highly specific ways. Ghost hunters, technically known as dissonance-energy para-resonators, comprised one of those groups of high-powered para-resonators.

The term *ghost hunter* described quite accurately what most of them did for a living. Their psychic abilities, while certainly impressive, were not what anyone would call multifunctional or flexible skill sets. Career options were limited.

As far as anyone knew, the only practical application of a hunter's talent was in controlling and destroying the highly volatile, potentially lethal balls of fiery, acid-green psi energy formally known as UDEMs. The acronym stood for unstable dissonance energy manifestation. They were known as ghosts because they drifted like so many lost specters through the endless network of underground tunnels that honeycombed the planet. No one knew why the long-vanished aliens had built the catacombs in the first place. The UDEMs were just as much of a mystery.

Most of the experts assumed the ghostly green phantoms had been meant to function, along with the dangerous psychic illusion traps that also infested the tunnels, as some sort of high-tech security system. But, as was the case with all of the ruins, artifacts, and relics left by the vanished race of beings that had first colonized Harmony, the real purpose of the ghosts was a matter of sheer speculation.

One thing was indisputably true, however. The energy ghosts made exploration and excavation of the vast network of underground passages extremely hazardous. And, since exploration and excavation of the catacombs was not only big business but also a major focus of several private and government-funded labs and many academic institutions, the ability to destroy ghosts guaranteed a certain degree of job stability.

The Guilds contracted the services of their members to various academic, corporate, and privately financed excavation teams that explored the catacombs for study and considerable profit. Over the years the hunter Guilds, led by a series of shrewd, ambitious men, had become powerful, secretive operations bound by mysterious traditions and Guild Law. There was an old Guild saying — actually there were a lot of old Guild sayings — but the one quoted most often was, "Once a Guild man, always a Guild man."

Occasionally an article appeared in one of the women's magazines touting the fact that there were some female ghost hunters. But statistically speaking, the vast majority of hunters were male — something to do with their particular psi talents being linked to certain male hormones, according to the experts. That meant that men ran the Guilds. And men in groups, as Elly's mother frequently pointed out, were strongly inclined to develop a pack mentality, complete with an alpha male at the top.

No doubt about it, the Guild Hall dripped testosterone, Elly thought. And the stuff was even thicker up here in the ornate, richly decorated offices of the Aurora Springs Guild executive suite.

"All right, Elly," Cooper said quietly. "It's obvious you're upset. Why don't you sit down and tell us what's wrong."

"Gosh, I'm afraid I don't have time to go into all of the details." She kept her voice very even, very cool. It wasn't easy, because you needed to breathe properly in order to control your voice, and breathing was getting hard. She felt a little feverish. "It would take much too long, and I know you're a very busy man. I certainly don't want to interrupt important Guild business."

Her father gave Cooper a quick, uneasy look and then took a step toward Elly. "Uh, honey, maybe we should go downstairs to the cafeteria, have a cup of coffee, and talk about whatever it is that seems to be bothering you."

"Forget the coffee, Dad." She did not take her eyes off Cooper. "I came here to ask the boss of the Aurora Springs Guild a couple of questions, and I'm not leaving until I get the truth."

Cooper's jaw tightened fractionally. "I've never lied to you."

Careful, she thought. *You do not know this man. You only thought you did.*

"Technically, that is probably a true statement," she agreed. "But you haven't always bothered to fill me in on all of the facts, have you?"

Cooper walked around the slab of rectangular green stone that formed the surface of his imposing desk. He lounged back against the edge of the massive chunk of quartz and folded his arms.

"What are your questions?" he asked calmly.

She swallowed hard and steeled herself. She was about to piss off the most dangerous man in Aurora Springs. Maybe she should have given herself twenty-four hours to cool down after she heard the gossip this morning.

Then again, an extra day of brooding would have changed nothing. *Might as well get it over with and get on with your life,* she told herself.

"There is talk going around the campus that a couple of months ago, shortly after you and I met, just before you were offered the position as head of the Guild, you challenged Palmer Frazier to a ghost-hunter duel down in the catacombs." She took a deep breath. "Is that true?"

Out of the corner of her eye she saw her father stiffen. His reaction told her everything she needed to know. The rumor *was* true. Her heart sank. For the first time she acknowledged to herself that she had been hoping against hope that Cooper would deny the story.

Cooper's expression, unlike John's, never altered. "Who told you that tale?"

"Oh, no you don't," she said swiftly. "I'm not about to give you the name of the person who repeated the story to me. Who knows what you might decide to do in retaliation."

"I'm only interested in plugging a possible security leak," Cooper said mildly.

"Got news for you, you're way too late to plug any leaks in this case. It took a while for the word to get out, but it is definitely in the public domain now. My informant was only relaying gossip that everyone on campus has already heard." She swept her arms out wide. "In fact, I think I'm probably the last one in town to find out about it. Talk about adding insult to injury."

John scowled. "What do you mean by that?"

"Let's just say this incident isn't one of the Guild's better kept secrets, Dad. I'm amazed you managed to hush it up this long." She turned back to Cooper. "But now that everybody's talking, I wouldn't be surprised if the story hits the tabloids this afternoon or tomorrow. Better warn that nice little man in that broom closet downstairs that you like to call your public relations department to brace himself. He's going to be a little overwhelmed when the local media starts calling."

"What, exactly, did you hear?" Cooper asked. His voice didn't sharpen, but his eyes did.

I definitely have his attention, Elly thought. But it didn't take parapsych senses to figure out that this was probably one of those be-careful-what-you-wish-for situations.

She was committed now, though. There was no turning back.

"Everyone is saying that the reason Palmer Frazier disappeared for several days a while back was because he needed time to recover from the psychic injuries he received in a duel with another hunter. They're also saying that's why he resigned from the Guild Council to — How did your PR department put it? Oh, yes, to pursue other interests in Frequency City."

"I see." Cooper looked thoughtful.

She wanted to scream, but she clamped her back teeth together, instead. She would not lose it here in front of this overcontrolled man. She had her pride.

"They say that you were his opponent, Cooper, and that you won."

Cooper continued to look meditative.

"This is most unfortunate," John murmured.

"Certainly struck me that way, Dad," she said. "According to the gossip that's going around, the only witnesses allowed were the other members of the Guild Council. That means you were there."

John winced uneasily. "Now, see here, my dear —"

She switched her attention back to Cooper. "Guess what, Cooper. Gossip flows through the Guild Hall as quickly as it goes across the campus. In fact, the news is all over town. And this is a small town, in case you've forgotten. Do you know what that means? It means I can't even go grocery shopping without people talking about me behind my back."

"This will all blow over in a month or two," John announced in forceful tones. "Frazier is fine. It was his decision to leave town and move to Frequency City."

"He would hardly want to hang around Aurora Springs after he'd been humiliated by losing a duel and being forced off the

Council," she shot back.

Cooper studied her with a considering expression. She knew that he was trying to decide just how much of the truth to reveal.

"I regret that there has been gossip and that it got back to you," he said slowly.

"For heaven's sake, you could have been seriously injured or even been killed."

Cooper's brows drew together above the rims of his glasses in a slightly baffled expression. "There was no danger of anyone getting killed."

"A sanctioned ghost-hunter duel is a formal ritual," John said quickly. "It's used only as a last resort to deal with challenges to the existing power structure of the organization. The strongest hunter wins. The members of the Council witness the results, and that's the end of the matter."

"You make it sound so simple," she retorted, thoroughly exasperated. "But everyone knows ghosts are terribly, terribly dangerous. Sure, hunters have some immunity, but one miscalculation, and we're talking a major disaster. When you're dealing with high-energy ghosts, there's always the possibility of serious psychic trauma."

"Nothing went wrong," Cooper said quietly. "The issue that had arisen was formally settled according to Guild Law. There should have been no gossip."

"Well, there is gossip, Mr. Guild Boss."

"It doesn't involve you," he said quietly.

"I have another news bulletin for you. Everyone is saying that I was the reason the duel was fought."

He frowned. "Who said that?"

"*Everyone.* Aren't you listening? My colleagues in the Department of Botany stared and whispered when I walked through the faculty lounge. You should have heard the giggling when I went into the women's restroom."

There was a short, heavily weighted silence at that news. The discussion was going downhill fast, and her heart was breaking into smaller and smaller pieces. She only had one last, frail hope to cling to.

"Elly," John said, placating. "You're the daughter of a Guild family. You know how important our traditions are."

"For heaven's sake, Dad, I've got nothing against a few institutional traditions. But we're talking about a full-blown *duel.*" She flicked a glance at Cooper. "In case neither one of you has heard, that sort of thing is considered archaic, primitive, uncivilized, and way over the top by modern, educated, sophisticated people such as my colleagues."

"Your father's right; the gossip will die down," Cooper promised.

"That remark only goes to show how out of touch you both are with mainstream society." She started to pace. "It's all very well for you not to worry, but let me tell you a few facts of academic life. This may come as a stunning shock, but it turns out that figuring at the center of a stupid, mega-macho duel between a couple of hunters — one of whom happens to be a Guild boss — is *not* the kind of thing that will help me get promoted to assistant professor."

"Calm down," Cooper said, his voice gentling.

"Calm down?" She stopped and swung around to face him again. "If you don't care about the risk you took with your own life or your parapsych profile, how about considering the damage that you did to my career?"

Cooper's mouth thinned. "What occurred was Guild business. It will not affect your career. I give you my word on that."

She resumed pacing. The only other alternative was to pick up a few of the smaller alien artifacts that decorated the chamber and start hurling them around the room. That would be undignified.

"Guild business," she repeated coldly.

25

"You know, somehow I just knew you were going to say that."

"The incident will not affect your career at the college."

"Pay attention, Mr. Guild Boss. Members of the faculty have been dismissed from Aurora Springs College for less than this."

John's snowy brows bunched. "No one is going to fire you because of this."

"Don't bet on it, Dad." She stalked past the full-length portrait of her several times great-grandfather, John Sander St. Clair, the first chief of the Aurora Springs Guild. "The Academic Council has a very strict Code of Conduct. Article One, Section a, Paragraph 1a, forbids every member of the staff from, and I quote, 'engaging in any type of behavior that might embarrass the college or reflect badly upon this institution. Such behavior shall be grounds for a formal reprimand, or, in the most serious cases, dismissal.' "

For the first time, Cooper showed an expression other than cool patience. It wasn't much of a show of emotion, to be sure, only a slight increase in the intensity of his unusual blue eyes, but she had been around him enough in the past two months to sense that he was starting to get irritated.

"Your father is right," he said very evenly.

26

"There's no way the Academic Council can blame you for an incident that involved only the Guild Council."

She came to a halt in front of another large portrait of a former Aurora Springs Guild boss. Albert Roy St. Clair was a great-uncle on her mother's side.

"You're missing the big picture here," she said. "I don't have to be guilty of anything. All I have to do is embarrass the college. In academic politics, perception is everything. Good grief. When I think of how hard I've worked to convince my colleagues that the Guild has changed over the years, that it isn't really an organization that is only half a step above a criminal mob, I could just spit. Talk about a complete waste of time and energy."

"You won't lose your position at the college," Cooper said without inflection. "Don't worry about it."

It was her turn to raise her brows. "Why? Because you'll make a few phone calls and intimidate the Academic Council?"

"If there's a problem, I'll take care of it," he said.

"Don't even think about trying to do any such thing, Cooper Boone. I will not tolerate you using your position to interfere in my career."

"I think you're overreacting here," Cooper said quietly.

"I'm furious. If you want to label that an overreaction, you're welcome to your point of view. Forget my little problem with the Academic Council. I'll handle my professional life my way. Let's get back to a more important issue."

His brows came together in a small frown of surprise. "There's a more important issue?"

"Yes." She braced herself. "You've as much as admitted that there was a duel. Let's move on to my second question. People are saying that I was the cause of that ghost-fight between you and Palmer Frazier. Is that true?"

Cooper exchanged a look with her father. She knew that he was making his decision, deciding how much of the truth to tell her. Did he realize that their entire future together hinged on what he said next? Probably not. He was a Guild boss. It wouldn't occur to him that this situation had escaped his control.

Cooper unfolded his hands. He took off his glasses with a deliberate air and set them down on the desk.

Slowly he walked across the room to stand at one of the tall windows. For a moment or two he studied the view of the ruins of the ancient alien town site that had been deserted thousands of years before humans had arrived on the planet.

"Frazier is a very ambitious man, Elly," he said quietly. "He was attempting to use you."

"We dated for a while," she said icily. "We had some fun together. He did not *use* me."

"He intended to marry you. He was going on the assumption that once you were his wife, he would be able to forge a natural alliance with your father. That would have given him a critical edge on the Council."

She felt the floor start to dissolve under her feet. So much for the one frail thread of hope that she had been clinging to so tightly for the past few hours.

"I see," she managed in a voice that was no more than a whisper. "This was all about the Guild."

John inclined his head in a sage manner. "It's true, Elly. Frazier was determined to marry you. I warned him off privately, but he ignored me. If he had succeeded in convincing you to contract a formal Covenant Marriage with him, I would have been placed in an untenable situation, forced to choose between supporting my son-in-law for the sake of my daughter and her future offspring, or voting against him and risking an irreparable rift in our clan. It is very likely that, in the end, I would have had to step down from the Council to avoid being caught in the middle."

"Which," Cooper said, turning back to face her, "would have tipped the balance of power on the Council in such a way that it is entirely possible Frazier would have become the new Guild boss. He certainly has the para-rez talent, the ambition, and the connections it takes to get the job. I can promise you, his leadership would not have been good for the future of this organization."

"Right," she said quietly. "Got it. You fought the duel to protect the balance of power on the Council."

"That's what we've been trying to explain, dear." John crossed the room to pat her on the shoulder. "How could you know about the political stakes involved in this affair? As Cooper just told you, it was Guild business."

She shook her head, smiling sadly at her own illusions. "Did it ever occur to either one of you to talk to me about the situation before you got involved in something as stupid as a duel?"

Both men looked taken aback by the question. Neither attempted an answer.

"I'm not a complete fool," she said wearily. "Nor am I the naive, sheltered little academic that everyone seems to think I am. Palmer Frazier isn't the first man who ever tried to get close to me in order to gain access to you, Dad. Let's get serious here. If I turned down dates from every man who was attracted to me at least in part because of my Guild connections, I'd have no social life at all. This is a small town. Everyone knows who you are and that I'm your daughter."

"I understand, dear, but Frazier is different," John said carefully. "He's very good at political maneuvering, and he's got excellent connections because he is descended from one of the founding members of the Frequency Guild. An alliance with our clan would have given him a great deal of power. When the two of you were dating it was obvious that he was trying to charm you. And you seemed to be getting rather serious about him."

"Maybe that was because he treated me as an equal," she said stonily. "He didn't put me into a little box that he could open or close whenever it was convenient for him. Sure, he was a charmer. But you know what? Palmer and I laughed at a lot of the same things. We liked to dance together. And here's a real stunner, he always showed up on time for every date. What a concept, hmm?"

Cooper's eyes tightened a little at the corners. "Where are you going with this, Elly?"

"When Palmer and I were dating, I never had to listen to a lot of excuses about how he had to cancel because of some last-minute Guild business," she said. "He was never late because of a meeting that ran too long. He never disappeared for an entire weekend with no explanation other than 'Something came up.' "

John was starting to look vaguely alarmed. "Now, see here, Elly —"

"I understood from the outset that Palmer's interest in me stemmed from the fact that he thought the two of us made a good match politically, financially, and socially." She shrugged. "He was right. As we all know, marriages have been arranged between Guild families since the founding of the organization for precisely those reasons."

John cleared his throat. "Marriages at the highest levels of the Guild involve a great deal more than just the two people who take the vows. Fortunes and the futures of entire families, not to mention the Guild, itself, are at stake. You know that, Elly."

"I sure do," she said. "But in this particular instance, it is all beside the point, because I never intended to marry Palmer Frazier." She paused a beat. "And if either of you two hardheaded hunters had bothered to ask me, I would have gladly told you that."

The office filled with a heavy silence.

"Mind if I ask why you're so certain that Frazier couldn't have convinced you to marry him?" Cooper finally asked in an eerily neutral tone. "Given that he was never late for a date and all?"

Because I had just met you, and after that there was no one else, she thought. But damned if she would say those words aloud now that she knew the truth about the duel.

"Certainly." She rezzed her brightest smile. "I'll be happy to tell you why I never wanted to marry Palmer Frazier. The reason is that I did not love him. What's more, I was pretty sure I would never be able to learn to love him. And you know what, guys? This may come as something of a surprise, but I wouldn't think of marrying a man who was only interested in using me to achieve his objectives in Guild politics."

Wariness flickered in Cooper's eyes.

John stared at her, astonished. "Now, hold on here, what is that supposed to mean?"

"I think we all know what it means, Dad." She gave her full attention to Cooper. "Talk about life's little ironies. I was never at risk of marrying Palmer Frazier, so that duel you two fought was all for nothing. But upon reflection, I realize that I owe you my sincere gratitude for getting involved in that challenge."

"Why?" he asked.

"Because if the duel had not taken place, and if I had not found out about it today, I probably would have continued to allow myself to be convinced that everything that was wrong between us would have been magically fixed after we got married. Talk about naive."

Cooper did not move. "What was wrong between us?"

"You're serious, aren't you? You really don't know how I've made excuses for you every time you were late for a date because of Guild business. You want to talk denial? I even went so far as to let Mom convince me that the fact that you've never shown any interest in doing anything more than kiss me good night very politely at the door was just your quaint way of demonstrating respect for my clan and the old courtship traditions. But that's not true, is it?"

"What are you implying?" Cooper asked without inflection.

"I'm not implying anything. I'm *saying* that your reasons for wanting to marry me are the same as Palmer Frazier's. You think I would make an excellent Mrs. Guild Boss. And, by golly, you're right. Not only can I bring you top-of-the-line family connections within the Guild, but I've got one foot in the mainstream world as well because of my academic career."

"Elly," John snapped. "That's enough."

"You liked the fact that I was involved in the world outside the Guild, didn't you, Cooper?" she said. "Because the status of the Guilds has been slipping for years, and that's a real problem."

"Elly," John repeated, sounding a little desperate this time.

"More and more people are coming to the conclusion that the Guilds are relics of another era," she continued tightly. "That they no longer serve any real purpose aside from supplying guys who can fry ghosts. Folks are asking themselves if that rather limited job description really warrants the kind of power and influence that the Guilds have acquired through the years. It's safe to say that if the organizations don't find a way to become a part of mainstream society soon, they are going to become anachronisms."

"The city-states will never forget that it was the ghost hunters who saved the colonies during the Era of Discord," John declared in ringing accents.

"Old news, Dad. Sure, there's still some macho glamour left, but let's face it, most educated, well-informed people view hunters as so much hired muscle. More and more young hunters are leaving the Guilds early. They join up just long enough to make some good money, and then they move on to more respectable professions in mainstream society. If the Guilds don't remake themselves and learn to operate like modern business corporations instead of closed, secretive societies, they're going to get left in the dust of history."

She broke off, exasperated.

Neither Cooper nor Elly's father said a word. They just looked at her as if she was one of the long-gone aliens who had returned unexpectedly to demand the return of the Guild boss's big quartz desk.

"Believe it or not, I didn't come here to debate the future of the Guilds," she said quietly.

"You wanted answers to your questions about the duel," Cooper said. "You got them. Now what?"

She started tugging on the spectacular amber and gold ring that she wore on her left hand. "Now that I know the real reason you fought that duel, I have no choice but to end our engagement."

"Elly," John was clearly stunned. "What do you think you're doing?"

"Giving Cooper back his ring."

She walked across the vast chamber and put the ring down on the quartz desk. It made a small, final-sounding little clink as it settled on the hard stone.

Cooper watched her, saying nothing.

"Keep your Guild secrets and your Guild traditions." She went toward the door. "And keep the ring until you find the right woman to be your wife."

"We'll talk later when you've had a chance to calm down," Cooper said.

"I'm afraid that won't be possible," she said. "I'm going to be very busy for the next couple of days, cleaning out my office and packing up my things."

John bristled. "The Academic Council has asked you to leave already? You said the rumors had just begun to circulate around the campus. There hasn't been time for anyone to call a meeting. They have to give you a chance to defend yourself."

"Relax, I haven't been fired, Dad. I'm going to turn in my resignation to the head of the Department of Botany as soon as I get back to the campus. After that I will be making plans to leave town. I'm moving on with my life."

"This is crazy." John rounded on Cooper. "You're the Guild boss, damn it, do something."

Cooper did not do anything. He looked at the ring on his desk and then he looked at Elly as though he was suddenly seeing her in a strange, new light.

"There is nothing Cooper or anyone else can do, Dad," Elly said from the door.

"I'll have your mother talk to you," John vowed, falling back on the threat of last resort.

"Mom will understand." Elly put her hand on the massive doorknob.

"I have one question," Cooper said softly.

She chilled. It took every ounce of will she possessed not to yank open the door and flee the room. Instead she made herself look back over her shoulder.

"What is it?" she asked.

"What did you mean a moment ago when you said that now that you knew the real reason behind the duel, you had no choice but to end the engagement? I got the impression that I gave the wrong answer."

"You did."

"I'm a student of history. I like to learn from it when I can. Was there a right answer?"

"To be honest, no." She tightened her grip on the knob. "Settling matters with a duel is a particularly appalling example of the worst and most benighted traditions of the Guild. But I grew up in a Guild family. I understand how tenacious tradition can be. I would not have ended our engagement solely because you engaged in a duel."

"Why are you ending our engagement, then?"

"Because of the reason you fought it."

"I don't understand."

"I know," she said.

She opened the door and walked out of the historic chamber. She would not collapse in a puddle of tears, she vowed. Not yet, at any rate.

She had a new life to plan. One thing was clear; she had to put some distance between herself and Cooper Boone. This town wasn't big enough for both of them.

Chapter 1

She knew an illegal drug lab setup when she saw one.

Bertha Newell brought the aging utility sled to a halt near the vaulted entrance of the underground chamber. She was an old ruin rat who had been excavating the alien catacombs most of her life. She figured she had spent more time underground than all of the members of the faculty of para-archaeology up at the university combined. This wasn't the first time she had come across evidence of illegal activity in the ancient tunnels.

Ever since the founding of the colonies, the maze of glowing green quartz tunnels had offered a refuge, albeit a dangerous one, to an endless assortment of thieves, murderers, escaped prisoners, drug dealers, cult leaders, and others who did not want their activities exposed to the light of day.

Down here in the endless network of

mostly uncharted passageways there was always someplace to hide, provided you were willing to take the risks. One bad mistake in the catacombs could easily result in a death sentence or worse.

She hesitated, trying to decide how to handle the situation. Ruin rats, by and large, were a live-and-let-live bunch. They tended to be obsessive about their privacy and secretive by nature. Most were ephemeral-energy para-resonators, otherwise known as tanglers, who, for various reasons, had never been accepted into the elite Society of Para-Archaeologists.

Tanglers were the only para-resonators who could de-rez the dangerous illusion traps that guarded many of the chambers inside the catacombs. They were as necessary to exploration and excavation teams as ghost hunters. But unlike the hunters, who had organized in tough, secretive guilds, tanglers had early on developed a strong academic tradition.

Today, a tangler who hoped to work on a reputable, licensed research team was expected to have several degrees and be a member in good standing with the Society of Para-Archaeologists.

Tanglers like Bertha who had never had the opportunity to attend college, let alone get into the Society, often took up a career on the shady side of the ruin trade. They made their livings by slipping in and out of the tunnels through hidden holes-in-the-walls and staking out their territories in uncharted areas of the catacombs. They cleared the illusion traps on their own and did their best to avoid the occasional ghosts, all in hopes of finding a few relics and artifacts that could be sold to private collectors.

Ruin rats as a rule preferred to avoid contact with others in the catacombs. Bertha was no exception. She was willing to overlook the occasional stash of loot that had been hidden by a burglar. When she had come across a bag of stolen credit cards last month she had quietly disposed of them without going to the trouble of reporting the incident to the authorities. The last thing she wanted was a bunch of cops running around the sector of the catacombs that she considered her private preserve.

But she had a particular dislike of those who dealt in illegal pharmaceuticals. Years ago she had nearly lost her daughter to an overdose. Sandra had eventually recovered, gone into therapy, and was now leading a normal life. But the memory of that terrible time still haunted Bertha's dreams.

She got out of the sled, checking the

dimly glowing corridor in both directions to be sure there was no sign of the lab's owner. She also listened hard for the soft whine of a sled motor or voices, although she knew better than to depend on her hearing down here in the catacombs. The green quartz that the aliens had used to construct the vast network of tunnels and rooms underground possessed a number of odd properties, one of which was that it distorted sound waves.

Satisfied that there was no one around, she went to stand at the entrance of the green chamber. The interior was lit, like every other room and corridor underground, by the pale, eerie glow of the luminous quartz that the aliens had used to construct their surviving structures and artifacts.

The lab was furnished with a variety of what looked like commercial-grade chemistry apparatus. Glassware, a series of stills and burners, and an assortment of implements littered the surfaces of two collapsible stainless steel workbenches.

Across the room there was another opening in the wall. She could see a portion of an antechamber.

Giving the corridor another quick survey, she went past the workbenches to peer into the second room.

A number of bulging burlap sacks were heaped inside. A strong, faintly medicinal aroma came from the sacks. She did not recognize the smell, but it made her think of some of the scents that greeted her whenever she walked into Elly St. Clair's herb shop.

Bertha went to the nearest sack and quickly untied it. Inside was a large quantity of dried plant leaves. She scooped up a handful of the brittle material and sniffed cautiously. The acrid tang hit her nostrils with unexpected force. An instant later she felt a disturbing tingle through her paranormal senses. The chamber started to change shape.

Wrinkling her nose in distaste, she stepped back quickly and breathed deeply. The room returned to its former proportions.

When her head cleared, she took another breath, held it, and went back to the sack. Reaching inside, she grasped a small handful of the dried leaves and dropped them into one of the several pockets that decorated her trousers.

A strong sense of urgency enveloped her. Her years underground had taught her not to ignore that primal warning. Hastily she retied the sack.

She had the evidence she needed, she thought, patting the pocket that contained the leaves. She would lock the coordinates of the room into the amber-rez locator of the sled. When she returned to the surface, she would turn over the strange herbs along with the location of the chamber to the Cadence City cops, anonymously, of course. They could take it from there. Maybe that good-looking flashy dresser, Detective DeWitt, who was getting all the media attention these days, would handle the raid.

She sensed the presence in the doorway behind her and swung around, fighting a wave of raw panic.

But her fear metamorphosed into fury when she recognized the person hovering there.

"Well, shit," she said. "Don't tell me this is *your* lab?"

"You shouldn't be here, Bertha."

She stalked across the still room, waving a hand at the apparatus on the workbenches. "You're dealing drugs, aren't you? Is this that new crap I've been reading about in the papers? Enchantment dust, or whatever the hell they call it?"

"Stay away from me." The figure in the doorway edged back nervously. "This is none of your business, Bertha."

"People are dying from this stuff."

"It's not my fault if the users fail to take the drug responsibly."

"There is no responsible way to take it. They say it's hugely addictive."

The figure retreated farther into the hallway. "I'm warning you, don't come any closer."

"You're scum. Murdering, drug-dealing scum." Memories of how close she had come to losing Sandra flashed through her brain, inciting a kind of fever. "People like you deserve to rot in green hell."

With a low roar, she broke into a run, charging the rest of the way across the lab room. Hands made rough and powerful from years of tunnel work were outstretched in front of her.

"No." The figure in the doorway yelped in fear, turned, and fled down the hall to the left.

Bertha reached the opening and rushed out into the dimly glowing corridor. The drug maker had already vanished into the nearby six-way intersection.

Still in the grip of her fury, she ran several more feet before common sense returned.

She knew better than most just how futile it would be to search any farther without having a fix on the dealer's personal amber.

The corridors that branched off in all directions were each lined with an endless array of chambers, antechambers, and connecting passageways. Her quarry could be hiding anywhere.

This wasn't her job, she reminded herself. Let the cops handle it.

Breathing heavily, she turned to trudge back toward the utility sled.

Perhaps it was because her heart was still pounding from rage and her recent exertion, or maybe because she was now obsessed with getting back to the sled so that she could contact the police. Whatever the reason, she did not hear the faint shuffle of footsteps on quartz behind her until it was too late.

She half turned, but the drug maker had already burst out of a nearby chamber. She caught a glimpse of the large chunk of green quartz that he clutched a fraction of an instant before the stone slammed against the side of her head.

Pain flooded her senses. And then she was falling through waves of darkness.

For a few seconds the drug maker stood over the fallen woman, heart pounding. Bertha Newell was still breathing.

I should hit her again, just to be certain.

But the thought of inflicting another blow made him queasy. There was already so much blood on the floor.

It wasn't his job to take care of this kind of problem, he reminded himself. He was the chemist, not hired muscle. He had been given a number to call in the event of an emergency such as this.

Unfortunately, personal phones, like so many other high-tech devices such as guns, did not work properly down here in the catacombs. Something to do with the heavy psi energy that emanated from the green quartz.

He would have to go back to the surface to place the call.

He turned to make his way toward his secret hole-in-the-wall, but caution made him hesitate. He had a feeling that he should secure his victim in some fashion, just in case she recovered consciousness before security arrived. But he had nothing to use to tie her hands and feet.

He hurried to the utility vehicle and pawed through the assortment of tools and survival gear stored in it. He saw nothing that would serve the purpose, and he dared not waste any more time.

As a fallback measure, he jotted down the frequency of the sled's amber-rez locator. If she did come back to her senses and managed to take off on the vehicle while he was aboveground, she wouldn't get far. Security would be able to track her down.

Chapter 2

A Few Hours Later in the
Old Quarter of Cadence City . . .

Elly stopped at the last booth at the back of the crowded, noisy tavern.

Cooper sat alone, dining on a large sandwich, some greasy looking fries, and a bottle of Green Ruin beer.

She was startled to see that he was dressed like the other hunters around him. It was, she reflected, the first time she had ever seen him in khaki and leather. One of the reasons she had fallen for him in the first place was that he had seemed so different from the other hunters she had known all her life.

He wasn't wearing his glasses or Guild seal ring, either, she noticed. He was, in fact, doing an excellent job of blending into the crowd. But then, Cooper had a knack for making you see what he wanted you to see. She could personally testify to that. Back at the beginning of the roller-coaster ride that had been their relationship, she had actually believed that he was a librarian.

But even in khaki and leather, he still rezzed her senses in a way that no other man had ever been able to do.

Her pulse was racing, but she gave him her coolest, most composed smile.

"Welcome to Cadence," she said brightly. "Mind if I join you?"

She had to raise her voice to be heard above the loud rez-rock music, but she did not allow her brilliant smile to waver by so much as a fraction of an inch. Growing up in a family with three brothers and a father who were all ghost hunters had taught her a few things about dealing with the species. So had her mother. Rule number one, according to Evelyn St. Clair, was that a woman had to stand up for herself, or else she would get trampled beneath a lot of heavy ghost-hunter boots.

Cooper's boots were heavier than those of most hunters.

He looked up from his sandwich and beer, showing no sign of surprise. She knew that he had seen her enter the bar a moment ago and had tracked her progress through the crowd. Very little escaped Cooper's notice. He had a hunter's natural awareness of his environment.

"Elly," he said in the low, dangerously

51

soft voice that never failed to stir the hair on the nape of her neck. He got slowly, politely to his feet. "Nice to see you again. When I got your call a few minutes ago, I was surprised to hear that you were in the neighborhood." He indicated the rowdy tavern scene with a faint inclination of his head. "Not exactly your kind of place."

She set her oversized tote very carefully on the seat across from the one Cooper was using.

"When you're looking for a hunter," she said, slipping out of her coat, "you go to places where they tend to congregate. Unfortunately, the Trap Door is just that sort of dive. The big surprise here is you. Back in Aurora Springs you didn't spend a lot of time in the usual hunter hangouts. You're not wearing your seal ring, either. What's up? Are you here incognito or something?"

"Yes, as a matter of fact, I am." He took her coat and hung it on the hook at the front of the booth. "Guild bosses tend to attract attention. I'd like to avoid that on this trip. Luckily only a couple of people here in Cadence know me by sight."

She sat down beside the tote. "Why all the secrecy?"

"I'm in town on personal business, not Guild business." He lowered himself onto the red plastic cushion across from her. "I'd prefer not to be recognized. There are reasons."

Oh, damn. He's got a mistress here in Cadence. He's trying to protect her from the media. The tabloids loved to cover illicit Guild boss affairs and associated gossip.

Her heart plummeted. The fizzy feeling deep inside that had been bubbling like mad ever since she'd gotten the phone call from her mother that afternoon, suddenly went flat.

Should have considered the possibility that he was involved with someone else, she told herself. *It's been six months, after all. What did you expect? That he had been pining away over there in Aurora Springs, missing you?*

When her mother had phoned to tell her that she'd heard that Cooper was on his way to Cadence, she'd been unable to suppress the little jolt of hope and excitement. He was coming after her at last.

Except that he hadn't come after her. The drive from Aurora Springs took an hour and a half, at most, and probably a good deal less in Cooper's sleek, high-powered Spectrum EX. Guild bosses didn't worry a lot about posted speed limits. Cooper had no doubt been in town for hours, but he hadn't called or come by the shop. Now she knew that he had probably gone straight to his lover's place.

But if that was the case, why wasn't he with her tonight? It was after eight o'clock. Maybe she was married.

Pull yourself together, woman. You're here on a mission.

Still, she found she had to give herself a couple of minutes to adjust to being this close to him again. She had not actually forgotten the impact he made on all her senses. She relived it frequently late at night when she was alone in her bed. Nevertheless, when she had learned he was due to arrive in town today, she had convinced herself that, after all these months away from him, she would be able to handle the sexy thrill.

It was downright annoying to discover that she had not developed any real immunity to Cooper in the past few months. But being on her own here in the big city and running a business had taught her a few new social skills.

"How did you know I was in town?" Cooper asked.

"The Old Quarter here in Cadence is my neighborhood now," she said smoothly. "Let's just say I have my sources."

"Right." He nodded, evidently satisfied,

and picked up his sandwich. "Your mother phoned and told you I was on my way here to Cadence."

"Well, yes, as a matter of fact. She called me this afternoon to warn me."

He looked amused. "She thought that my impending arrival warranted a warning?"

"She's my mom. She didn't want me to be taken by surprise if you decided to show up at my shop."

"Should have remembered that moms are inclined to do things like that." He drank some beer and lowered the bottle. "So, how's life in the big city?"

His mesmerizing blue eyes were even more riveting without the transparent shield of his glasses, she discovered. Or maybe she had just forgotten how compelling they were.

"Life here is great," she said briskly. "A whole new world, in fact. I always knew that Aurora Springs was staid and conservative compared to a city like Cadence, but I didn't realize just how old-fashioned and behind the times the place really is until I got here."

"Been an enlightening six months for you, has it?"

"It certainly has. Did you know, for instance, that the local Guild is making a major effort to go mainstream like the Resonance City Guild? There's talk of turning it into a corporation."

He shrugged. "Mercer Wyatt will probably be able to make the Cadence Guild resemble a mainstream business enterprise. But I can guarantee you that when it comes to the inner workings at the top, things aren't going to change much."

"How do you know that?" she demanded. "Look at the Resonance City Guild. They say the former boss, Emmett London, managed to turn it into a respectable corporate entity before he resigned. It even has a representative on the Resonance Chamber of Commerce, for goodness' sake. Talk about mainstreaming."

"I've got nothing against taking the Guilds mainstream. Up to a point. Got a few plans of my own for Aurora Springs."

That stopped her. "You do?"

"Yes." He raised his brows. "But that doesn't mean anything will actually change much in the executive offices."

"Why not?"

"Because," Cooper said with an air of great patience, "although you can change some aspects of how the Guilds function and how they are perceived by the public, at their core, they are fundamentally different from mainstream corporate entities."

"Why?" she demanded.

"The Guilds are a cross between business enterprises and emergency militias. That mix requires a management style that is different from that of mainstream businesses. It also requires more emphasis on discipline, tradition, and a degree of secrecy that true corporations can't maintain."

"This is ridiculous." She sat back in the seat and flattened both hands on the table. "I don't know why I'm bothering to argue with you. Talk about a waste of time. If you want to keep the Aurora Springs Guild mired in outdated traditions, that's your problem, not mine."

"True," he agreed. "You gave up any right to comment on the subject when you threw my ring back in my face, didn't you?"

She stiffened. "I didn't throw it back. I just sort of set it down on your desk."

He shrugged. "We each have our version of events. Want some fries?"

She was suddenly and uncomfortably aware of the fact that she had not eaten dinner. That would put her last meal at shortly before noon, she reflected.

She looked at the fries, mouth watering. "No, thank you."

"Suit yourself." He ate another fry.

She cleared her throat. "Those things aren't good for you, you know."

"I've heard that." He smiled his unreadable smile again. "Worried that I might get fat?"

She felt herself redden. It was impossible to imagine Cooper Boone putting on weight. He was as hard and lean and tough as a ghost-leopard.

"I was thinking of your arteries, not your waistline," she muttered, wishing she had kept her mouth shut.

"Seeing as how you decided not to marry me, you don't have any long-term interest in my cardiovascular system." He paused, a fry halfway to his mouth, and gave her a polite, questioning look. "Or maybe you're hoping that the grease will do me in?"

She gripped the edge of the table with both hands. "Never mind. I'm here on business. Mind if we get to it?"

"No. Got to tell you, I've been damn curious ever since I got your call. Should I be touched that you kept my personal phone number all these months?"

"It was still in my address book," she mumbled, deliberately offhand.

Actually, it was still locked into her memory, along with so many other small details about Cooper, such as his bird-of-prey profile and the way he wore his dark hair brushed straight back from his high forehead.

"Okay, so much for the warm reunion," he said, biting off the end of the fry with strong, white teeth. "On to business. Why did you track me down here tonight?"

She took a steadying breath. "I need a hunter."

A dangerous light came and went in his eyes. "Is picking up hunters for an evening of fun and games a new hobby for you?"

She could feel the heat rising in her face and prayed that the weak illumination provided by the small candle on the table concealed her blush. It was no secret that a lot of women found ghost hunters extremely attractive prospects for occasional flings and one-night stands. Bars such as the Trap Door were popular stops for bachelorette parties and groups of single females out on the town in search of a little excitement.

Because of the nature of their work — they were, in essence, primarily expensive bodyguards in the tunnels — hunters tended to be in great shape physically. But it wasn't just their macho swagger and their rakish khaki-and-leather attire that drew the attention of women. Rumors abounded that ghost hunters were especially good in bed after they had de-rezzed a ghost. The hormone thing, Elly reflected.

"Here in Cadence I prefer to date outside the Guild," she said smoothly. "In fact, none of my friends know that I'm from a Guild family, and that's the way I intend to keep it."

"Ashamed?"

"Of course not," she shot back, infuriated by the accusation. "It's just that when I left Aurora Springs I was determined to make it on my own without the help of my family or Guild connections. Oh, never mind, I don't have time to explain. The important thing right now is that I need a hunter I can trust. I would also prefer one who is not affiliated with the local Guild."

"You trust me?" he asked.

"Yes."

"Got to say, that comes as something of a surprise, given our personal history."

"You and I certainly had our issues, Cooper. But I never, for a moment, doubted that you could be trusted. My father told me once that your word was good amber. I have no reason to believe otherwise."

The phrase *good amber* was an old one in the Guilds. Down in the catacombs everything depended on the quality of the tuned amber that was used to focus psi energy. Amber was necessary to navigate the endless, ancient tunnel complex. Badly tuned amber could lead a man or an entire excavation team astray, dooming those who relied on it to wander forever in the labyrinth belowground. Good amber was amber that could be relied upon when the going got rough.

"Tell me why you need a hunter," he said.

"I have to go into an off-the-charts area of the catacombs tonight, as soon as possible. It's a sector that I am reasonably certain has been cleared of illusion traps, but when it comes to ghosts, well, you know how they are. Unpredictable. I'd prefer to have a hunter along."

He put down the fry he had been about to eat. "Are you joking?"

"No."

"What the hell is this all about, Elly?" His eyes went hard and cold. "I can't believe that you've been foolish enough to get involved in illegal excavation work. But if that's the case, tell me now. I'll take care of it."

She had vowed that she would not allow him to push any of her buttons tonight, but this was too much.

"And everyone wonders why we broke

up." She spread her hands. "This is a perfect example of why marriage between us would have been a disaster."

He blinked. "What did I say?"

"You honestly don't know, do you? You haven't even got a clue. Never mind." She sat forward determinedly. "We don't have time for this. Don't worry, I'm not going to involve you in anything illegal. This is a straight search-and-rescue job."

"Who needs rescuing?"

"A friend of mine."

"Why not hire a professional SAR team?"

"The person who is lost would definitely not appreciate having a formal team sent in after her."

"In other words it's your friend who is involved in some illegal excavation work," Cooper said.

"Stop jumping to conclusions. Bertha Newell works under a legitimate private license. Years ago she applied for and received a permit to excavate a sector of the catacombs that neither the university nor any of the large exploration firms wanted to be bothered with."

"So this Bertha Newell is a ruin rat? How did you get involved with her?"

"I'll explain later."

"If I turn you down, you'll try to find another hunter, right?"

She straightened her shoulders. "No. If you don't come with me, I'll go down alone."

"Like hell you will."

"Well, not entirely alone," she amended quickly. "I've got a friend who will go with me."

"A hunter friend?"

"No."

Cooper exhaled slowly. "Looks like I don't have much choice. If something happens to you down there in the catacombs, I don't want to have to face your parents with the news."

"I am aware," she said through her teeth, "that I have placed you in a somewhat difficult position."

"But you're going to do it anyway."

"I don't have any choice, either. Bertha may be in very serious trouble."

"All right," Cooper said.

She felt her spirits lift. If anyone could help her find Bertha tonight, it was Cooper Boone. "It's settled, then. You might as well meet the third member of our team."

He did not look pleased. "Someone else is involved in this thing?"

"Yes." She opened the large tote, reached inside, and gently lifted out a ball of shapeless gray fluff. "This is Rose."

Rose batted her baby-blue daylight eyes. The second set of eyes, the ones she used for hunting at night, remained discreetly hidden in her tatty fur.

Cooper looked at the small beast. "You've got a pet dust bunny?"

"She showed up on my back doorstep shortly after I opened my shop. She came back every day around closing time. I fed her. We've become roommates."

"What's she got around her neck?" Cooper asked.

"One of my bracelets. Turns out Rose has a thing for jewelry. Like any good roommate, she borrows my stuff."

"Not sure the Public Health Department would approve of allowing a dust bunny into an eating establishment, even a hunter bar."

"That's why I carried her in the tote," Elly explained.

Rose rumbled in an inquisitive manner and made it clear that she wanted to be put down on the table. Elly looked around to be sure that no one was paying any attention to the booth at the rear of the tavern, and then she released Rose.

The dust bunny scampered halfway across the table, her six legs invisible in her lintlike fur. She paused and sat up to examine Cooper with great interest.

"Does she bite?" Cooper asked.

"Of course not," Elly said quickly. "She's just a little thing. If you provoked her or scared her, she might nip your finger, but that's all."

"I've always heard that by the time you see the teeth, it's too late."

"That's just an old story. There is very little known about dust bunnies, so ridiculous tales like that have tended to be perpetuated."

Cooper extended his fingers. Rose sniffed delicately and appeared satisfied. She switched her attention immediately to the sandwich and fries.

Cooper picked up a fry and then paused to look at Elly with polite inquiry. "Okay to feed her one of these, or are you worried about her arteries?"

"There isn't much information available about dust-bunny nutrition, so I let Rose eat whatever she wants," Elly admitted.

"Lucky bunny."

Rose accepted the fry with great delicacy and started munching.

Somewhere behind Elly a barstool crashed to the floor. Glass shattered. A man roared in outrage.

"Son of a bitch. I saw her first."

"She doesn't want to dance with you. Can't you get that through your thick skull? She wants to dance with me."

"The hell she does."

There was a sickening thud, followed by a howl and several drunken shouts. Chairs scraped the floor. Small flickers of acid-green ghost energy lit up the gloom. Elly sighed. When ghost hunters got excited, they tended to unconsciously summon little bits and pieces of whatever stray dissonance energy happened to be in the vicinity. There was plenty of the stuff available here in the Old Quarter. Like other forms of psi power, it leaked from the invisible cracks and crannies in the massive walls that encircled the Dead City of Old Cadence and seeped upward from the underground tunnels.

"Looks like it's time to leave," Cooper said, getting to his feet.

"Very observant of you." Elly slung the strap of her tote over one shoulder. She scooped up Rose, plunked the dust bunny down on her other shoulder, and slid out of the booth. She grabbed her coat.

Cooper wrapped his fingers around her wrist and hauled her toward the back door.

"So, do you come here often?" he asked as they went past the rancid-smelling kitchen.

There was another loud crash and a lot more yelling. Elly saw two cooks in heavily stained aprons grab heavy pots and charge toward the front of the tavern. They looked like they'd had some experience breaking up bar fights.

"My first time," she said. "But, gosh, if I'd known how much fun I was going to have, I'd have stopped in sooner. You know, until I moved here to Cadence, I had no idea just how boring life was back in Aurora Springs."

Chapter 3

In hindsight, all he could say was that it had seemed like a good idea at the time, Cooper thought, hauling Elly past the restrooms and out the rear door. But things were not going as planned.

He should have known better. If recent history had taught him nothing else, it was that his best laid plans never worked the way they were supposed to when Elly was involved.

This latest strategy gone bad was a perfect case in point. It had looked so simple, so foolproof, when he'd concocted it six months ago. All of them, her parents and her brothers included, had agreed that it was nothing short of brilliant. Give Elly six months in the big, bad city, and she would have a change of heart.

Let her kick over the traces imposed by her small-town, academic life for a while. Give her a chance to find out just how hard the world outside the ivory tower really was. Let her discover how difficult and exhausting it was to run a business with its endless paperwork, long hours, difficult customers, and precarious financial issues.

To say nothing of her career. She was devoted to the study of botany. She would soon come to miss the intellectual challenges of the classroom and the stimulation of her colleagues' conversation and the attractive, tranquil grounds of the college campus.

And what about her precious personal greenhouse? he had reasoned. In Aurora Springs the private conservatory attached to her quaint post–Era of Discord cottage was larger than the house itself. You couldn't have a greenhouse that size in the Old Quarter of a big city. There wasn't room.

In the opinion of everyone involved, Elly had been born for the academic realm, not the tough, ghost-fry-ghost world of small business. After six months on her own in Cadence, she would be more than happy to come home, resume her position in the Department of Botany at Aurora Springs College, and marry him.

He had planned to surprise her by walking into her shop first thing in the morning when he was rested, showered, shaved, and dressed in the new shirt and jacket he had bought for the occasion. He had wanted to make a good impression.

It had surprised the hell out of him when she had phoned while he was eating a late dinner to say that she wanted to see him immediately. He had told himself that was a good sign. Okay, the first meeting after all these months wasn't going to go quite as he had planned it, but he had nevertheless experienced a surge of satisfaction bordering on triumph. The let-Elly-rez-her-untuned-amber-in-the-big-city strategy had worked, just as he had intended. She couldn't wait to see him.

When she walked into the Trap Door tonight, though, he had gotten a real bad feeling about his so-called brilliant strategy.

For starters there were the sexy clothes. Elly had never worn her skirts that short back in Aurora Springs. The minuscule black number splashed with exotic green leaves cut so high he was sure he could have fit both of his hands in the space between knee and hem.

She had never worn any tops as snug-fitting as the black knit thing that she had on, either. He would have remembered. The garment framed her elegant, apple-sized breasts in a way that had made every hunter in the room want to take a bite.

Her dark brown hair still glowed with natural amber-colored highlights but, like the skirt, it was cut a lot shorter than it had been back in Aurora Springs. She no longer wore the conservative, academic-looking twist she had favored back home, either. Instead, the new look was sleek and sassy. It skimmed her jawline and accented her delicate features and exotic green eyes.

In fact, the only thing that looked familiar about her attire were the amber-and-gold earrings. He remembered them well. She had never been without them back in Aurora Springs. She had told him once that they had been a gift from her parents and had great sentimental value.

The biggest shocker though, was the smile. Damn. If he hadn't been sitting down, he probably would have fallen flat on his face. It wasn't just the dazzling brightness of those pretty little white teeth she had flashed at him; it was the attitude, the sheer female challenge. *Catch me if you can.*

And now he knew that the only reason she had tracked him down tonight was because she needed a bodyguard to accompany her on a somewhat less than legal trip into the catacombs.

It was a depressing end to a long day that had been filled with anticipation.

He paused to survey the alley. It appeared empty, but given the poor lighting and the fog, it was impossible to be certain. The shadows coiled heavily in several places between the back door of the tavern and the alley exit.

Cooper tightened his grip on Elly's wrist. "Where are you parked?"

"I took a cab. Didn't want to risk leaving my car on the street."

"I can see why you'd hesitate," he said grimly. "This isn't exactly an upscale section of town, is it?"

"Speaking of which, I was a little surprised to learn that you were eating at the Trap Door tonight," she retorted coolly. "Guild bosses usually dine in classier establishments."

"I told you, I'm not here in my official capacity. I came to Cadence on a private matter. Thought that if I stuck to places like the Trap Door, no one would recognize me."

"Oh, right. I keep forgetting your private business here. I have to tell you, though, it's awfully hard to imagine you involved in anything but Guild business."

"Are you saying I'm a workaholic?"

"I'm saying that you have no life outside the Guild."

"No life? What the hell is that supposed to mean?"

"Never mind. Let's get going. I want to find Bertha."

He wanted to argue about his life. He had spent years crafting it, shaping its course, and preparing himself to reach his goal. But he wasn't sure how to defend himself against a charge that he didn't completely understand in the first place, so he focused on the more immediate problem.

He looked down at her strappy, high-heeled sandals. He could see her toenails. She had painted them a brilliant shade of scarlet. They gleamed in the glow of the light above the door. Back in Aurora Springs, he had never seen her wear such blatantly sexy, open-toed shoes like the pair she had on tonight. Classic pumps had been more her style.

He thought about all of the hunters back in the bar who must have noticed her toenails when she had walked through the crowd to his table.

"You can't go down into the catacombs in those shoes," he said. "If you sprained an ankle, I'd have to carry you out."

She gave him a frosty smile. "I wouldn't want you to strain anything."

"Thanks. I appreciate the thought." This was not going well.

"As it happens, you have nothing to worry

about," she said. "I've got a second pair of shoes in my tote." She tapped the large bag she had slung over one shoulder. "We'll go straight to Bertha's shop and use her hole-in-the-wall to go into the catacombs."

"She showed you the location of her private gate?" He started toward the barely visible mouth of the alley, drawing Elly with him. "Never met a ruin rat who wasn't obsessively secretive about his or her hole-in-the-wall."

"Bertha trusts me, probably because she knows I'm not potential competition. I'm not a tangler or a hunter. I'm not even in the antiquities trade."

The words were spoken a little too evenly, he thought. He could hear the faint trace of wistful resignation in them.

Unlike everyone else in her family, Elly possessed only a normal amount of psi talent. Like the average person, she could rez a door lock or activate a dishwasher, but she lacked either of the two types of powerful para-rez talents that would have enabled her to make a career in alien archaeology. Without such talents, she had no need of genuine, highly tuned amber to focus her psi senses.

It could not have been easy growing up in a family of strong hunters with a mother who was a tangler, he reflected. Elly must have envied the freedom the others enjoyed to explore the strange underground world of the catacombs. More crucially, by watching the others in her clan, she would have understood intuitively that she was missing out on the satisfaction and sheer exhilaration that came with the exercise of strong psi senses down in the catacombs.

It had to be the equivalent of knowing intellectually what an orgasm was but not being able to achieve one, he decided. Damned frustrating.

"Have you got your friend's amber frequency?" he asked.

"Yes. I've also got the frequency of her sled's amber-rez directional locator. She gave both of them to me in case of an emergency."

"Are you sure this is an emergency? Those old ruin rats sometimes spend days down in the catacombs."

"I may be overreacting," she admitted. "It's true, Bertha is a pro. But this morning before she went underground, she ordered her usual month's supply of amber-root tisane and told me that she would pick it up this afternoon when she got out of the tunnels. When she didn't show up by closing time, I became concerned."

"You checked around to make sure she wasn't sick in bed or visiting relatives?"

"Yes. I called her antique shop and got the answering machine. I asked the florist who runs the shop next door to hers if he'd seen her, but he said no. She's just disappeared, and I'm afraid that means she ran into trouble down in the catacombs. She's tough, but she's not a young woman, Cooper."

Sirens wailed somewhere in the night.

"Someone called the cops," he said. "Just what we do not need."

He urged Elly to a faster pace. The heels of her stylish sandals echoed on the old paving stones.

"Guess it would be a little awkward to explain why the boss of the Aurora Springs Guild got picked up at a bar brawl, wouldn't it?" Elly said, ghoulishly cheerful.

There was just enough light to allow him to see that she was smiling again. It was a real smile this time, not that flashy, full-rez ray beam she'd used on him back in the tavern.

"If they pick me up, they'll probably grab you, as well," he warned.

"Good point." She increased her pace. "We certainly can't afford to be delayed explaining things to the cops tonight. Let's hurry."

"You know," he said, "there was a time when you would have been horrified at the idea of getting arrested. Now the only thing you're worried about is wasting the time it would take to converse with the police."

"Back in Aurora Springs I had to worry a lot about embarrassing my family and shocking the sensibilities of those pompous, narrow-minded blowhards on the Academic Council. But here in Cadence, I'm happy to say, those are no longer considerations."

"Is that right?"

"Yes." She was a little breathless now. "Here in the city I'm free in a way I've never been before in my life."

Pompous, narrow-minded blowhards. It didn't sound like she was longing to return to her former position at Aurora Springs College.

One by one, Cooper thought, the premises upon which he had constructed his master strategy were crumbling before his very eyes.

The sirens were closer now. He heard the rear door of the tavern slam open. He glanced back over his shoulder and saw a heap of men in khaki and leather briefly jam the opening. A few managed to squeeze through. Boots thudded on the old stones.

Luckily, the fleeing hunters chose to run in the opposite direction.

He brought Elly and Rose to a halt at the juncture of the alley and the street. To the left the massive green quartz walls of the Dead City rose into the night, bathing the scene in a faint chartreuse glow. The aliens had vanished centuries ago, but they had left the lights on.

When he looked toward the corner at the other end of the block, he could see a couple of police cruisers closing in on the front entrance of the Trap Door.

"We've got a little problem here," he said. "If we try to approach my car from this direction, the cops will probably stop us. They'll be picking up everyone who happens to be wearing khaki and leather."

"I've said for years that ghost hunters need to realize that there is a price to be paid for being so desperately fashion challenged."

He opted to ignore that. "Our best bet is to circle around and approach my car from another direction. Make it look like we're returning to it from one of the cafés down the street."

"Sounds like a plan."

"How fast can you run in those fancy high heels?"

"Fast." She let the tote slide off her shoulder and reached inside to extract a pair of sporty-looking athletic shoes. "But not as fast as I can run in these. Here, hold Rose."

She transferred the dust bunny to his shoulder, braced one hand on his arm, and bent down to change shoes. Cooper was very conscious of the warm weight of her fingers as she balanced against him and stepped out of one high heel.

He caught a fleeting glimpse of a dainty, elegantly arched bare foot before it disappeared into one of the running shoes. Something low and deep inside him tightened and hardened. It had been a long six months, he thought.

Actually, it had been a good deal longer than six months if he counted from the first time he had seen Elly walking into the Guild Archives. And he was definitely counting from that point, because that was the moment he had decided that she was just what he had been looking for in a wife.

It had been a very long eight months and five days, to be precise.

Elly took her hand off his arm and straightened. "I'm ready." She sounded unsettlingly enthusiastic about what they were about to attempt. "Where, exactly, are we headed?"

"Across this street and through the alley in the next block. When we reach the far end, we'll walk up to the cross street and then mosey back to my car."

"Just a couple of innocent onlookers." She retrieved Rose.

"You got it."

He guided her into the second alley, pausing at the entrance to open all of his senses to the night. The faint green glow from the walls did not reach into the deep shadows of this cramped passage.

He took another look at Rose. Her baby-blue eyes were wide open, but she was fully fluffed and munching contentedly on the last bit of fry.

Cooper dug a flashlight out of one of the flapped pockets of his trousers and gave it a little pulse of psi energy to switch it on.

Elly muttered something he didn't quite catch. She sounded disgusted.

"What's wrong?" he asked.

"These shoes are going to be ruined," she said.

"They're athletic shoes. They're made for getting dirty."

"That's beside the point. Do you have any idea how much they cost? I paid a fortune for them, and I never intended to wear them through whatever was in that slimy puddle back there."

"Now, see, if you were wearing a pair of sturdy hunter boots made out of genuine chroma-snakeskin, you wouldn't have to worry about the contents of alley puddles or anything else you happened to step in. Good boots will go anywhere, I always say."

She turned her head slightly to look at him. He could not see her expression in the shadows, but he got the feeling that he had surprised her.

"I'll keep that tip in mind next time I shop for shoes," she said without inflection.

He was brooding on the fact that Elly seemed nonplussed by the possibility that he might have a sense of humor when he noticed the outline of Rose's small body change abruptly.

In the blink of an eye, the shapeless ball of fur thinned into a sleek, taut shadow. The dust bunny opened a second set of eyes and turned to look at one of the doors in the alley wall.

"Damn," Cooper said softly.

The heavy door crashed open. Cooper caught the unmistakable whiff of ghost energy. He reacted without even thinking about it, halting and spinning on his heel to face the threat. Simultaneously he used his grip on Elly's wrist to whip her to safety behind him. Out of the corner of his eye he saw Rose cling to Elly's shoulder with all six legs.

The ghost materialized swiftly, a small inferno of swirling, seething energy that flared and pulsed. It moved closer, forcing Cooper, Elly, and Rose into a corner formed by a large, rusted-out trash container and the brick wall.

"Big," was all Elly said.

She was right, Cooper thought, the sucker was large for a ghost generated outside the catacombs. But it was not a very powerful UDEM. Showy, but no real strength at the core.

He studied the fiery green mass for a couple of seconds, probing for the pattern with his psi senses. The waves of dissonance energy in the UDEM were only marginally under control. The hunter who had created this ghost was either rezzed on drugs or a little crazy. It was fortunate that the guy wasn't powerful enough to summon more energy, Cooper thought.

The UDEM drifted closer. Even when they were summoned and manipulated by a skilled dissonance-energy para-rez, standard-issue ghosts were never fast-moving. Top speed was usually somewhere in the neighborhood of a rapid walking pace. But the hunter operating this one knew what he was doing. It probably wasn't the first time he had used a ghost to trap his victims between the trash container and the wall.

This was a classic back-alley mugging.

A skeletal figure loomed in the opening, its bony frame dimly outlined in the weak glow of the light burning behind him.

"Anyone moves, and you're all fried." The mugger's voice was frayed at the edges. "I'm not warnin' you twice."

Definitely a crazy, or an over-rezzed doper, Cooper thought. Sanity had probably become a somewhat remote concept for him.

"Take it easy," Cooper said quietly. "Nobody's moving."

The jittery mugger made his way slowly down the two steps to the pavement. He was so unsteady on his feet that he had to brace himself against the brick wall. In the backwash of the light cast by his ghost, his skull-like features were etched in sickly green.

"Your wallet, rings, amber, watch, anything you got on you," he muttered. "I need it all. You hear me? I need money for the chant."

"No problem," Cooper said. He sent psi energy through the amber he carried on the end of his watch chain. "Okay if I reach for my wallet?"

"Do it slow."

"Sure." Cooper reached one hand toward his back pocket.

Generally speaking, you fought ghost fire with ghost fire. The problem here, he decided, was that if the mugger realized that a second UDEM was being formed in the vicinity, he was likely to lash out with his own ghost before the new one could be used against him.

One brush of ghost light rezzed all of the victim's senses to the point of extreme psychic pain. That phase was followed by a period of unconsciousness that could last for hours.

He needed a distraction, Cooper thought.

He was about to create one when the agitated robber switched his attention to Elly. In the green glare Cooper saw the skull-like face scrunch up with confusion. A sheen of sweat coated his face.

"What in green hell? You got a rat on your shoulder, lady? "

"Rose is not a rat," Elly said. "She's a dust bunny, and you're scaring her with your ghost. Please don't hurt her."

Elly's voice was gentle and calming. She understood that they were dealing with a dangerous, unpredictable doper, Cooper thought. And whatever else she was, Rose sure wasn't scared. In the pulsing light he could see the dust bunny's teeth; a lot of them.

"I don't give a damn about the varmint." The mugger used the back of his sleeve to wipe his mouth. "Drop the big purse, lady."

"Whatever you say," Elly agreed. She slowly lowered the tote, taking her time about it. "I have to put it down carefully, though. There's a very expensive relic inside."

The man's eyes widened with feverish excitement. "Alien or Early Colonial?"

The guy might be a crazed dope fiend, Cooper thought, but he knew his antiquities. Probably a Guild man who had spent time underground before he had fallen into the clutches of the drug.

"Alien," Elly assured him briskly with the air of a professional saleswoman about to display an expensive item to a customer. "Would you like to see it?"

"Take it out. Real slow."

"Of course." She reached down into the tote. "It's a very fine piece."

The jittery mugger watched her with a desperate air of anticipation. He was so focused on visions of the pharmaceuticals he planned to buy that he never noticed the small ball of ghost fire Cooper summoned behind him.

The little UDEM drifted toward the back of the mugger's head. Cooper was well aware that what he intended had to be done carefully. He did not want to kill the doper, just knock him out for a while.

Elly started to remove something from the tote.

"Let me see that," the man said, taking a step closer. "Throw it over here."

Cooper let the leading edge of the small ghost brush ever so gently against the mugger's head.

The skeletal figure stiffened abruptly, arms jangling, mouth opening on a silent scream. He jerked violently a second time and then collapsed to the ground, unconscious.

The mugger's ghost winked out instantly as the psi energy abruptly ceased. Underground, the UDEMs were fueled by the ambient power of the catacombs. Aboveground, however, it took a trained hunter to keep one together.

Cooper dissolved his own UDEM. The last of the green light disappeared, leaving only the thin beam of the flashlight.

"Nicely done," Elly said. She dropped the

high-heeled sandal she had partially re-moved back into the tote and surveyed the fallen man with a slight frown. "I hope you didn't use too much energy on him, though."

Cooper crouched beside the unconscious man and checked for a pulse. He found it immediately.

"He'll wake up in a few hours with a bad headache and no clear memory of what hap-pened." Cooper rose and urged her toward the mouth of the alley. "Are you okay?"

"For heaven's sake, I was raised in a hunter family, remember? It isn't the first time I've seen ghosts."

"Just checking. Thanks for distracting that SOB with the story about having an alien artifact in your bag, by the way. He never even realized that I was working ghost light behind him."

"You're good, aren't you?" she said, giving him a thoughtful, sidelong glance. "That little ghost was very intricate, very ef-ficient, very tightly constructed. Not many hunters could have generated one like that."

"I've had a fair amount of experience," he said.

"You've got more than experience. You've obviously got both a lot of raw power and a high degree of control."

"Yeah, well, I'm a Guild boss, re-member?" he said, trying to keep things light. "I'm supposed to be good."

She fell silent beside him. Probably not a good sign, he thought.

At the mouth of the alley, he turned right, steering Elly and Rose toward the intersection. At the corner they all paused and looked back up the street toward the Trap Door. The bar was in the middle of the adjacent block. Directly in front three police cruisers had come to a halt, lights flashing. He could see some cops going through the door. A crowd was coalescing to watch the excitement.

"We're in the clear," he said. "My Spectrum is at this end of the street. Everyone is looking the other way. If we're careful, no one will notice us. From here on we walk, we do not run. People tend to notice folks who are moving too fast."

"Understood. But I suggest we walk at a very brisk pace, if you don't mind."

"Fine by me."

They were only a few steps away from the Spectrum when a patrol car glided up beside them. The hard-eyed officer behind the wheel nailed them in the beam of his flashlight.

"Where are you two going?" he asked,

most of his attention on Cooper.

"Home," Elly said before Cooper could respond. "As quickly as possible."

"Not from around here, huh?"

"My friend is from out of town. I brought him down to the Old Quarter to show him the sights. We just finished dinner at a charmingly quaint little café up the street and were walking back to the car when all of a sudden there were police cars everywhere."

The officer switched the beam to Elly's face. "What's the name of the café where you had dinner?"

"The Emerald Wall," she said without missing a beat. She produced a card from the pocket of her coat. "My name is Elly St. Clair. I own St. Clair's Herbal Emporium. I specialize in custom-blended tisanes, teas, and tonics. If you ever need anything in that line, be sure to stop in at my shop. I know police work is very stressful. I have a special moonseed tisane that can do wonders."

The officer scowled at the card and then looked at Cooper. "Where are you from?"

"Aurora Springs," Cooper said.

The officer looked amused. "Come to the big city to visit the lady and see the bright lights, huh?"

"That was the idea," Cooper said.

The officer switched off the flashlight.

"All right, you two, go on, get out of here."
He gave Elly one last glance. "Is that a dust
bunny on your shoulder?"

"Yes," she said. "Her name is Rose."

Cooper noticed that Rose had gone back
to doing a good imitation of something that
had rolled out from under a bed. Only her
innocent blue eyes were showing.

"Heard they can be dangerous," the officer said, playing the light on Rose, who appeared not to notice.

"That's a silly urban legend," Elly said.
"The most she might do is nip a finger, and
she would only do that if she was seriously
provoked."

"If you say so. Go on, you two. You don't
want to hang around this neighborhood."
He gave Elly a stern look. "Next time you
want to show a visitor a good time, I suggest
you take 'em to a better part of town. Don't
want to give tourists a bad impression of
Cadence."

"Thank you for the advice," she said.

The officer drove off down the street.

"You heard the man," Cooper said,
opening the Spectrum's passenger door.
"We don't want to hang around here. This
is a bad neighborhood. Surprised you'd
bring an innocent tourist like me to a place
like this."

"Thought it might give you something to talk about when you went back to Aurora Springs. Not like there's much else of interest going on back there."

"Not since you left town," he said.

Chapter 4

She gave him a quick, startled look and then, evidently choosing to let the remark go, she slipped into the front seat. She moved quickly and gracefully, but he nevertheless got a tantalizing glimpse of the inside of one softly rounded thigh. He felt his blood heat. *Definitely a dangerous neighborhood.*

He went to the other side of the car, got in beside her, and rezzed the ignition. Flash rock melted, and the powerful engine purred. He pulled slowly, sedately away from the curb.

"What's the address of your friend's place?" he asked.

"Number Twenty-six Ruin Lane. Not far from my shop. Turn right at the next corner."

Rose hopped from Elly's shoulder onto the back of the seat and sat up to take in the view of the night-shrouded streets.

Cooper drove to the corner and turned down another narrow street lined with the dark, gloomy, old-fashioned buildings the

First Generation colonists had erected two hundred years earlier.

The newer sections of Cadence were optimistic and energetic in style. But here in the Old Quarter, the structures fashioned by the settlers reflected a grim determination to survive. The buildings hunkered down like gargoyles, creating a maze of narrow streets, crooked lanes, and dark alleys. *Atmospheric* was about the only positive word that could be used to describe this part of town.

The dark, brooding structures of the Old Quarter stood in stark contrast to the elegant, airy, alien towers and spires that rose inside the massive green quartz walls. Cadence, like the other three major city-states on Harmony, had been established around the ruins of one of the four major ancient dead cities that had been discovered shortly after colonization. Although the mysterious aliens who had originally settled the planet had vanished thousands of years ago, their strangely ethereal urban landscape and the dangerous labyrinth of underground tunnels they had built defied time and the elements. Cooper sometimes wondered if the human cities would last as long.

On the other side of the car Elly cleared her throat.

"Are you okay?" she asked.

"Why wouldn't I be okay?"

"Just wondering," she said a little too lightly. "That was a very tightly wound ghost you used against that mugger."

It hit him that this was the first time she had actually seen him work ghost energy. He tightened his grip on the wheel.

"What's the matter? Are you afraid I'm going to turn into a raging sex fiend?" he asked politely. "Don't worry. I usually save that for a full moon."

She wrapped her arms very tightly around herself and angled her chin. "Don't be ridiculous."

"Look, Elly, I'm sure you're well aware that every hunter rezzes ghost light a little differently. No two do it quite the same way. My patterns have always been complex. It's the way my psi energy resonates." He didn't even pause as he gave his standard explanation. He'd been using the line for years, ever since it had become obvious in his teens that his para-senses were not the same as those of other hunters. "Doesn't mean I exerted an unusual amount of power. I didn't melt amber."

"Right." She shot him a quick, assessing look and then turned back to stare fixedly ahead at the street scene. "Nevertheless, everyone knows that working a ghost, even a small one, has a certain, uh, pronounced effect on a hunter. Turn left here."

The conversation was going downhill fast. "Don't tell me that you actually believe all that garbage about ghost hunters becoming sex-crazed after they work ghost light."

"No offense, but I've got three brothers, remember? They can't wait to find a date after a day spent working ghost light down in the catacombs."

"Most guys your brothers' ages, ghost hunters, or not, are seriously interested in sex. Goes with the territory of being male."

To his surprise, her mouth curved a little at that. "But men like you who are older and wiser are no longer at the mercy of their hormones, is that it?"

Was she teasing him? "Relax, I'm no more of a threat to your virtue now than I was before I rezzed that damned ghost back there in the alley."

"I see," she said, perfectly neutral.

That hadn't come out quite right, he reflected. The unfortunate fact was that he was semiaroused, and she had obviously sensed it. What she did not know was that the ghost work had little to do with his current condition. He'd been feeling this way since she'd walked into the Trap Door.

"Look, I'm not saying that summoning ghosts doesn't have some side effects," he plowed on, going for reasonable. "But as you get older, you learn how to handle the rush. I'm not going to throw you over my shoulder and haul you off to the nearest bed."

She tilted her head slightly. "You're starting to sound a little testy. That's part of the syndrome."

"Testy?"

"Short tempered, irritable. You know, *testy*. I've noticed that ghost hunters often get that way after they've fried a ghost."

"Is that so?" he said, very polite, but through his teeth.

"If they don't get rid of the adrenaline overload in some other way, that is. When they can't get a date, my brothers go to the gym, instead."

"You really know how to rez a man's amber, don't you?"

"Like I said, three brothers. I've had oodles of experience."

He got a cold feeling. No doubt about it, leaving her alone here in Cadence for the past six months was proving to be one of the biggest miscalculations of his life. He didn't make many mistakes, but when he made them, they tended to really resonate.

"What have you been doing for fun here in Cadence?" he asked, determined to change the subject.

"I've been pretty busy." She patted Rose again. "You'd be amazed at how much work it takes to open up a small business and get it running at a profit."

"As a matter of fact, I'm not the least bit surprised," he said, putting a not-so-subtle emphasis into the words. "I run the Aurora Springs Guild, remember? It's a very *big* business. Requires even more work and time than a small business."

"Forget it, that logic isn't going to fly with me. There's a vast difference between being interested in your work and being obsessed with it."

"And you know where that line is?"

"Yes, I do." She paused deliberately. "You know, in hindsight, you owe me, big time."

"How do you figure that?"

"What if we had actually gone through with a Covenant Marriage? Just think how miserable you would have been by now. I'd be nagging you, rezzing your amber, as you put it, constantly, day in and day out. To escape, you'd be spending even more time at the office. What were you thinking, anyway, going straight for a full Covenant? If we were going to try any kind of relationship at all, we should have gone for a limited Marriage of Convenience."

"Thought I knew what I was doing," he said.

The marriage laws had been relaxed slightly in the past two centuries, Cooper reflected, but not a whole lot. The rigid rules had made sense two hundred years ago when the colonists had found themselves abandoned on Harmony.

The settlers' primary goal in those dangerous early years had been to establish a strong, cohesive social fabric. The personal happiness of individuals had been a distant second. The social scientists, philosophers, and elected leaders had known that the basic building block of any society was the family. They had concluded that if the small, fragile colonies were to stand any chance at all of survival, the social structure had to be founded on strong family units.

The desperate, determined Founders had drawn up a Constitution and a series of laws designed to ensure that families remained intact, regardless of the price that had to be paid. Hence, the institution of the Covenant Marriage, a bond which, generally speaking, could be severed only by death or an act of the Federation Council.

But the Founders had also understood the need to provide an alternative for those who were not ready to take the big leap. The Marriage of Convenience was a legally recognized arrangement that had to be renewed regularly by both parties involved. It could be terminated at any point. There were pitfalls, however. Couples had to be particularly careful about birth control. The arrival of a baby automatically converted the short-term status of a Marriage of Convenience to that of a permanent Covenant Marriage.

Families encouraged their offspring to experiment with MCs while they were young and more at risk of being swept away by the glittering lures of romance, passion, and plain, old-fashioned lust.

Covenant Marriages were supposed to be carefully thought out business and social arrangements reserved for those who were more mature and ready to settle down.

Guys like him, Cooper thought. He'd had it all so carefully planned.

"Well, don't blame yourself too much." She patted his shoulder in much the same way that she had just patted Rose. "After all, I accepted your proposal. I thought I knew what I was doing, too. And Guild tradition is a powerful force. Guess we both had a narrow escape."

"Guess so." Conjugal relations was the last subject he wanted to think about just now. But he couldn't seem to move on. "You ever tried an MC?"

"Who? Me? Nope. Left at the next corner."

"Why not?" he asked, unable to stop himself.

"Let's just say that an MC is easier said than done in a small town where everyone knows that you're the daughter of one of the members of the Guild Council. I always had to worry about the real motives of the men who showed an interest in any sort of arrangement with me, short- or long-term."

"Men like Palmer Frazier, do you mean?"

"I think we'd better avoid the topic of Palmer Frazier." She paused. "What about you? Ever been in an MC?"

"No."

"Why not? Too busy working your way up through the Guild?"

He moved one hand slightly on the wheel. "That was one of the reasons."

"Are there any others?"

"None that I'm prepared to discuss tonight."

"Oh." She sounded chagrined. "I don't

have the right to ask those sorts of personal questions, do I? Turn right."

He followed directions obediently. There was no reason to mention that he already knew how to get to Ruin Lane because he had cruised past St. Clair's Herbal Emporium earlier today, immediately after he had arrived in town.

As was the case with all of the other major city-states, Cadence had grown rapidly, pushing out into the surrounding countryside. Predictably, the Old Quarters had been treated with benign neglect. Over the years many of the neighborhoods near the great walls had became home to the down-and-out and those who lived on the margins of society, as well as a varied selection of nightclubs, bars, and taverns.

But due to their close proximity to the ancient alien metropolises, the Old Quarters all possessed one strong, vibrant, economic underpinning that kept them from sliding into complete decay: a lively trade in alien antiquities, both real and fake.

Interspersed with the cheap apartment houses, dives, and forlorn storefronts here in the cramped streets of Cadence's colonial neighborhoods, Cooper saw small shops purporting to offer relics from the Dead City and the Early Colonial era.

When he had made quiet inquiries a few months back to assure himself that Elly was not living in a dangerous neighborhood, he had been told that her shop was in one of the newer, recently gentrified sections of the Old Quarter. Today when he had driven slowly down Ruin Lane, he had been relieved to find out that his information had been solid.

True, the area wasn't as neat and tidy as the street where she had lived back in Aurora Springs, but he didn't see conventions of drug dealers, cop cars, and prostitutes on the corners, either.

"There's Bertha's shop," Elly stated. "Go around the corner. We'll park in the alley."

"I seem to be spending a lot of time in alleys tonight."

"They're considered a scenic attraction here in the Old Quarter. Very atmospheric."

He eased the Spectrum slowly into the narrow service lane behind Newell's Relics, parked, and climbed out. The fog was getting thicker, he noticed.

Elly, with Rose on her shoulder, emerged from the front seat before he could get around to the passenger side.

She removed a key from the depths of her tote and went quickly toward the rear door of Newell's Relics.

"Hang on a second," he said quietly. "I want to be sure the Spectrum is still here when we come back."

He sent out a little pulse of psi power through his amber, using it to grab some of the ambient energy drifting through the night. Concentrating briefly, he formed a tiny ghost and anchored it to the rear license plate of the Spectrum. The little UDEM flared to life, illuminating the plate in a faint, green glow.

"That should do it," Elly said dryly. "Can't imagine anyone dumb enough to steal that car now."

He shrugged. "In my experience, it's excellent insurance against grand theft auto."

Okay, so it was a little flashy, he conceded silently. Very few dissonance-energy pararezzes were strong enough to anchor a ghost, even a small one, outside the catacombs. But replacing the Spectrum would be both expensive and inconvenient. The little UDEM sent an unmistakable message: *Touch this car, and the owner will hunt you down and fry your brains.*

Elly opened the door of the darkened shop and switched on the lights.

He followed her inside and found himself in a back room filled with small green quartz artifacts. There was nothing that looked particularly valuable, as far as he could see. Most of the relics were the sort of simple tomb mirrors, undistinguished urns, and unexceptional vases that were found in low-end antiquities shops in every Old Quarter.

"Where's her rat hole?" he asked.

"Same place mine is, in the cellar. Stairs are over there."

"You've got an entrance to the catacombs beneath your shop?" he asked, surprised.

"Yes. Pretty cool, huh? Doesn't do me much good, of course, but I let my friend Doreen use it. She takes me down with her sometimes."

"Who's Doreen?"

"She's another ruin rat. A tangler. Very fashionable. She went shopping with me shortly after I arrived and helped me pick out a new wardrobe."

"I did notice the new clothes," he said neutrally.

"Doreen has a shop and apartment directly across the street from mine."

"I see."

He followed her down a cramped flight of steps into the depths of a damp, dark cellar.

"You know, this isn't how I had planned

to spend my first night in the big city," he remarked.

"That's the trouble with you Guild bosses, you're not spontaneous," she said.

Chapter 5

The rush hit him before he got out of the catacombs, rezzing all of his senses, making him fully aware of his power.

It had been a close call tonight. Thanks to the stupid, weak-stomached chemist, the old woman had nearly escaped. Those damn ruin rats were hard to kill.

By the time he had arrived on the scene to clean up the mess, Bertha Newell and her utility sled had vanished, leaving only a pool of blood on the green quartz floor. The woman had evidently come back to her senses long enough to climb aboard the sled and drive off into the maze of tunnels. She had probably been terrified to return to the surface, fearing that someone would have been waiting for her. She had been right. Now that they knew she had seen the lab, she could not be allowed to live.

Luckily, the chemist had noted the frequency of the amber-rez locator on Newell's sled. It was the only smart thing the fool had done tonight.

He tightened his grip on the wheel of his

sled. If it weren't for the fact that the chemist was the only one who knew precisely how to transform the psi-bright herbs into enchantment dust, he would have gotten rid of him long ago. But without the damn chemist, the herbs were just so many dried weeds.

It had not been difficult to track Newell's sled through the tunnels. Unfortunately, by the time he had caught up with her, she had abandoned her utility vehicle and crawled off into a corridor laced with myriad chambers, antechambers and mazelike passages.

He had hoped to find a trail of blood leading from the sled to the woman's hiding place, but there had not been one. She had somehow stopped the bleeding long enough to conceal her trail.

In the end, he had been forced to abandon the hunt.

He regretted the fact that he had not been able to make absolutely certain that Newell was dead, but he had used his para-rez talent to ensure that, even if she did survive, she would never be able to return to the surface.

There was little possibility that anyone would send a search-and-rescue team in after her, he told himself. Ruin rats were notoriously secretive. Most eventually became full-blown paranoids. They worked alone, rarely trusted anyone with their personal amber frequencies, and never told others about their excavation locations for fear of being ripped off by the competition.

But even if, by chance, someone did miss Newell and send a team in to search for her, there wouldn't be a problem. The amber-rez locator on the woman's sled no longer functioned. Not that anyone was likely to attempt a search-and-rescue operation. Who would give a damn about a lost ruin rat?

He left his sled in the green quartz chamber where he always stored it and headed for the surface as swiftly as possible. He was really on fire this time. He had been forced to use the blue stuff. The afterburn was tearing through him in hot, thrilling waves.

He had to find a woman before the crash came. He couldn't have *her,* not yet at any rate, and the other one was out of town.

He would have to make do with a street whore, he thought, climbing swiftly up the steps to ground level.

He found just what he was looking for a short time later in a twisted little lane. She was a cheap-looking blonde in a skimpy red dress, huddled in a dimly lit doorway, pulling on a synch-smoke cigarette.

He was desperately thankful for the fog, which was so heavy now that even if someone noticed him talking to the woman, he could not possibly be identified from a distance.

With a supreme effort of will he managed to summon enough control to conceal the feverish lust beneath his public mask. It wasn't easy.

"You look cold," he said, walking toward her.

She lowered the cigarette and gave him a professional perusal.

"You want to warm me up, handsome?" she asked.

"It would be my pleasure."

"It'll cost you seventy-five bucks. Cash up front."

He reached into his pocket for a small packet. "Got something better than money."

She took the packet, opened it, and inhaled gently. In the pale light of the vestibule he could see the sudden anticipation that animated her once-beautiful features.

"The chant will cover it, all right." She rose and opened the door. "What do you say we go upstairs to my place?"

"I'm in a hurry," he said, following her

through the doorway.

"I know. They all are."

He barely made it back to his hiding place before he collapsed. The effects of the bad afterburn made him feel like a vampire. After the initial euphoric rush of heated lust came the inevitable crash into a deep, heavy slumber that could not be denied.

When he awoke the next morning, he reached for his journal. It was time to make another modification in the elaborately detailed plan he had constructed several months ago.

But first he made a careful note of the two recent deaths. He put a little question mark beside Bertha Newell's name because, although he was certain that she would not make it out of the catacombs alive, he had not actually seen the body. He liked to be precise.

He had no doubts about the fate of the hooker, however. The dose of chant that he had given her had been especially prepared by the chemist to be used in case of just such an emergency. No one could have survived it.

Chapter 6

Elly rezzed in the code of the high-tech lock that Bertha had installed on the concealed steel door. There was a faint snick of sound as it released.

"I'll get it." Cooper shifted the flashlight to his left hand, grasped the heavy handle with his right, and pulled the door inward. The hinges groaned. "This thing is old. Looks like it might be Early Colonial."

"My rat hole dates from Colonial days, too," she said. "All the buildings on Ruin Lane were put up around the same time."

They went through the steel door and down another long flight of steps. At the bottom a familiar green glow rimmed a jagged opening in the green quartz wall of the tunnel.

Elly knew that nothing human had created the rips and tears in the nearly indestructible green quartz. Some experts assumed that the openings had been made by the aliens themselves, using the same machines that they had used to construct the catacombs. The other theory was that at some point in the planet's past, massive earthquakes had done the damage.

An invisible current of psi energy flowed out of the opening. It whispered across all of her senses. On her shoulder, Rose stiffened with anticipation.

Cooper examined her curiously in the emerald light. "You can feel it, too?" he asked. He sounded surprised.

"Of course. I can sense psi power when there's a lot of it around," she said briskly. "Most people can. Why do you think the Old Quarters of the cities have all the most popular nightclubs, casinos, and restaurants? Tourists love the little buzz they get from psi energy."

"Is that how it feels to you? Like a little buzz?"

"No," she said, reaching into her tote for an amber compass. "If you want to know the truth, it feels like I'm looking through a dark mirror. I can sense shapes and shadows moving on the other side, but I can't quite see them. It's frustrating. That's one of the reasons I haven't used my own hole-in-the-wall very much. I've gone into the tunnels a few times with my friend, Doreen, but that's about it."

"You never talked about what it was like not having the same kind of strong parapsych profile that everyone else in your family has."

"There were a lot of things you and I never discussed, Cooper." She started toward the rip in the wall.

"I'll go first." Cooper eased her aside and moved through the opening ahead of her.

Typical hunter, she mused. Get one underground, and he immediately took charge. Then again, that's what they were all trained to do, she reflected. The safety of the exploration and excavation teams depended on the strong-willed hunters who, in an emergency, could deal with the impressive egos and the research fever that often overtook the academics they were hired to protect.

She followed Cooper into the dimly lit green hallway.

Cooper contemplated the seemingly endless corridor that stretched out in front of them, assessing the multitude of vaulted openings and branching passageways.

"Let me see that frequency number that your friend gave you," he said, drawing a small, palm-sized amber-rez locator out of his pocket.

No hunter worth his amber went anywhere without an amber compass and an amber-rez locator, Elly thought wryly. Her father and brothers even carried them when they dressed for formal occasions.

She handed the slip of paper to him and waited while he coded the frequency of Bertha's utility sled into the device.

"I'm not getting anything," he said, frowning. "Are you sure about the frequency?"

"Yes. But maybe the sled's locator was disabled for some reason." She rummaged in her tote. "Bertha also gave me the code for her personal amber."

"Let's try that."

She read the second frequency number to him.

He entered it and nodded once, looking satisfied.

"Got a fix," he said. "Not too far away."

"Thank goodness."

"Let's go."

He went forward, all business now, moving so quickly that Elly had to hurry to catch up with him.

The jagged opening in the wall behind them vanished after they made the first turn. Elly looked back over her shoulder, startled, as she always was when she went underground, to realize how quickly the catacombs became a disorienting maze. The softly glowing labyrinth distorted all sense of direction. Even though they had only traveled a short distance, the odds were good that, without amber, they would never be able to find their way back to Bertha's cellar or any other exit for that matter.

In spite of the stimulation of the psi energy that emanated from the tunnel walls, a shiver tightened the skin along her spine.

"Whenever I get a chance to come down here, the experience always makes me think about that children's book, *The Adventures of Alice in Amberland*," she confided.

Cooper checked his compass and turned a corner. "Never read it."

"You're kidding. It's a classic. It's supposed to be based on an old Earth story. It's about a little girl who falls down a dust bunny hole and winds up having lots of adventures in the catacombs. Didn't your mother read the book to you when you were a boy?"

He turned another corner. "Maybe that was the year she read me Nishikawa's *A History of the Closing of the Curtain*."

"No offense, but that's one of the biggest, dullest books ever written. Not exactly childhood reading material."

"I liked it." He led the way into a long, curving corridor. "But then I'm a Guild librarian, remember? History is my thing."

"Once upon a time you were a librarian," she said coolly. "Now you are a Guild boss. And I'd sure like to know how you made that jump, by the way."

"You know how I got the job. Your father and the other members of the Council elected me to the position."

"I've never, ever heard of a Guild librarian getting promoted into the executive office."

"First time for everything. If you had such a big problem with my promotion, why did you agree to become engaged to me?"

"Because we had already started dating, and I thought I knew you well enough to take the risk."

He turned his head to look at her. "Are you sure it wasn't because your parents and everyone else in your clan pressured you into agreeing?"

She was temporarily shocked speechless. It took her nearly three full seconds to find her tongue.

"Don't be ridiculous," she snapped.

He shrugged. "You said, yourself, that high-ranking Guild marriages are usually arranged for reasons of politics and connections. Having a daughter enter into a Covenant Marriage with a Guild boss would be considered a good move by most clans."

"I'm not saying my family wasn't wildly enthusiastic about the idea of the two of us marrying, but if all they cared about was having an alliance with the head of the Guild, they would have pushed me to accept a date with your predecessor."

That got his sudden and complete attention. "Haggerty wanted to date you?"

"I think he was angling for a Covenant Marriage, if you want to know the truth. After his last Marriage of Convenience expired he made it clear that he was looking for a permanent replacement and that he considered me an excellent option."

"Your father didn't go for it?"

"No, and neither did anyone else in the family. But most of all, I wasn't interested."

"Mind if I ask why? Haggerty was the right age. Old Guild family. Strong pararez. Well educated. Polished." He hesitated. "I was under the impression that women liked him."

She grimaced. "And he liked women."

"That's a bad thing?"

"It wouldn't have been if he'd had anything resembling a moral compass. But it was no secret that Haggerty was a dreadful womanizer. In the five years that he was in charge of the Guild, he contracted three Marriages of Convenience, each with a different woman. Heaven only knows how many mistresses and lovers he had on the side." She shuddered. "He was definitely not what my family or I considered good husband material."

"Huh."

"You seem to be having a small problem processing that data," she observed. "Did you really think that the only reason I agreed to get engaged to you was because my family was putting pressure on me?"

"After you left town," he said quietly, "I wondered."

"Well, stop wondering. I agreed to the engagement because, for a while, I thought we were meant for each other."

"But you changed your mind."

"Only after I realized that the Guild would always come first for you."

"Tell me," he said, "does it ever occur to you that you might have gotten the wrong impression about me?"

"You clarified whatever false impression I might have had the day you told me why you fought that duel with Palmer Frazier."

"About that duel —"

"Forget it. Old history. Let's change the subject. Speaking of dedicated Guild men, do you ever wonder what really happened to Haggerty?"

He glanced at her, frowning. "What do you mean? Everyone knows that he went down into the catacombs, had a heart attack, and died."

"Oh, sure, that's the official story." She gave a dainty little snort. "But between you and me, I've got another theory."

"Yeah? What do you think happened to him?"

"It occurred to me at the time that he might have been done in by one of his mistresses or an ex-wife," she said, warming to her personal conspiracy theory. "That possibility makes a lot more sense, if you ask me. Because up until then, Haggerty appeared to be in excellent health."

"They say that the first warning of heart trouble is often a heart attack."

"I know, but I'm still convinced that Haggerty didn't die of natural causes."

"Where in green hell did you get the notion that he was murdered by an ex-wife or a mistress?"

"Came up with it all on my own," she said, not without some pride.

He stopped in the middle of the glowing hallway, caught her by the arm, and turned her so that she had to meet his eyes.

"Just how well did you know Haggerty?"

"I told you, he tried to put some pressure

on my family to contract a Covenant Marriage."

"That doesn't answer my question."

She shrugged. "We met at several Guild functions. Talked a few times. He thought he could charm me the way he did all of his other female conquests. He made a pass. I told him in no uncertain terms to keep his hands to himself and that I was definitely not interested in marrying him. That was the end of the matter."

"Haggerty made a pass?"

"Yes. I never mentioned the incident to Dad because I was afraid he might confront Haggerty about it. Besides, as I keep pointing out to everyone who will listen, I'm quite capable of dealing with men who only want to marry me because of my Guild connections."

"Damn," he said very softly. "I never heard about that."

"There's no reason you would have heard about it. You weren't even living in Aurora Springs at the time. You didn't move there until a month or so before Haggerty died." She frowned. "Try to stay focused here, Cooper. We're looking for Bertha."

He exhaled deeply. She got the feeling he was exerting himself to exercise some serious self-control. He started forward again with long, impatient strides.

"One more thing about Haggerty before we leave the subject," he added.

She had to jog a little to catch up with him. "What about him?"

"That theory of yours? About how he might have been murdered?"

"What of it?"

"Keep it to yourself," he said.

The mag-steel that resonated in the words startled her. It wasn't a suggestion, she thought. Mr. Guild Boss had just issued an order.

Hmm. Now this was an interesting development.

She was trying to think of a clever way to question him further when she heard a low rumble of warning in her left ear.

"Rose?" She turned her head quickly to look at the dust bunny.

Rose was no longer a ragged ball of dryer lint. She had gone sleek and wiry again, showing all four eyes, six paws, and wickedly sharp teeth. Her attention was fixed on the upcoming intersection.

Elly opened her mouth to warn Cooper but saw that he had already halted in midstride. He, too, was focused on whatever lay around the corner. The prowling tension in him was unsettlingly akin to what she sensed emanating from Rose.

A couple of battle-ready predators, she thought.

She studied the intersection. It was similar to several they had already passed through. The entrances to five glowing green corridors branched off from a circular point.

"What is it?" she asked.

"Ghost energy." Cooper said. "A lot of it. Stay behind me."

She sighed. "Here we go again with the unnecessary orders. Don't worry. I know the drill. I won't do anything stupid."

"Good plan."

Without warning Rose sprang from her shoulder onto Cooper's.

"What the — ?" Cooper began, then he smiled, showing a few teeth of his own. "Okay, gorgeous, I don't mind having backup for this one."

Cooper went forward, Rose on his shoulder.

"Be careful, you two," Elly called.

She trailed a respectful distance behind the pair, but she wasn't unduly concerned for their safety. If anyone could handle a catacomb ghost, it was the very powerful chief of the Aurora Springs Guild. Her real worry was that the UDEM up ahead would turn out to be the reason why Bertha had not made it back out of the tunnels.

When he reached the point where the five other corridors came together, Cooper turned into the nearest without any hesitation. She followed with appropriate caution.

Cooper stopped so suddenly that Rose had to use all six paws to keep her perch.

"What is it?" Elly asked.

"Got a problem," Cooper said softly, looking into the tunnel.

She reached the circular intersection and turned to see whatever it was that had riveted him.

She sensed the new psi energy before she saw the source.

For a few seconds the only thing that registered was the wrongness of the light flooding the passageway. Cooper and Rose were bathed in the odd, pulsating glow. It wasn't the familiar acid green that she associated with ghost energy and the quartz walls. Instead it was an eerie, unnatural blue that produced a deeply disturbing effect on her senses.

Was this what vertigo felt like? she wondered.

She was looking into a whirling vortex of energy. It was like gazing into the heart of a tornado or a water spout.

The vortex appeared to have opened in the floor. It spiraled downward to an invisible vanishing point. Lightning sparked. The angry, seething light swirled in a wide pool of dissonance energy waves that completely covered the floor of the wide tunnel, wall to wall.

Aside from the occasional crackle of the miniature lightning strikes, the blue tornado made no audible sound. But Elly's psi senses were rattling and shaking like windowpanes in a violent storm.

"What's wrong with the floor?" she asked, dumbfounded.

"Blue ghost," Cooper said.

"No." She shook her head, uncomprehending. "It can't be. There is no such thing. Blue ghosts are just old hunters' tales. Everyone knows that."

But it was definitely a form of dissonance energy, she thought. There was no mistaking the wild, flaring power.

"Is that your friend's sled?" Cooper asked.

She managed to jerk her gaze off the vortex and spotted the familiar shape of Bertha's aging utility sled. It was perched on the far rim of the pulsing, rippling vortex. The energy storm lapped at one rear wheel, as though trying to suck it down into the heart of the whirlwind.

There was no sign of Bertha.

"Dear heaven," Elly whispered. Horror threatened to close her throat. "That ghost got her. No one could survive a close brush with that thing. But where's the body? *There's no body.*"

Chapter 7

Cooper looked at Elly's horrified face. In the pulsing blue light she looked a little like a ghost, herself, the old-fashioned, supernatural kind.

"Don't panic on me," he said, automatically falling back on the tone of icy command that he had learned to use in the days when he had worked the catacombs as a hunter. "Save the hysterics for later. We don't have time for them now."

"I am not panicking," she snapped, irritated. "I'm worried sick about what has happened to Bertha. There's a difference."

The cold anger in her voice reassured him. "Good to know. All right, there's not much option here. I'm going to de-rez this thing. Then we'll look for Bertha."

Elly's eyes widened. "You can handle this monster?"

"Yes."

"Wow. Okay, I'm impressed, Mr. Guild Boss."

He was privately amazed that she had accepted his statement as fact. In her shoes, a lot of people would have refused to believe his claim.

"Cooper?"

He studied the blue ghost, probing carefully for the patterns. "Yeah?"

"Do you . . . do you think that blue UDEM somehow swallowed up Bertha and . . . and *incinerated* her?"

"Ghost energy doesn't burn hot enough to destroy flesh and bone. It can scorch and singe, but that's about the limit. Mostly it fries the psi senses. You know that as well as I do."

"But this is a *blue* ghost. No one knows much about them. They're not even supposed to exist."

"Let me get rid of it, and then we'll see what we've got." He lifted Rose down off his shoulder and handed the dust bunny to her. "Here, take gorgeous. Things might get a little tricky here. I don't want her to get caught in the backwash."

"No." She took Rose, cradling her protectively in her arms.

"Go stand in one of the other tunnels," Cooper added. "It will give you some protection in case things get out of hand."

She obeyed, retreating to the cover of a vaulted passageway.

When he decided she was safely out of the

reach of the blue storm, he went to work, using his psi senses to snag ambient blue dissonance energy out of the air.

The stuff was invisible to the eye at first, but as he forced it to coalesce into a tight, flaring ball, it took on a blue hue.

He manipulated it into a vortex. For some reason, that was the way blue ghost fire came together most naturally. He adjusted the dissonance wave patterns, emphasizing those that resonated in opposition to the patterns of the one that swirled on the floor.

The level of psi power in the confined space rose swiftly. He had to concentrate harder and harder to keep it contained. If it escaped his control, the fierce waves of energy would swamp not only his senses but possibly reach as far as where Elly waited, partially sheltered.

When he had achieved the shade and patterns that he needed, he began the process of merging his ghost with the blue vortex that blocked the corridor.

This was the most dangerous part of the process. The idea was to use his ghost to cancel out the energy patterns of the one on the floor. A mistake could easily result in an explosion that would send violent waves of psi power splashing outward, swamping his senses.

There was so much flaring light in the passage now that it was difficult to see. He squinted against the glare. *Should have brought along a pair of dark glasses,* he thought. He'd have to remember that the next time he went out on a date with Elly. His new motto was *be prepared.*

The two ghosts came together in a senses-jarring flare of light and energy.

The flames winked out with a suddenness that was disorienting.

"It's gone," Elly whispered. "That was absolutely amazing."

"You okay?" he asked.

"Yes. Rose and I are fine." She moved quickly toward him. "What about you?"

"I'm all right." *For a while,* he thought. *And then I'm going to be in real trouble. Got to get out of here before the burn-and-crash hits me.*

He did another quick frequency check. "According to this, we're almost on top of your friend."

"But she's nowhere in sight. There's only the sled."

"At least we now know why its frequency didn't resonate on the locator. The blue ghost fried it." He looked around. "We've got fifteen minutes, no longer. After that, we have to start back toward our entry point."

Elly looked at him with sudden concern. "You melted amber to deal with that blue ghost?"

"Yes."

Tuned amber didn't physically melt when you pushed an unusual amount of power through it, but if it was overworked, the stuff lost much of its ability to sustain an intense, highly concentrated psi focus.

He went forward quickly, watching the readout on the locator. When he passed a narrow doorway he got a sharp ping.

He stopped and looked into the room. Like all of the myriad rooms that branched off the endless corridors, the proportions felt a little off, not quite human. This particular chamber was too high and too narrow. The angles where the walls met didn't look right.

The motionless figure of a woman lay sprawled on the glowing floor. She was somewhat past middle age, dressed in a long-sleeved sweater, overalls, and sturdy boots. She had a stocking cap pulled down over her short, gray hair.

"Here she is," he said. He went into the room and crouched beside the still form to check for a pulse. "She's alive."

"Thank God." Elly rushed across the room. *"Bertha."* She went down on her knees. "She's unconscious."

"Not surprising. Probably got brushed by that blue before she made it into this room. Lucky the burn didn't kill her."

"She didn't get fried, or at least that wasn't her only problem." Elly gently touched the stocking cap that covered Bertha's head. "Look. It's wet with blood. She must have hit her head when she fell. We've got to get her out of here."

He checked his watch. Time was slipping away fast.

"We'll use her sled," he said. He paused at the doorway and met her eyes. "One more thing. Very important."

"What's that?"

"When she wakes up, she probably won't have any clear memory of what happened just before she hit her head. And if she did get brushed by that ghost, it's a sure bet she'll have a case of amnesia that will wipe out the events of the past several hours."

"I know. So?"

"So we're going to tell her that she had an encounter with a ghost. But we're not going to tell her it was a blue. Let her think it was a routine UDEM."

Elly got slowly to her feet. "She probably wouldn't believe she ran into a blue, anyway."

"Something else," he added quietly.

"What's that?"

"It's okay to tell her that I'm from Aurora Springs, but I don't want her to know about my connection to the Aurora Springs Guild."

Elly wrinkled her nose. "It's not just a connection. You're the Guild boss."

"I don't want her or anyone else here in town to know who I am. From now on, I'm Cooper Jones."

"Why?" she asked.

"It's complicated."

"Let me guess," she said. "Guild business?"

"Yes."

"Gosh, what a stunning surprise."

He ignored that and went out into the hallway to get the utility vehicle. The blue was more than just routine Guild business. It was a potential public relations disaster, one that could threaten the future of all of the Guild organizations.

As far as the public was concerned, blues did not exist, and neither did hunters like him, who could de-rez them. Ever since their founding, the Guilds had gone to extraordinary lengths to keep the secrets of the blues buried deep in the archives. The effort had paid off. Over the years, the unusual blue ghosts and those who could summon them had receded into the realm of myth and legend.

There was a good reason for concealing the truth, he thought. People were inclined to get nervous when myths and legends came to life.

Chapter 8

Bertha stirred and opened her eyes. Elly exhaled a sigh of relief.

"Bertha, it's me, Elly. You're safe."

"Elly?" Bertha's voice was hoarse. Her gray eyes were dazed. "What are you doing here?"

"My friend, Cooper, and Rose and I came looking for you. You're okay. You had a brush with a ghost, and you must have hit your head when you went unconscious."

Bertha screwed up her face. "Can't remember . . ."

"Don't worry about it." Elly patted her shoulder. "You know how it is after an encounter. You'll be all right in a day or so. That's all that matters."

Cooper de-rezzed the engine and got off the vehicle. His face was hard and taut. "Let's get her into the sled."

"No problem," Bertha said, sitting up cautiously. She put a hand to her head. "Got a headache, but that's all that's wrong. Be right as tuned amber tomorrow."

Cooper helped her to her feet.

"I think you should go to the emergency room," Elly said.

"No," Bertha replied. "No doctors. I'm okay, I tell you. Got some supplies in the sled. Just need to clean up the mess and put a bandage on my head."

They got Bertha into the back of the sled. Elly climbed in beside her and opened the first-aid kit. She was relieved to see that Bertha's wound, although bloody, was not as bad as she had feared.

Cooper started to get into the driver's seat. She saw him hesitate, and then step down from the vehicle.

He walked swiftly to where the blue vortex had been whirling a few minutes earlier. She watched him lean down to pick up a small, narrow object that was lying on the floor. Sliding it into a pocket, he loped back to the sled.

Before she could ask him what he had found, he was rezzing the engine.

She could question him about whatever it was he had picked up some other time, she thought. Right now she had to focus on cleaning Bertha's wound.

Ten minutes later, sporting the bandage that Elly had applied over the disinfected wound, Bertha managed to stagger up out of the cellar and into the darkened back room of her shop. She swayed a little, but she stayed on her feet.

"Need to sleep it off," she mumbled, rubbing her temples with her thumbs.

"If you won't go to the ER, you're going to come home with me," Elly said firmly. "I'm not leaving you here by yourself tonight."

For a few seconds she thought Bertha would refuse.

"Okay, okay," Bertha finally grumbled.

Cooper rechecked his watch and then draped one of Bertha's arms over his shoulders.

"Let's go," he ordered, obviously still in full hunter-in-charge mode.

"Whatever," Bertha said groggily. "Just need some sleep."

"You and me, both," Cooper added.

Elly watched him with growing concern as he maneuvered Bertha outside into the alley and eased her into the front seat of the Spectrum. Elly had not one but two people who were in imminent danger of collapsing on her, she thought. She had to get them both back to her apartment as quickly as possible.

"I'll drive." She held out her hand, palm up.

"Not necessary," Cooper growled.

"You are in no shape, and you know it."

"Your shop's in the next block, right?"

"The keys, Cooper."

He looked annoyed, but displaying the decisive thinking that had no doubt been responsible for taking him all the way to the top of the Aurora Springs Guild, he handed her the keys.

"Be careful," he warned. "The car belongs to a known Guild boss who won't be happy if it gets dinged up."

"Yeah, I've heard those guys can be real touchy," Elly said.

She tossed the Spectrum keys into the air. Was she nonchalant in the face of danger, or what?

Unfortunately she missed the catch. The keys clanged on the paving stones.

"Oops," she mumbled.

Cooper watched her scoop up the keys.

"This will probably be interesting," he said.

She drove the powerful car very gingerly through the alley. The headlights penetrated only a few feet into the heavy fog. Every trash can was a major hazard.

She made it across the narrow street that separated the blocks and drove cautiously into the alley that ran behind her own shop.

She was sure she heard a deep sigh of relief when she stopped at the rear door of St. Clair's Herbal Emporium and de-rezzed the ignition.

"See?" she said, handing Cooper the keys. "No problem."

He pocketed the keys without comment. With Rose hunched on his shoulder, he climbed out of the backseat, opened the passenger door, and reached down to assist Bertha.

Elly de-rezzed the heavy new lock that she had recently installed and opened the back door of the shop. The familiar scents and a pleasant trickle of psi energy wafted over her, soothing and comforting all of her senses.

She rezzed the lights, revealing the ranks of herbs and flowers that hung upside down from the ceiling and filled an array of baskets.

"My apartment is on the floor above the shop," she said. "We need to get Bertha up those stairs."

Bertha grunted. "I'm not a total invalid here."

She grasped the handrail and trudged up the steps.

Elly left Cooper standing at the foot of the stairs while she piloted Bertha down a short hall into the darkened bedroom.

Bertha balked in the doorway, scowling ferociously at the neatly made bed.

"This is your room," she complained.

"Don't worry, I'll sleep on the sofa."

"Can't take your only bed."

"Yes, you can and you will," Elly said. "Please, Bertha, don't go into stubborn mode on me tonight."

"Can't." Bertha lurched into the room and collapsed on top of the bed, eyes closing. "Feel like a building fell on top of me."

"I don't doubt it." Elly tugged off Bertha's heavy boots. "Do you remember anything at all about what happened?"

"Not much." Bertha rubbed the nape of her neck. "Can't think. Maybe in the morning."

"Do you feel nauseated?"

"No."

"How many fingers am I holding up?"

Bertha peered at her hand. "One. G'night."

She started snoring.

Elly covered her with a spare blanket and left the bedroom, closing the door behind her. Patient number one was under control, she thought. Now to deal with patient number two.

Rose tumbled up the stairs and drifted into the kitchen in search of her food dish.

Elly went to the landing and looked down. Cooper was still standing at the foot of the staircase. It seemed to her that he was gripping the end of the banister much too tightly.

He watched her with stark, hot eyes. An unfamiliar tension radiated from him.

A chill of awareness swept through her. "Cooper?"

"Remember, don't tell her who I am."

"Yes, I know." She wrinkled her nose. "Guild business."

"Yeah, and it just got a lot more complicated."

"What's that supposed to mean?"

"I'll explain in the morning." The words sounded ragged around the edges. "Just wanted to make sure you understood how important it is that you don't tell her about the blue."

"I won't."

"I need to get out of here." He shoved himself away from the banister and started toward the door.

"I don't think so." She hurried down the stairs. "You're not in any shape to drive, especially given the fog. You'll have to stay here tonight."

"Bad idea. I'll be back in the morning."

"I'm not going to let you leave."

"Be okay." He kept walking toward the door.

"Like heck you will." She rushed past him and flung herself in front of the door, barring his path. "Stop right where you are. I mean it. You cannot possibly intend to drive that Spectrum anywhere tonight. You're a danger to yourself and others."

He blinked a couple of times and then nodded, reluctantly acknowledging the obvious.

"You're right. I'll sleep in it, instead," he said.

"You will do no such thing. This isn't the most dangerous neighborhood in the Old Quarter, but it isn't exactly Ruin View Drive with lots of private security patrols, either. One of the shops in this very block was broken into just a few days ago. Trust me, you do not want to sleep in the back of a car in that alley. That would be asking for trouble."

He shook his head. "Can't stay here."

"Look, we both know that you're going to crash big time after that energy burn. I've got a perfectly good sofa upstairs. Why not use it?"

His eyes went very, very blue. "Because

even though I'm going to crash in a little while, right now I'm burning up, that's why."

"You've got a fever?" Alarmed, she stepped forward and put her palm on his forehead. "Oh, dear, you do feel warm."

"Not that kind of fever. Get out of my way, Elly, I'm warning you."

He jerked away from her hand, moved around her, and yanked open the door.

"Warning me about what?" she asked, following him out onto the small back stoop.

He circled the Spectrum to open the door on the driver's side and paused to look at her over the roof of the vehicle. In the dim glow of the light above the doorway his face was an implacable mask.

"Remember what I told you earlier after I summoned that small ghost to take care of that mugger we ran into?" he said evenly. "About how I could handle the rush before the crash?"

"Yes."

"Well, that was true for routine ghosts. But this one was a blue."

"And you melted amber to deal with it," she whispered, comprehending at last. He was in a state of intense lust. And he was trying to protect her from himself.

He scrubbed his face with one hand. "As much as I hate to ruin my macho Guild boss image, I gotta tell you, it has been a very long eight months and five days. Not that I'm counting."

He slid into the driver's seat.

Eight months and five days. He *was* counting, Elly thought.

She felt her heart rate escalate.

"Cooper, wait."

She went down the steps, yanked open the passenger side door, got in beside him, and slammed the door shut.

"Cooper, are you saying you haven't dated anyone since I left Aurora Springs?"

He gazed straight ahead through the windshield. "Get out of the car, Elly, for both our sakes."

"Not until I know why you haven't slept with anyone in the past eight months and five days."

He turned, one arm stretching along the back of the seat of the car.

"I haven't wanted anyone else," he said. "Just you."

The fog closed in around the Spectrum. The close confines of the interior of the front seat seemed almost unbearably intimate.

Careful, Elly thought, *you're over-rezzed*

*yourself tonight. All that adrenaline earlier
and now the man who has been invading
your dreams for the past few months is
telling you he wants you.*

*And you want him. You've wanted him
from day one. That's why you seized the
excuse of knowing he was in town tonight
to track him down to ask for his help.*

"Cooper —"

"Get out of the car."

She ignored that. "I didn't think you felt
that way about me."

"You were wrong. Now, please, get the
hell out of the damn car."

Her blood fizzed in her veins. She felt
light-headed. Anticipation heated her insides. She touched the side of his stone-hard
face.

"I'd rather kiss you," she said, feeling
more daring than she had ever felt in her
entire life.

"Bad idea. If you kiss me, I can't promise
that I'll be able to stop."

"Who said anything about stopping?"

She leaned toward him and kissed him
lightly on the mouth.

For a fraction of an instant, Cooper went
utterly still. In the next heartbeat, he
claimed the kiss with a rough groan,
crushing her against the back of the pas-

senger seat. His mouth was fierce and hot and ruthless.

Energy — sexual, not psi — flashed inside the front seat of the Spectrum, engulfing her senses.

Cooper moved closer, pushing hard against her. Heat came off of his body in waves. His mouth shifted to her throat. She felt his hand glide up under her sweater. Somehow he got her bra undone. She could feel his fingers shaking a little. Or maybe she was the one who was trembling.

The next thing she knew, his thumb was scraping lightly over her nipple. She almost screamed at his touch. Her skin had never felt so incredibly sensitive.

"Cooper."

He raised his head to look down at her. He was breathing heavily.

"Did I hurt you?"

"No, *no.*"

Her head tipped back against the seat. She braced herself against the onslaught by clamping her hands on either side of his lean, solid chest. He was hot, so hot. And so was she.

He grabbed a fistful of her skirt and shoved the garment up to her waist. Her panties vanished in the next instant.

He propped her right foot on the dash,

opening her. His fingers stroked deep. She was suddenly aware that she was already very damp.

"Talk about melting amber," he whispered.

He moved in the shadows, turning them both so that he was the one sitting in the passenger seat. Somehow she was astride him.

She could no longer see anything at all through the Spectrum's windows. It wasn't just the thick mist outside that limited the view. The glass itself was seriously fogged on the inside.

So much heat. Exhilaration and urgency made her shiver in Cooper's arms.

His hand moved between her thighs. Everything inside her was growing tighter.

She reached down and unfastened his trousers. His rigid erection surged into her hand.

He gripped her hips, cupping her buttocks in the palms of his hands. Positioning her where he wanted her, he slowly, carefully eased her downward.

When she felt the size of him, her body tensed involuntarily against the sensual invasion. Her fingers clenched around his shoulders, and she froze.

"Open for me," he whispered, his voice

husky with need. "Got to be inside you. Waited so damn long."

She felt herself precariously balanced on the bright line between pain and pleasure.

"This may not work," she gasped.

He took one hand off her thigh and did something to the delicate, exquisitely sensitized little nubbin between her legs. Without warning her climax rolled through her, stealing her breath and her voice.

"It'll work," he said.

He took advantage of the delicious distraction that he had created to thrust deeply into her. Her body accepted him fully this time, thrilling to the intense sensation. Gloriously satisfying contractions throbbed through her.

Cooper uttered an exultant, half-muffled groan. His release roared through him in heavy, pounding waves that she could feel deep inside.

For a short eternity Elly could not envision anything of importance existing beyond the realm encompassed by the front seat of the car. Everything she needed was right here, she thought. She could live in the vehicle for the rest of her life so long as Cooper was with her.

Eventually it dawned on her that Cooper was no longer moving. The realization brought her back to full awareness with a start of anxiety.

"Cooper?"

His head was resting against the back of the seat. She could see that his eyes were closed. His breathing was steadying rapidly.

First the burn and then the crash, she reminded herself. She had to get him inside before he went out like a de-rezzed light. She eased herself away from him, wincing a little. Her entire lower body felt tender. The muscles of her inner thighs were jelly.

"Cooper?" She shook him, gently at first and then with more force. "Wake up, Guild Boss. We have to get you inside. I told you that you couldn't sleep out here in the alley tonight. It's just too dangerous."

"Huh?" His dark lashes lifted slightly. His sleepy smile was the essence of male satisfaction. "Can't remember the last time I had car sex. Going to have to do this more often."

"Out." She reached across him and pushed open the door. Chilly, damp air spilled into the vehicle. "Move, Boone. There's no way I can carry you."

"I'm fine right here." The words were slurred. He closed his eyes again.

"I'm not going to leave you out here, and that's final."

When that reminder elicited no response, she climbed awkwardly over him and got out of the car. Her sweater was still hiked up over her breasts. Hastily, she yanked it down.

The light over the back door of the shop barely reached the Spectrum. On the positive-rez side, she thought, if any of her neighbors were still up they might not notice her getting out of a strange car with her clothes in disarray and a near-unconscious man in the front seat. Not that folks here in the big city paid attention to that sort of thing, she assured herself. This wasn't a small town where everybody loved to gossip.

"You know," she said to no one in particular, "I never had problems like this back in Aurora Springs."

"Neither did I," Cooper mumbled.

"At least you're not completely asleep yet."

She leaned back inside the car, gripped his right arm, and tried to drag him bodily out of the vehicle.

"Out," she said in her sternest tones, trying to cut through the veil of heavy sleep that she knew was crashing through him. "Right now."

"Nag, nag, nag."

But Cooper rolled slowly out of the front seat and actually managed to stand on his own two feet, although he had to lean heavily on her and the car door to do so. It said a lot for his stamina that he was still able to move at all under his own steam in this condition, she thought.

She got him up the step and through the doorway. Rose tumbled toward her in an agitated manner.

"He's okay," she said. "At least, I think he is."

Cooper opened one eye. "That's it. I'm inside. I'm going back to sleep."

His knees buckled. She couldn't hold his weight, but she was able to control his collapse to the floor so that he did not hit anything important on the way down.

She went back outside to secure the Spectrum. Suddenly remembering her missing panties, she opened the passenger door and checked the front seat. The little triangle of red lace dangled off the gearshift. She snatched up the underwear and locked the car.

Cooper hadn't had an opportunity to hang a ghost on the license plate. She could only hope that the expensive vehicle would still be there in the morning.

She hurried back into the shop and rezzed

the new lock. Cooper was still sprawled, faceup, on the floor, eyes closed. He did not stir when she shoved a pillow under his head and covered him with a blanket.

When she was satisfied that she had done all she could, she de-rezzed the light, collected Rose, and climbed to the upper floor. A heady mix of weariness, astonishment, and nervy excitement hit her full force halfway up the stairs.

What had she just done?

She'd had sex with Cooper Boone, that was what she had done. In the front seat of his car, no less.

When she emerged from the bathroom a short time later, having showered and changed into a nightgown, she went into the kitchen. Rose was sitting on the windowsill next to the little vase that held the strange green flower.

Her mother had given her the vase. Evelyn St. Clair had found it years ago while working as a tangler para-archaeologist for a private exploration team.

There was no way of knowing if the small, gracefully shaped vessel had been intended to hold flowers, of course. As was the case with virtually all of the alien artifacts, its original purpose remained a mystery. But it worked very well as a vase. It also functioned as a dim and slightly eerie nightlight. Like all green quartz artifacts brought out of the catacombs, the stone emitted a faint, residual glow after dark.

Elly went to stand at the window. Rose sidled along the windowsill, getting closer to her hand. Taking the hint, she petted the dust bunny gently somewhere in the vicinity of the top of her head. Together they looked out at the view of the green-tinged fog.

"The thing I have to keep in mind here is that nothing that happened tonight can be considered normal," Elly said to Rose. "I definitely should not make any assumptions about the future based on what just occurred down there in the front seat of the Spectrum."

Rose rumbled softly. Elly couldn't tell if she was agreeing or not. Rose appeared to be a fairly worldly dust bunny. Nevertheless, it was unlikely that she understood much about the potential emotional ramifications of human passion.

"Melting amber always hits a hunter hard, you know," Elly explained. "And that was a for-real blue ghost that Cooper de-rezzed tonight. There's no knowing exactly how that kind of psi drain will affect him. It's quite possible that, come morning,

Cooper won't even remember having hot sex with me."

Rose made another vaguely comforting noise.

"Wouldn't be surprised if he wakes up with no recollection at all of what happened." Elly pondered that for a moment. "It would certainly make things simpler if he happened to develop a convenient case of amnesia regarding the events of the past half hour."

Rose sat up on her hind legs and playfully batted the stalk of the green flower, causing the bloom to bob lightly.

"The thing is, I'm not sure that I *want* him to forget. I'm certainly not going to be able to forget, and I'm afraid that is going to really, really complicate things."

Rose blinked her big blue eyes a couple of times and looked concerned in a dust bunny sort of way.

Elly reached out to cup the elegantly shaped, emerald flower. The velvety soft petals felt delightful against her skin. But that wasn't the only sensation she experienced when she was this close to the blossom. A frisson of unusual energy gently sparked her paranormal senses.

The sensation was not unfamiliar to her. Ever since she was a girl, she had been able to detect a delicate psi buzz from plants of all kinds. In her experience each species had a distinctive energy pattern in the same way that it had other distinctive characteristics such as fragrance and color and petal design.

The problem, of course, was that, as far as anyone knew, the flora of Harmony did not give off any psi energy, at least not in a wavelength that humans could detect with their para-senses or their high-tech gadgets. The fact that she could detect the resonating frequencies of plants made her different and, when it came to parapsych abilities, being different was not generally considered a good thing. The result was that her unusual talent had been kept a deep, dark family secret.

But because of her ability, she knew that there was something very unique and possibly extremely important about the strange green flower on her windowsill. Unfortunately, she knew of no one she could talk to about the matter. If she took the specimen to a botanical research lab and explained what was going on, the scientists and technicians would very likely refer her to a parapsych therapist for counseling.

"Let's go to bed, Rose."

Chapter 9

Cooper awoke to a world of exotic scents and the sound of footsteps overhead.

He opened his eyes and saw a mass of dried herbs and flowers hanging over him.

Rose sat on his chest, watching him with an expectant air. She wore a different bracelet around her neck this morning. He could see sparkly pink stones here and there in her lintlike fur.

"Hello, gorgeous. Do you have to go outside? Am I supposed to open the door? I'm not familiar with the personal habits of dust bunnies."

Rose skittered around in small circles and drifted down to the floor. She was either in high spirits or else she had to go outside in a real hurry.

"Okay, okay, give me a minute, here. Been a while since I slept off a ghost burn."

He sat up slowly, wincing a little, and climbed to his feet. The sight of his face reflected in a small mirror on the wall made him groan.

"I look like the kind of guy you'd expect

to meet in a dark alley at midnight," he said to Rose. "I need a shower." He rubbed the stubble of his morning beard. "I also need a razor. Let's go see if my car is still outside in the alley."

He opened the back door. Fog once again cloaked the Old Quarter, muffling street sounds and turning daylight into twilight.

The Spectrum was still in the alley, right where he had left it.

"Wheels and all," he said to Rose. "Neighborhood isn't as bad as Elly thinks it is."

Rose hovered on the threshold, showing no signs of wanting to go out.

"Don't ever say I didn't give you your chance," Cooper said.

He went down the step, opened the trunk, and removed the small overnight kit that he always carried. The duffel bag containing most of his clothes and travel supplies was in his hotel room where he had left it after checking in yesterday.

He closed the trunk and went back into the shop. Rose waited for him in the doorway. He scooped her up and made for the staircase.

When he reached the landing he followed the low murmur of voices and the tangy scent of freshly sliced oranges to the doorway of a small, cozy kitchen. He suddenly realized he was very hungry.

Elly didn't notice him immediately because she was leaning into the interior of the refrigerator, searching for something on one of the shelves. Her hair was pulled back into a ponytail. She wore a stretchy red pullover and a pair of sleek-fitting jeans that hugged the curves of her sweetly curved rear.

A hunger that had nothing to do with breakfast ripped through him.

Rose tumbled out of his arms and drifted across the room. She bounced up onto the windowsill and took up a position next to a green quartz vase that held a single flower.

Bertha hunkered over the table near the window, a mug in one beefy hand. It looked as though the bandage on her head had been replaced with a fresh one.

She saw him, gave him a quick once-over, and then nodded.

"You must be Cooper Jones," she said in her gravelly voice. "You sure look like a guy who melted amber in the past twenty-four hours. Elly, here, tells me I owe you. Thanks for hauling my ass out of the catacombs last night."

"No problem," Cooper said. "Not like Elly and I had anything better to do."

Bertha chuckled and gave him a knowing

wink. "Now that's a bald-faced lie if I ever heard one. Got a hunch you had other plans for the evening. Have to tell you, until this morning, I didn't know Elly had any serious boyfriends."

"For heaven's sake, I never implied that Cooper was a boyfriend." Elly straightened abruptly and closed the door of the refrigerator with great precision. "I said he was a friend."

"Right. Got it." Bertha's gray brows bounced up and down. She hid a smile behind her mug.

Elly swung around to face Cooper, a ripe orange in her hand.

"Good morning," he said.

She gave him the same bright, confident smile that she had used on him last night.

"How are you feeling?" she asked.

"Like I need a shower and a shave." He indicated his overnight kit. "Mind if I use your bathroom?"

"Help yourself," she said. "Bertha and I were just talking about last night. She can't recall much."

Bertha heaved a sigh. "Got a vague memory of driving my sled toward a new sector where I've been doing some excavating in the past few weeks. I remember feeling that something was wrong. You

158

never ignore that sensation when you're underground."

"No," Cooper agreed.

"But damned if I can recall what happened next."

"You have no memory of the ghost that zapped you?" Cooper asked.

"Nope." Bertha shook her head. "Elly tells me it was a big one, though. I've always heard that in the case of a major ghost burn you almost never remember exactly what happened."

"In your case, you also managed to hit your head," Elly added. "Between the blow and the burn, I doubt if you'll ever remember exactly what happened last night."

"Probably not," Bertha agreed. "Sure glad you two came along when you did."

"It was a good thing that you gave Elly the frequency of both your sled and your personal amber." Cooper propped one shoulder against the doorjamb and folded his arms. "She probably told you that the sled's amber-rez locator got fried by the ghost."

Bertha nodded. "Yep. Gonna be expensive to get it replaced, too. That sled is old. Parts are hard to get."

"You're sure you don't want me to take you to a doctor this morning?" Elly asked with a concerned frown.

"Hell, no," Bertha said fervently. "I'll be okay. Takes a lot more than a big, bad ghost to fry this old tangler. This special tea of yours is making me feel better by the minute. Like Cooper, here, mostly I need a bath."

"Are you sure you don't want to use my shower?" Elly asked.

"Thanks, but I'd rather go back to my own place to get cleaned up." Bertha looked down at her rumpled shirt and trousers. "I want to put on some fresh clothes." She scowled. "Damn, these overalls were brand-new. Now look at 'em. Little bloodstains all over the place."

"Scalp wounds tend to bleed a lot," Elly said.

"Probably have to throw them out. Real shame, too. Had all these pockets organized just the way I like 'em." She patted one of the pockets in question. "Huh."

"What?" Elly asked.

"There's something crunchy in this pocket. I don't recall putting anything in there." Bertha undid the flap and reached inside. "Well, I'll be. Don't remember picking this up."

Cooper watched her put a handful of plant residue on the table. "Looks like a bunch of dried weeds."

"Now, where in green blazes did I find that stuff?" Bertha shook her head, baffled. "And why did I save it?"

Elly put down the orange she had been about to slice. Cooper saw that her attention was riveted on the crumbly plant material.

She walked to the table and picked up a pinch of the dried leaves. She studied them for a long, considering moment.

"I'll have to check my collection of herbals to be certain, but I think these are dried psi-bright leaves."

"Never heard of psi-bright," Bertha said.

"It's a wild herb that is native to the tropical zones," Elly said. "It was discovered about a hundred years ago by botanists on the Second Tropical Expedition. It has some unusual pharmacological properties. For a while researchers thought it might prove useful in the treatment of certain types of parapsych disorders. But in the end the research was abandoned because it was extremely unpredictable as a drug."

She stopped talking and looked at Cooper.

"What's the matter?" he asked.

"According to the newspapers, the new drug on the streets, the one they call enchantment dust, or chant, is derived from psi-bright," she said slowly. "In fact, there was another overdose reported in the papers this morning."

She picked up the newspaper on the kitchen table and handed it to him without another word.

Cooper removed a black case from his pocket, opened it, and unfolded his glasses.

He studied the paper's masthead and saw that he was looking at a copy of the *Cadence Star.* The story of the overdose was front-page news.

Woman Found Dead
in Old Quarter

The body of Bonnie May Stevens was discovered in her Old Quarter apartment at approximately two a.m. this morning. Her roommate, who declined to give her name, reported the death. Police records indicate that traces of a white powder were found near the deceased. A spokesman for the department said that an autopsy and an analysis of the powder would be done as soon as possible to determine the cause of death.

The roommate suggested to journalists that Stevens had a long history of drug use and prostitution. She added that Stevens appeared to have been badly beaten, perhaps by one of her clients, shortly before her death. "She was roughed up real bad," the roommate said. "I think somebody killed her."

Detective Grayson DeWitt, the head of the new Drug Task Force, will be in charge of the investigation into Stevens's death.

"We've taken a few of the biggest dealers off the streets in recent weeks," DeWitt told reporters. "But we're not going to stop until we nail the drug lord who is manufacturing and distributing the chant."

Anyone with information pertaining to the death of Stevens is urged to contact the Drug Task Force unit of the Cadence Police Department immediately.

A picture accompanied the article. It showed a lean, square-jawed man in his early thirties standing on the steps of the Cadence Police Department building. He looked so resolute and photogenic in a flashy, hand-tailored silver gray, pin-striped suit that Cooper assumed he was an anchor for one of the local television stations.

The caption informed him that the man in the picture was Detective Grayson DeWitt.

He lowered the paper, took off his glasses, and looked at Bertha. "You're sure you can't remember where you got this?"

Bertha shook her head. "Sorry. It's all a blank. I'll tell you one thing, though. Nothing I hate more than drug dealers."

"I think we're going to have to go with the theory that you discovered that psi-bright around the time you got fried by the ghost," Cooper said.

Elly watched him very intently. "You think Bertha stumbled into a drug ring, don't you? And someone tried to kill her."

"I think it's a very real possibility, yes," Cooper said.

Bertha's expression tightened in alarm. "If I take those herbs to the cops, they'll want to know where I found them. I can't tell them because I don't know. They might not even believe me without concrete proof. No one trusts ruin rats. That Detective DeWitt has made a lot of high-profile arrests lately. What if he decides to throw me in jail for the possession of psi-bright?"

"It's worse than that, I'm afraid," Cooper said quietly. "Whoever tried to silence you the first time will probably try again if he discovers that you made it back out of the catacombs."

"Ghost-shit." Bertha slumped in her chair. "What in green hell am I going to do?"

Alarmed by the change in the mood of the room, Rose tumbled off the windowsill and bounced onto the table. She nuzzled Bertha's big hand in a comforting manner.

"Don't worry, Bertha," Elly said. "It's going to be okay."

Bertha raised her head. "How do you know?"

"Because you're in good hands," Elly said calmly. "Cooper, here, will take care of everything."

Bertha straightened slowly. She turned her shrewd, seen-it-all eyes toward Cooper. "And just who are you, Cooper Jones, that you can take care of everything?"

"I hadn't planned on telling you, but under the circumstances, I think you should know," he said. "I'm the head of the Aurora Springs Guild. And I'd take it as a favor if you kept that information to yourself."

"Well, damn," Bertha said, brightening. "You mean this is Guild business?"

"Yes, ma'am," Cooper said.

"Then there's some hope at the end of

this damn tunnel, after all. What happens next?"

"I'm going to make a call," Cooper said.

Chapter 10

Within ten minutes a dark Coaster with heavily tinted windows pulled into the alley behind St. Clair's Herbal Emporium.

Cooper made another phone call to check the IDs of the two hunters inside and then bundled Bertha into the backseat.

"You'll be okay at the Guild safe house, Bertha," he said. "I'll let you know as soon as we've got this thing under control."

She nodded brusquely. "I appreciate this, Mr. Boone."

"Trust me, you're doing the Guild a favor by cooperating," he said.

"Yeah?" Bertha smiled slightly. "They say the Guild never forgets a favor."

"That's true. I don't want you making any phone calls, but if you remember anything that might be useful, let one of these gentlemen know. They can get the message to me."

"Sure, but I wouldn't be too hopeful, if I were you." Bertha heaved a sigh. "I'm not likely to ever remember what happened in the few minutes before the burn."

167

"You never know." Cooper stepped back and motioned to the driver. "Take good care of her," he said to the man. "Ms. Newell is a friend of the Guild."

"Yes, sir, we'll make sure she doesn't come to any harm." The man behind the wheel inclined his head. "By the way, Mr. Wyatt said to tell you welcome to Cadence."

"Thanks."

He waited until the big car had turned the corner at the end of the alley and vanished into the fog. Then he went back upstairs to Elly's small apartment and stopped in the kitchen doorway.

"Bertha's off to the safe house," he said. "She'll be fine."

"That's a relief." Elly paused in the act of squeezing an orange. "It's obvious she stumbled into something very nasty last night."

"I think so. By the way, I didn't see any other vehicles parked in the alley. Where's your car?"

"In a private garage at the end of this block. Those of us who have shops and apartments on Ruin Lane rent space there."

"I see. Think there's any room for the Spectrum?"

"No. There's a waiting list."

"Guess I'll just keep hanging ghosts on the license plate, in that case."

She searched his face. "You must be half starved. Hurry up and shower. I'll have breakfast waiting when you get out."

He nodded, started to turn, and then hesitated.

"Everything okay with you?" he asked, feeling his way.

"Certainly," she said, very brisk and matter-of-fact. "Why wouldn't it be?"

"Well," he said, "neither one of us is a teenager, anymore. Car sex can be strenuous for adults."

Her cheeks turned a hot shade of pink. She stopped squeezing the orange and faced him with both hands on her hips.

"I think you'd better take that shower," she said. "Right now."

"You thought I wouldn't remember, didn't you?" He studied her flushed cheeks. "No, you *hoped* I wouldn't remember."

She cleared her throat, picked up another orange, and got very busy with it. "What occurred in your car last night was an aberration. A complete anomaly. An abnormal reaction to a highly unusual and extremely stressful situation. I think it would be best if we both pretend it didn't happen, don't you?"

"Aberration? Anomaly? Abnormal?" He straightened out of the doorway and started toward her. "We're talking about the hottest sex I can recall having in years, probably in my whole life."

The stain in her cheeks deepened. "Really, Cooper?"

"Yes, really, Elly." He kept moving toward her. "You know, I promised myself I'd be a gentleman this morning. It occurred to me that you would probably be feeling a little shy after what happened between us. I wanted to demonstrate some respect for your delicate feelings. Didn't want you to think I was some kind of low-life hunter who got over-rezzed melting amber and used the most convenient female at hand to satisfy himself."

"I never thought that," she said quickly, taking a step back.

"You're sure?"

"I'm positive." She fluttered her hands at him in a warding-off gesture. "Look, there's no need to get upset about this. What happened last night was just one of those things. No harm, no foul."

"To you, maybe, but not to me." He closed the distance between them.

She took another step back, but the small space offered little room for retreat. She came up hard against the wall. "We can talk about this after you come out of the shower."

He leaned in close and flattened both hands on the wall on either side of her head, caging her.

"We're going to talk about it now," he said.

"There's nothing to discuss," she said, a little breathless. "I mean, car sex is all very nice, of course, but —"

"Very nice? That's all you can say about what went on downstairs in my car last night?"

Somehow, trapped as she was between him and the wall, she still managed to bristle. Her fine, lilting brows snapped together in a glowering frown.

"Well, it doesn't exactly imply a deep, meaningful relationship, now does it?" she said very evenly. "Especially when we both know that the impulse was artificially generated because you melted amber."

"Oh, no, you don't." He leaned closer. "You're not blaming this on me. What happened in that alley was not my fault. I tried to leave before things went too far. But you wouldn't let me go, remember? You wouldn't even let me have some privacy so that I could sleep off the afterburn in my own car."

"I was worried you might get mugged down in that alley."

"Guess what? I'm starting to think maybe I did get mugged. By an innocent-looking little herbalist who wanted to find out what it was like to have hot sex with a hunter after he'd melted amber."

"That's not true." She stared at him, appalled. "You know it isn't."

"You sure about that?"

"Of course, I'm sure." She folded her arms and narrowed her eyes. "I was there, if you will recall."

"Huh."

"And just what is that supposed to mean?" she demanded.

"If you didn't take advantage of me in my ghost-burned condition, are you, by any chance, implying that I took advantage of you?"

Her mouth tightened. "I never said that."

"Good. We've established that the encounter was consensual."

She cleared her throat. "I never said otherwise."

"Moving right along, let's go back to your earlier comment, the one about how our episode of hot car sex did not imply a meaningful relationship."

"I think you've pushed this far enough."

"Honey, I haven't even begun to push. What I want to know is, didn't last night mean anything at all to you?"

She got a haunted look. "I'm warning you . . ."

"Or is having car sex with ghost-burned hunters a casual, sophisticated form of entertainment for you now that you've moved to the big city?"

"You know damn well that isn't true!"

"So we can now state unequivocally that last night did have some meaning for you."

He knew he'd gone too far an instant before the outrage flashed across her face.

"Son of a bitch," she shrieked.

She moved so fast that he didn't even realize her intention until she had ducked under his left arm. By then it was too late. She had the pitcher of freshly squeezed orange juice in one hand and was upending it over his head.

He winced as the sticky juice drenched his face and chest and splashed onto the floor.

A shocked silence descended.

"Sorry," he said, wiping his face on the sleeve of his shirt. "You were right. I did push it a little too far."

"Why did you do it?" she whispered.

"Because last night meant something to

me, and I didn't want to think that it had been completely meaningless to you. You hurt my feelings, if you want to know the truth." He shrugged. "Go figure."

"I hurt your feelings?"

"Guild bosses have feelings, too."

She blinked. And then she started to giggle. The giggles turned into laughter. He watched, fascinated, as she wrapped her arms around herself and doubled over with the force of her mirth.

It had been over six months since he'd heard her laugh, he thought. He knew he'd missed it. He just hadn't realized how much until now.

"I don't believe it," she finally managed to get out.

"What? About Guild bosses having feelings?" he asked.

"No, that you managed to make me laugh about last night." She shook her head, smiling wryly as the laughter subsided. "Go take your shower, Guild Boss."

He looked down at the orange juice that saturated front of his shirt. "That would probably be a good idea. Too bad I don't have a change of clothes in my kit bag. Most of the stuff I brought with me is back in my hotel room."

He started toward the kitchen door.

"One question," she said a little too smoothly.

He paused and looked back at her. "Yeah?"

"Where did you learn to argue like that? You sounded a lot like a lawyer cross-examining a witness."

"I took some law classes when I attended Resonance City University."

She tilted her head slightly, letting him know he had surprised her.

"You wanted to be a lawyer?" she asked.

"No," he said, "I had other career plans. Figured some background in law would be good preparation."

"Really?" Curiosity lit her face. "Did you want to go into business or one of the professions? So few dissonance-energy para-rezzes ever look beyond ghost-hunting as a career. It's such a narrow field. No intellectual stimulation at all, really, and most hunters have to retire early when they start losing their edge. A lot of middle-aged hunters end up just sitting around the Guild Hall all day, collecting their pensions and swapping ghost stories."

"The profession has its moments."

"Why the law classes?"

"Like I said, figured it was good background for my future career."

"But you were a Guild archivist before you became a Guild boss."

"The history and information retrieval studies were part of the preparation, too."

"For what?" she asked blankly.

"From the time I was nine years old, the only thing I wanted to be when I grew up was boss of the Aurora Springs Guild."

She stood, unmoving. The last of the laughter faded from her expressive face.

"Good grief," she said, clearly stunned. "Most of the men who make it to the top of the Guilds rely on their natural para-rez talents, family connections, and a very wide streak of ruthless ambition. I've never heard of one actually *studying* to prepare himself for the job."

He gripped the edge of the doorway. "Something you should understand about me, Elly. Almost every move I've made and almost every step I've taken in my life has been designed with two goals in mind: to become a Guild boss and to keep the job for as long as I wanted it."

She tapped one crimson fingernail against the countertop. "I always knew the position was important to you. I just didn't realize how important."

"Something else you should know. I said *almost* every move and every step was designed to achieve those objectives. But there have been a couple of notable exceptions, one of which was what happened in the front seat of the Spectrum last night."

Her eyes widened.

He pushed himself out of the doorway before she could get her mouth closed and went down the hall to take a shower.

Chapter 11

Elly tossed the beaten eggs into the pan when she heard the door of the bathroom open. She was okay now, she assured herself. In the length of time it had taken him to shower and shave, she had cleaned up the spilled orange juice, organized breakfast, and gotten her emotions back under control.

His booted footsteps sounded softly in the hall. She was unable to suppress the little chill of excitement that swept through her. She was about to serve breakfast to Cooper Boone after a night of wild sexual abandon in his arms.

Don't get carried away here, she told herself, sprinkling fresh herbs onto the eggs, *that little scene in the Spectrum lasted just long enough for him to get your clothes off. We're talking at most maybe fifteen minutes, after which he went right to sleep. We are not talking about an entire night of passionate sexual abandon.*

In addition she must not forget that the fact that he had wanted to have hot sex with her while he was in the midst of a major burn-and-crash was not exactly a ringing testimonial to her seductive powers. Any man who had melted amber would have been in the mood for sex.

Cooper walked into the kitchen. She blinked.

"What now?" he asked.

"Your shirt."

"What about it?"

She cleared her throat. "You forgot to put it on."

He looked down at his naked chest. "It was soaked with orange juice, remember?"

"Oh. Right." She concentrated on stirring the eggs and tried not to think about the fact that she was going to serve breakfast to Cooper Boone and that he was naked from the waist up.

Rose chortled cheerfully, tumbled off the windowsill, and drifted across the floor to greet Cooper for the second time that morning.

"Hello, gorgeous." Cooper scooped her up and held her in one hand. "You'd think I'd been away for a week."

Elly moved the eggs off the heat. "Ready to eat?"

"Oh, yeah. I'm hungry enough to chew green quartz."

His body needed fuel after the heavy psi drain last night, she told herself. Good thing she had scrambled every last egg left in the carton.

"Back to your windowsill, gorgeous." Cooper set Rose down next to the vase and flower. He took a closer look at the green blossom. "Never saw a flower like this before," he remarked. "What's it called?"

She watched him covertly. Cooper was nothing if not a very powerful para-resonator. Was he picking up any trace of the psi buzz?

"I don't know," she admitted. "Rose started bringing them to me shortly after she moved in. I hunted through my reference books, but I couldn't find any flower matching its description. A few weeks ago I finally showed one to Stuart Griggs."

"Who is Griggs?"

"The florist who has the shop next to Bertha's place. I would have gone to him sooner, but he's not very friendly. Honestly, given his general attitude, I don't know how he manages to stay in business. At any rate, he said he didn't recognize the species, either. He suggested that it was probably an orchid hybrid of some kind."

"Odd shade of green," Cooper observed. "At first I thought it was an artificial flower carved out of imitation alien quartz."

He hadn't felt a thing, she thought, not even a tingle.

"No, it's a real flower," she said. "It will wither in a few days, just like the others. They seem to last a little longer if I keep them in that green quartz vase."

"So where is Rose getting them?"

"I've got a nasty feeling that she is filching them from someone's private hothouse. They're probably a local orchid grower's pride and joy. Those guys can be obsessive."

"Yeah?"

"Trust me, you don't want to mess with an orchid person. My biggest concern is that the grower might catch Rose in the act of swiping the flowers and take after her with a rake. You know, like in that children's story, *The Tale of Dickie Dust Bunny*?"

"Never read it."

"You can't have missed that one, too. Think back, Cooper. Little Dickie Dust Bunny's mother tells him that he mustn't go into Mr. McAmber's garden because his father had an accident there and ended up in a pie. But, naturally, little Dickie can't resist the idea, so he disobeys and goes into the garden."

"What happens?"

"He has all sorts of adventures, nearly gets caught, and barely makes it out alive. There are some very charming illustrations that accompany the story." She paused. "Does that resonate at all?"

He reflected briefly. "I remember Mom and Dad giving me an illustrated copy of Littleton's *Founders of the Harmonic Colonies* when I turned five. Does that count?"

She sighed. "Never mind."

Cooper scratched Rose in the general vicinity of her ears. "I wouldn't worry about Rose getting caught, if I were you. Got a hunch she's way too smart for that. Besides, who would want to eat dust bunny pie?"

Elly glared. "You know, you have a tendency to interpret things a bit too literally at times."

"I prefer to deal with facts, if that's what you mean," Cooper said. He lost interest in the flower and sat down at the table. "Speaking of which, we need to talk about this blue ghost situation."

"Right." She poured him a mug of her specially blended rez-root tea and carried it to the table. "We're talking Guild secrets here, aren't we?"

He took the mug from her hand. "Afraid so."

"Sheesh. And the Guilds wonder why they make mainstream society so nervous."

"The existence of blue ghosts has historically been one of the most closely guarded of all Guild secrets."

"Why?" She went back to the stove and spooned the creamy scrambled eggs onto a plate. "I admit it looked awfully scary, but you de-rezzed it successfully."

"The reason the Guilds don't want to go public with the truth about the blues is because they're not part of the natural landscape down in the catacombs."

"What do you mean?" She added toast to the plate and went back to the table. "I saw it, myself. It was a highly unusual ghost, but it was definitely a ghost."

"No wild blues have ever been encountered floating randomly through the tunnels. As far as anyone knows, it takes a human to pull blue ghost light." He took a swallow of the tea and lowered the mug. "Someone like me, for instance."

"That monster vortex was rezzed up by a person? A hunter?"

"Yes."

"You're sure of that?"

"Trust me." He picked up a fork and started in on the eggs with enthusiasm. "I'm sure."

She grappled briefly with that. "But we didn't see anyone else down there. Hunters, even strong ones, can't summon ghosts from any great distance. Besides, large, human-generated ghosts disintegrate very quickly once the hunter stops feeding it psi power through amber. Dissonance energy is inherently unstable."

"Some hunters can make ghosts hang around for quite a while, even after the hunter himself has left the scene."

"Oh, sure, small, simple ghosts, maybe, like the ones that you attach to your license plate to protect your car. But that's not what we're talking about here. That blue firestorm wasn't some uncomplicated little UDEM. It was very complex."

"How do you think I do that trick with the ghosts and the license plates?"

She shrugged. "I just assumed you could do it because you're a very strong para-rez. It's not that unusual. My dad and my brothers can pull off the same stunt."

"No hunter, not even a strong one, can make any kind of ghost stick unless he has a chunk of amber to anchor it."

She frowned. "So how do you attach one to your license plate?"

He smiled slightly. "I'll let you in on an old hunter secret. You install a chunk of amber behind the plate or under the fender of the vehicle. Once that's in place, any hunter who is strong enough can get a ghost to stick for a while."

She groaned. "To think that all these years I let my brothers convince me they were super macho para-rezzes because they could make dumb little ghosts stick to things like license plates or the canopy of my bed."

He paused, the fork halfway to his mouth. "They attached ghosts to your bed?"

"It only happened once. One night when I was nine I woke up and found a little UDEM hovering over my bed. Scared the you-know-what out of me. I was afraid to move. But I screamed bloody murder. Mom and Dad came running in, and Dad zapped the ghost."

"What about your brothers?"

She grinned. "Dad took all three of them down into the catacombs the next morning. When Logan, Matt, and Sam returned, they looked as if they'd all seen *real* ghosts. I got deeply sincere apologies from each of them. Suffice it to say I didn't wake up to any more ghosts." She returned to the counter and poured herself a mug of tea. "Let's get back to that blue vortex. How did the hunter who summoned it make it stick in the corridor? I didn't see any amber around it."

"You're forgetting the amber-rez directional locator in the dash of Bertha's sled."

"Oh, right."

"I'm betting the hunter knew the frequency. That's probably how he was able to chase her through the catacombs."

She sat down across from him and wrapped both hands around her mug. "He found the sled, but he didn't find Bertha."

"Probably didn't have the frequency of her personal amber."

"Thank goodness. She must have realized at some point that he was tracking her using the sled's amber. She abandoned the sled and managed to hide in a chamber until he was gone."

"I think so, yes."

"But if that's the case, how did she get the ghost-burn?"

"Maybe she waited until the hunter left and then tried to retrieve the sled. Blues are more volatile than greens. All she had to do was get a little too close to that vortex, and she would have been singed."

"After she got zapped she maintained consciousness long enough to crawl into the nearest chamber, and then she passed out."

"That's my take on it, yeah." Cooper munched some toast.

Elly exhaled deeply. "It fits with your theory that she stumbled into a drug-making operation."

"That's sure how it looks to me."

She leaned back in the chair and stretched her legs out under the table. "One thing I don't get here. Why have the Guilds been so anxious to keep the blues a secret all these years?"

He chased the last of the eggs around the plate with a piece of toast. "Two reasons. First, unlike greens, blues can be manipulated with far more precision and speed. Even a small one can be used to kill."

"They can be turned into weapons more easily than greens?"

"Not only that, a hunter who knows what he's doing can convert a blue vortex into a sort of psi-seeking missile that will home in on a specific piece of tuned amber."

"In other words, it combines the elements of a weapon with those of an amber-rez directional locator or a compass?"

He nodded. "You have to know the frequency of the target amber, but if you've got that —" He let the sentence end, unfinished.

"And last night, the amber in Bertha's sled was the target?"

"Looks like it."

She shuddered. "Okay, I can see where that information would make the general population a bit more nervous about hunters."

He drank some more tea and lowered the mug. "The good news is that blue energy is only effective underground in the catacombs. You can create some splashy fireworks with it aboveground if you're very strong and if you know what you're doing, but there's not enough of it up here to manipulate into a vortex, which is what's needed to turn it into a weapon."

"What's the other reason the Guilds have tried to keep blues hushed up?"

"Does the name Donovan Cork resonate?"

"The serial killer?" Startled, she set her mug down hard on the table. "The guy who used to lure women down into the catacombs and murder them? He could rez blues?"

"Yes. That's how he killed his victims. Death by blue looks a lot like a heart attack."

She frowned. "He murdered a number of prostitutes before they finally found his body in the tunnels. No one could figure out exactly how he had killed the women. They assumed it was some sort of fast-acting poison. As I recall, the authorities concluded that Cork, himself, had taken the poison when he feared that he was about to be arrested."

Cooper watched her over the rim of the mug. "How about Stewart Picton? Ever heard of him?"

"Well, of course. He's in all the history books. Forty years ago he set out to blackmail several members of the Federation Council. If they didn't pay off, he murdered them and their spouses. He was finally stopped but not before he had killed at least four people."

"J. Herbert Harris?"

"Another serial killer," she said. "Very famous case a couple of years ago. There were several best-selling true crime books written about him." She paused, frowning. "They found his body in the tunnels, too."

"There have been others over the years."

"Are you telling me that they were all hunters who could rez blue ghost energy?"

"Yes. Fortunately, most blue freaks are identified as problems early on and removed before they become notorious."

A small chill slipped down her spine. "Blue freaks? Is that what they're called?"

His mouth tightened at the corners. "Yes."

"So who removes these guys when they become problems?" she asked carefully.

"You know the old saying about how the Guild polices itself?"

She made a face. "Everyone knows that. Frankly, most people assume that's the Guild's way of avoiding having to deal with local law enforcement."

"The Guilds don't mind letting local cops take care of the run-of-the-mill criminals in the ranks. For the most part it's good for the image. Says we don't consider ourselves above the law."

"Not everyone believes that, but never mind. Go on."

"Image issues aside, the cops don't have the resources to track down and neutralize a rogue hunter who can pull blue ghost energy," Cooper said. "Even if they could track one through the tunnels, which is where guys like that tend to retreat if they're in danger of getting caught, they wouldn't have the firepower to bring him down. You know how it is down in the catacombs. Like most other high-tech devices, guns don't work well there."

"Okay, I think I see where you're going here. Let me guess; it takes a blue hunter to stop one of these blue freaks, right?"

"Yeah, that's pretty much what it comes

down to in the end."

"Wow." She propped her elbows on the table and cradled her chin on her hands. "Those guys must be the mysterious *enforcers* I used to hear my brothers whispering about from time to time."

"Enforcers?"

"That's what they called them. They would never tell me exactly what an enforcer did, of course. Big Guild secret, you know. Probably weren't exactly sure, themselves."

"I'd like to think that was the case," Cooper said dryly. "Only members of the Guild Councils are supposed to be aware of the blues and everything that goes with them. But now that I've learned how gossip runs through the Guild halls, I won't hold my breath."

"I told you once before: Never underestimate the power of rumor and gossip."

His jaw tightened. "Believe me, I haven't forgotten."

She got up and went back to the counter to pour herself another cup of tea. "So the Guilds have these secret enforcers to deal with blue freaks?"

"That is more or less the job description." He paused a beat. "The hunters who pursue that particular career path prefer the title of investigator, I believe. Enforcer sounds like a hit man."

She waved that aside. "I suppose the reason I haven't heard more gossip about the blues and the enforcers over the years is because we never had any problems of that sort in the Aurora Springs Guild. One of the advantages of being a small-town organization, no doubt. Lower crime rates."

"Got news for you." He watched her very steadily from the other side of the table, "The Aurora Springs Guild did have a problem with a blue freak a while back. He went into the murder-for-hire business. Sold his services for nearly a year quite successfully before someone on the Council realized what was going on. The freak was always careful to take contracts out of town in one of the big cities so as to lower the risk of drawing attention to himself at home."

"Are you serious?"

"I never joke about Guild business."

"True," she agreed. "Well? Who was he? You've told me this much, you have to tell me the rest."

He shrugged. "The freak was Haggerty."

"Haggerty?" She couldn't believe her ears. "Douglas Haggerty, the former Guild boss? Your predecessor?"

"Yes."

"That's amazing. He was the boss of the Aurora Springs Guild for over ten years. Good grief, the man made a pass. He wanted to *marry* me."

Cooper raised his brows. "Your father was the Council member who first became suspicious of him. That was one of the reasons John made sure Haggerty didn't get anywhere near you."

"Holy dust bunny." She whistled softly. "This is incredible. So that's the reason Haggerty disappeared, huh? The Council brought in one of those enforcers to get rid of him?"

"They voted to bring in an *investigator* who worked undercover for a while, figuring out exactly what was going on and gathering evidence."

"Undercover?" She shook her head. "Real cloak-and-dagger stuff, I guess."

"Well —"

"Who was the enforcer?" she asked. "Is he still hanging around the Guild Hall back in Aurora Springs, or did he ride off into the sunset after getting rid of the bad guy?"

"As a matter of fact, he's here in Cadence."

"What's he doing here?" she demanded. "Or is that top secret?"

"At the moment he's having breakfast.

Hoping for a second cup of tea."

She closed her eyes and sagged back against the counter. "You."

"Afraid so."

She opened her eyes and smiled wryly. "And to think that I mistook you for a genuine Guild librarian."

He got up abruptly, heading toward the kitchen counter. "I *was* a genuine Guild librarian. Still am, for that matter." He picked up the teapot. "Just because I'm now the chief exec of the Aurora Springs Guild doesn't change the past or my training."

She had managed to put a dent in his icy self-control with that last comment, she realized. He had not liked the implication that he had misled her.

"You just said you were an enforcer," she reminded him.

"Investigator." He splashed tea into his cup. "But since an investigator invariably has to do his work undercover, it means he has to have a real job that provides a legitimate cover."

"So you became a real librarian?"

"I like the work." He put the pot down on the hot plate. "I believe in learning from history. And the profession provided convenient camouflage for my investigations, regardless of the location. Every Guild has a historical archive. It never ceases to amaze me how people are inclined to underestimate folks who work with books and manuscripts."

"Well, I suppose your old job description isn't the issue any longer. You are now a Guild boss with a talent for raising blue ghosts. Last night we discovered that a blue freak tried to kill Bertha, presumably because she uncovered his drug operation. Obviously we have a situation here."

"Afraid so."

"What happens next?"

"I'm going to do some preliminary background work today. Then, tonight, you and I are going to dinner at the home of a friend of mine."

"You've got a friend here in town?" she asked.

"You don't have to look at me like that. Just because I'm a Guild boss doesn't mean I don't have friends."

"I didn't mean . . . oh, never mind." She raised her eyes to the ceiling and sighed. "What's the name of this friend?"

"Emmett London. He and his wife, Lydia, have a town house in another section of the Old Quarter."

"What?" She straightened. "We're invited to dinner at the home of *the* Mr. and

Mrs. Emmett London?"

He raised his brows. "Is that a problem?"

"They were all over the newspapers about three months back. Emmett London took over as Guild boss here in Cadence for a while when Mercer Wyatt was hospitalized."

Cooper looked amused. "I heard that."

She ignored the interruption. "Emmett and Lydia were local celebrities for a short time. The tabloids made a big deal out of their relationship. It was so romantic. And the wedding was spectacular. I saw the photographs in the papers. Lydia wore the most gorgeous gown."

"When the invitation was extended, I happened to mention Rose. I was told that you should feel free to bring her along."

"Really?"

"Evidently Lydia London also has dust bunnies."

"Good heavens," Elly said. "This is the first time Rose has been invited out for dinner. She'll probably spend hours choosing the right bracelet for the occasion."

Chapter 12

Shortly after eleven o'clock that morning, Elly saw the door of Thornton's Alien Antiquities open. Doreen Thornton, the proprietor, emerged. She was cutting-edge trendy, as usual, in a tight, tiny pink skirt and snug green sweater that showed off her hourglass figure to advantage. Fishnet stockings and pink-and-green heels finished the look.

Doreen's tight black curls framed pretty, dark-brown features and riveting dark eyes. She wore an amber pendant around her neck.

Elly knew that the amber in Doreen's pendant was genuine. The stone was of good quality and professionally tuned. Doreen had spent a lot of money on it.

Like Bertha, Doreen was an ephemeral-energy para-resonator, a tangler who could handle the dangerous illusion traps that peppered the catacombs. Like Bertha, she had never had the advantages of a college education and therefore had never qualified to join the exclusive Society of Para-

Archaeologists. Drawn to the world under-ground, as were so many with her type of parapsych abilities, she had chosen to eke out a living as a ruin rat.

It was either that or get a job as a cocktail waitress, she had explained to Elly.

Doreen had been one of the first on Ruin Lane to welcome Elly to the neighborhood. Elly had been grateful for both the friend-ship and the fashion advice. Until she met Doreen she had not realized how sadly un-stylish her Aurora Springs wardrobe was.

Doreen darted across the mist-bound street and opened the door of St. Clair's Herbal Emporium. The bell tinkled.

"Man, I don't think this fog is ever going to lift," she announced, closing the door. "I know this is the season for it, but I can't re-member the last time it hung around for so long. Not good for business, that's for sure."

"Tell me about it," Elly said, leaning on the counter. "I've only had two customers all morning."

Rose, crouched over her little box of bracelets at the end of the counter, chortled a greeting.

Doreen patted her affectionately. "You are looking fabulous today, my little fashionista." She peered more closely at the strand of green stones that sparkled in Rose's gray fur. "New bracelet?"

Rose preened.

"She helped herself to it out of my jewelry box this morning," Elly explained.

"Give the girl credit. She knows what looks good on her."

"Maybe, but at the rate things are going, I'm not going to have any bracelets left," Elly said.

"So take Rose shopping."

"I may have to do that. How was the visit to the parents?"

"The usual. Dad coughed up a small loan to help with the rent on the shop this month." Doreen made a face. "Had to listen to another lecture from my mom and my aunt on the subject of getting serious about a Covenant Marriage. I drove back here as fast as I could very early this morning."

Elly went to the hot plate and poured two mugs of the herbal tisane that she had made earlier. The aromatic blend of Harmonic honey, redstick spice, and amber root made a pleasant contrast to the damp, gray day.

"Did you tell them about the new boyfriend?" she asked, carrying the mugs back to the counter.

"No." Doreen picked up one of the mugs

and inhaled the fragrance with an air of delight. "Figured they would just start asking questions, and I really can't talk about him yet. I gave him my word that I would keep our relationship quiet until after he's finished with this new assignment."

"Must be hard dating a cop."

"The hours are weird, that's for sure." Doreen grinned. "Kind of exciting, though. He's such a hunk, and he sure doesn't dress like the average detective. The man has a sense of style like you would not believe."

"I can't wait to meet him."

"I'll introduce you as soon as he's off this current case. He says that until it's finished, he has to keep a very low profile, especially in the Old Quarter. He can't risk being seen by the bad guys. So, what's up with you? I heard you had a visitor last night."

Elly winced. "Word travels fast."

"Especially on Ruin Lane. I got the story from Phillip and Garrick first thing today. They said they saw a black Spectrum EX parked in the alley behind your shop last night and that it didn't leave until after eight this morning. Can you confirm or deny?"

"Uh-huh."

"I'll take that as a confirm." Doreen grinned. "Well?"

"There's not much to tell," Elly mumbled. "Just a friend from out of town. I let him stay overnight at my place. No big deal."

"How can you say that? He spent the whole night."

"Not in my bed," Elly said.

It was always nice to be able to tell the truth.

Chapter 13

Both the blue vortex and the utility sled were gone.

Impossible.

Shaken, the killer stared at the section of the catacombs where he had rezzed the blue and anchored it to the sled.

He checked his amber for the fifth or sixth time, wondering if he had taken a wrong turn somewhere in the catacombs on his way back to this place. But when he pulsed a little psi power through the navigational device he got the same reading. This was the precise spot where he had nailed Newell's sled.

There was no way the woman could have de-rezzed the blue. She was a tangler, not a hunter, let alone a blue hunter.

Nothing and no one could have destroyed the vortex except another dissonance-energy para-rez who could do what he could do with energy from the blue end of the spectrum. That kind of parapsych talent was so rare that it had become the stuff of myth and legend.

There was no escaping the obvious: Another blue had de-rezzed his vortex. Coincidences of this magnitude were even more scarce than hunters who could raise blue ghosts.

That damned blue freak, Cooper Boone, was in town. Somehow he had found Bertha Newell last night.

Chapter 14

"When it comes to barbecuing fish, the first rule is to make sure the grill is clean and well-oiled." Emmett London made an adjustment to one of the gleaming knobs on the giant outdoor grill. "That's what keeps the filets from sticking, falling apart, and dropping into the fire."

Cooper lounged against the deck railing, drink in hand, and surveyed the massive grill. Flames leaped and smoke roiled out across the deck, mingling with the fog.

"That thing is as big as a car," he said.

"Sure is," Emmett said, looking pleased. "Mercer Wyatt gave it to us for a wedding present. You should see the manual."

"Tricky to operate, huh?"

"It is more than merely tricky," Emmett said. "Grilling is an art, my friend, one that requires innate talent, practice, a passion for perfection, and the ability to work under pressure."

"I can see the problem with the pressure," Cooper said. He glanced at the three dust bunnies perched on the railing beside him.

The one introduced as Fuzz and his small companion, who went by the name of Ginger, wore little satin ribbons on top of their furry heads. Rose hovered next to them, glittering like a high-class showgirl in the green-stone bracelet she had selected to wear for the evening.

None of the bunnies had seemed surprised to see each other tonight. Cooper got the feeling they had all been previously acquainted. The fluffy beasts supervised the grilling process with close attention.

"In my admittedly limited experience, dust bunnies are big on barbecue," Emmett said. "Probably because they are not what you'd call vegetarians."

"How did you end up with two of the little guys?"

Emmett glanced at the bunnies wearing the bows. "One's a girl, I think. She's Fuzz's friend. He started inviting her to dinner a few weeks ago. Got a bad feeling I'm going to look under the bed one of these days and find a bunch of baby dust bunnies."

"You know, until I arrived here in Cadence yesterday and discovered that Elly was rooming with Rose, I never knew anyone who kept a dust bunny as a pet."

"Until you and Elly showed up with Rose tonight, my wife was the only person I knew who lived with one. Lydia once told me that it was Fuzz who initiated the association. Just appeared on her balcony one evening and made himself at home."

"Elly says that's how it was with Rose. Brings flowers every so often, and in exchange, she likes to wear Elly's bracelets."

"I'm not sure what's going on between Lydia and Fuzz, but I've got a hunch there's some kind of psychic bond."

"The experts say there's no such thing as a true psychic bond between animals and humans," Cooper reminded him.

"Tell that to Fuzz and Lydia."

Cooper smiled. He was enjoying the evening, in spite of the complications of the last twenty-four hours. He hadn't intended to have the blue ghost problem turn into a social visit with an old friend, but that was where the phone call to Mercer Wyatt, the chief of the Cadence Guild, had led.

If we're dealing with a blue," Wyatt said, *"we've got to keep a low profile. Whoever he is, he may be anywhere at or near the top of the organization. I don't think you and I should take the risk of being seen meeting to talk about the problem. This is a secure line, but we both know that there is no such thing as perfect security."*

"This is your town," Cooper said. *"How do*

you want to handle the situation?"

"I know you're not officially an enforcer any longer, but it's not like there're a lot of guys with your kind of talent I can call on. You know that as well as I do."

"Had a feeling you were going to say that."

"In addition, you've already got a jump on this thing because you were first on the scene last night," Wyatt added. "Will you do me a favor here and take care of the business?"

It never hurt to have the chief of one of the other Guilds in the position of owing you a favor, Cooper thought, but he wasn't in town to make nice with his opposite number in the Cadence City Guild. He'd had other plans.

Nevertheless, the freak had to be uncovered and dealt with as quickly as possible. Bad press of the kind that a criminally minded blue was capable of generating would be devastating for all of the Guilds, not just the Cadence organization.

"I'll look into it," Cooper said, reluctant but resigned.

"Emmett will be your contact. Now that he's no longer officially associated with the Guild, no one in the organization is paying any attention to him. With luck, that in-

cludes our blue freak. You two should be able to communicate without arousing any suspicions."

Emmett London was the former head of the Resonance City Guild. He had held the position for several years, during which he had made great strides toward transforming it into a legitimate, respected, damn near mainstream institution. Satisfied with what he had accomplished, he had stepped down from the position to pursue a career as a business consultant.

A few months back he had moved to Cadence, met and married Lydia Smith, and settled enthusiastically into domestic life.

Cooper envied him. Sure, there had been a few problems for Emmett along the way, small details like a couple of dead bodies and a murderous madman who had tried to become a dictator. But those distractions aside, Emmett's life looked very good.

The Londons' town house was in one of the newly renovated, upscale neighborhoods of the Old Quarter. From where he stood on the deck Cooper could see the dark expanse of a park and the fog-reflected green glow of the Dead City Wall.

After bringing drinks out to the men a short time earlier and declaring barbecuing to be men's work, Elly and Lydia had disappeared back into the warmly lit town house.

"Another thing to keep in mind with fish," Emmett said, making more adjustments to the grill's controls, "is that you don't want to go poking and prodding the filets with a spatula after you've got them on the fire. That way lies disaster."

"I'll try to remember that," Cooper said. "You know, I'm impressed. Never realized you knew how to barbecue."

"It's a skill you don't pick up until after you get married, settle down, and stop eating out in restaurants."

"Guess that explains it. I'm still eating in restaurants a lot."

"Meant to talk to you about that." Emmett moved upwind of the smoke. "You were supposed to be married by now. Had my tux all pressed and ready to wear to the wedding. What the hell happened?"

"Things got complicated."

"Women do tend to have that impact on a man's life," Emmett said, looking knowledgeable.

"I heard that," Lydia said loudly from the doorway.

She walked out onto the deck carrying a flat, rectangular glass dish that contained the fish. When she passed beneath the lamp, the light gleamed on her red hair.

Elly trailed a couple of steps behind her, a glass of wine in each hand.

Emmett smiled winningly at his wife. "But life would sure be boring without a few complications of the female sort," he said. "Isn't that right, Cooper?"

Cooper caught Elly's eye. She turned away very quickly and got very busy setting one of the wineglasses on the table.

"Right," he said.

Lydia smiled approvingly. "Just so you know."

Emmett gave her a quick, possessive kiss and took the dish from her. Lydia picked up the wineglass that Elly had placed on the table and took a sip.

"Pay attention, here," Emmett said to Cooper. "In spite of your recent little set-back, you may have need of this information someday. I don't give out my grilling secrets to just any visiting hunter who drops in for a free meal."

"I'm watching every move you make, London," Cooper said.

Elly looked thoughtful. "You two have known each other a long time, I gather?"

"Met a few years back when I was running the Resonance City Guild." Emmett examined the marinated fish with the air of a brain surgeon preparing to operate.

"Brought him in to handle a little problem we had at the time."

"Really?" Elly smiled benignly. "Would that have been a problem in your Archives Department, by any chance?"

"How did you guess?" Emmett said smoothly. "Never knew anyone who could whip an Archives Department into shape faster and with less bad press than Cooper, here." He looked at Cooper, spatula at the ready. "You ready to watch the master at work?"

"Not sure I'm up to this," Cooper said. "I tend to faint at the sight of blood."

"You know the old saying, the ghost that doesn't kill you makes you stronger." Emmett used the spatula to convey the fish onto the grill. "So, you got a plan to track down our blue freak?"

"Not sure you could call it a plan," Cooper said. "More like an extremely thin lead." He reached into the pocket of his shirt and removed the object he had retrieved from the floor near the scene of the blue vortex. He held it up so that they could all see it.

"Looks like a fancy swizzle stick," Lydia said, taking a closer look at the little plastic sword.

"It is," Cooper said. "Ever heard of a club

called The Road to the Ruins?"

Lydia looked interested. "That's your lead?"

Cooper looked at her. "It's all I've got at the moment. What do you know about it?"

"Well, for starters, The Road is the most exclusive nightclub and casino in town. It's located in the Old Quarter, right up against the wall. It's a private club with a special VIP entrance. If you don't have a pass, you have to stand in a long line with all the lesser beings and hope that the bouncers will eventually let you in. I admit that I can't give you any firsthand observations of the place, because Emmett tends to be extremely straitlaced about some things."

"I'm a married man," Emmett declared piously. "Married men don't join clubs like The Road to the Ruins unless they're doing deals with underworld figures or having torrid affairs with their best friends' wives."

"Excuses, excuses." Lydia exchanged a meaningful glance with Elly. "Beware. This is what happens after you get married. All of a sudden they want to stay home every night and grill fish instead of taking you out for a good time."

"I'll remember that," Elly said politely.

She sat down on a deck chair and crossed her legs. Cooper was suddenly keenly aware that the little violet-colored dress she was wearing was even shorter than the skirt she'd had on last night.

"They say the food is great," Lydia continued. "And I've heard the entertainment is first-rate, if a little on the raunchy side."

Cooper looked at Emmett and shook his head in a mockingly sorrowful manner. "And to think you never take your wife there."

"Call me boring." Emmett used the spatula to transfer the filets to the grill. "But I guarantee you, it isn't the kind of place you'd take the respectable daughter of a high-ranking member of the Aurora Springs Guild, either."

"I think he's talking about me," Elly said to Lydia.

Lydia nodded. "Yes, I did get that impression."

Emmett ignored both of them. "The owner is a guy named Ormond Ripley. Said to have discreet ties throughout the underworld and also in the political sphere. He's been smart enough and sufficiently well-connected to stay out of trouble with the law, which is saying something, given that he's operating a casino. Used to be a Guild man."

"I get the picture." Absently, Cooper

swirled what was left of his drink. "Now, all I have to do is find a way to get inside the club." He raised one brow at Emmett. "Got any suggestions?"

"Wyatt can pull some strings and get you in," Emmett said. "I'll give him a call in the morning."

Elly rezzed up a suspiciously bright smile. Cooper got a sinking feeling in the pit of his stomach.

"No need to call the local Guild boss," she said airily. "I go to The Road a lot. I know some people. I can get Cooper inside. We can go tonight, if you like."

Chapter 15

After dinner Cooper and Emmett went inside the house to put together a detailed plan for dealing with the blue freak.

Elly and Lydia stood at the edge of the deck and watched the men walk away, talking in low tones.

"Guild business," Lydia intoned darkly.

"Don't remind me," Elly said.

For a while they stood silently together, looked out over the mist-shrouded park. At the far end of the railing, Rose, Ginger, and Fuzz sat munching quietly on pretzels.

"Did you see the look on Cooper's face when I told him that I could get him into The Road?" Elly asked after a while.

Lydia laughed. "Priceless. Typical Guild-boss-caught-flatfooted expression."

"Doesn't happen often."

"Enjoy the moment."

"Thanks, I will."

Lydia tipped her head a little to one side. "Do you really know someone who can get you a pass into that club?"

"I have a couple of friends who have been

members for quite a while. They own a very successful antiques business on Ruin Lane. I blend special tisanes for both of them, and in return they've invited me to go with them to The Road a couple of times. I'm sure they'll let me borrow their pass tonight."

"Under other circumstances, it sounds like it would be a fun evening."

"Yes." Elly leaned her forearms on the railing and linked her fingers, absorbing the night. "I get the impression that Cooper is sort of stuck having to take care of this problem for the Cadence Guild."

"Emmett told me earlier that blue freaks don't come along very often. Neither do the unique kind of dissonance-energy pararezzes who can handle them."

"When you think about it, it's my fault Cooper got involved in the first place. If I hadn't asked him to help me find my friend in the tunnels last night, he would never have known about that blue vortex."

"Was it really as scary as Emmett and Cooper implied?" Lydia asked.

"I've never seen anything like it, that's for sure, and I've been into the catacombs on several occasions with my family. It looked spooky and very powerful, although I don't think I took it as seriously as I should have because Cooper was able to de-rez it so quickly."

"Emmett says he's good."

"I must admit, even though I was raised in a Guild family, I've always assumed that blues and enforcers were mostly hunter legends."

"Well, you're way ahead of me. I'd never even heard of blues or enforcers until today."

"Goes to show what a good job the Guilds have done keeping their secrets down the years."

"I know it isn't any of my business," Lydia said, "but Emmett told me earlier that you and Cooper had been engaged for a while. He said you called off the wedding."

"Yes."

"Let me guess, the job got in the way?"

Elly smiled sadly. "You're very astute."

"Not really. It's just that I've been there and done that. There was a time when I was worried sick that Emmett was going to become the permanent head of the Cadence City Guild. I wasn't sure if I could handle it. Luckily, it turned out that he didn't want the job."

"Unfortunately, Cooper does want the job," Elly said. "He's made it clear that being the head of the Aurora Springs Guild is very, very important to him."

"And you've decided you can't deal with being Mrs. Guild Boss?"

"When we first met I didn't know that he was even a candidate for the job." She unlinked her fingers and spread her hands. "I thought he was a librarian, for heaven's sake."

"A librarian?"

"He was brought in from out of town to organize the Aurora Springs Guild Archives. Or, at least, that's what everyone claimed. He has all kinds of degrees in history and archival research and information retrieval. But it turned out that the academic background, although genuine, was just cover for his real position as an enforcer."

"Ah."

There was a world of understanding in the simple exclamation.

Elly sighed. "Right after I started dating him, the old Guild boss, Haggerty, disappeared, and the next thing I knew the Council had appointed Cooper as the new chief. He asked me to marry him before I had a chance to adjust to the change in the situation."

"Got to watch out for those librarians," Lydia said.

"You can say that again. Well, to make a short story even shorter, I soon found out how important the job was to him. Cooper started showing up late for dates or even breaking them altogether at the last minute. He evaded any discussion that involved Guild business. It dawned on me that maybe the only reason he wanted to marry me was because of my family connections."

"Connections?"

"He doesn't have any of his own," Elly explained. "His people are all non-Guild. Very distinguished academic types for the most part. They don't even live in Aurora Springs."

"I see."

"I think Cooper also liked the fact that I was an instructor at Aurora Springs College. He wanted a wife who could give him some good contacts with respectable, mainstream institutions in the community."

"You're sure those are the only reasons he wanted to marry you?" Lydia asked.

Elly winced. "Yesterday he admitted that almost every move he's ever made in his life since the age of nine was aimed at establishing himself as the head of the Aurora Springs Guild."

"Why?"

Elly hesitated. "You know, I haven't

asked him that question. I've been too busy being offended by the glaring possibility that he saw me as just another step to his ultimate goal."

"Well, I can't blame you for not wanting to be a stepping-stone."

"For a while, after I found out he was going to be made the head of the Guild, I was able to convince myself that we could still have a good marriage. Dad kept going on and on about how Cooper was the new, younger face of the Guild, a leader who would guide the organization into the future. I certainly believe that mainstreaming is a worthy goal. I told myself that I could be a partner in the effort, blah, blah, blah."

"Blah, blah, blah." Lydia nodded. "I know exactly what you mean."

"Give me a break, I was falling in love with the man, and you know how it is. You can talk yourself into just about anything when you think you're in love."

"True," Lydia said. "Been there and done that, too. So, what happened? Why did you decide it wasn't going to work after all?"

"I found out Cooper had engaged in a hunter duel."

Lydia groaned. "You've got my full sympathy on that issue. I can't believe that in this day and age supposedly smart, intelligent, well-educated Guild men still conduct occasional duels. It's such a stupid, immature way to settle matters."

"I couldn't agree more."

Lydia looked at her curiously. "What was the duel about?"

"Cooper challenged a member of the Aurora Springs Guild Council named Palmer Frazier. Palmer and I had dated for a while before Cooper and I got serious. According to the Aurora Springs tabloids and the rumors on the campus where I worked, I was the reason the duel was conducted."

"Two men fought a for real duel over you?" Lydia whipped around to face her, eyes wide and fascinated. "Oh, my gosh, that is so incredibly romantic."

"Not exactly."

"Okay, okay, so we agree that dueling is totally immature, retrograde, and outdated masculine behavior. But I gotta tell you, Elly, I've never before met any woman who actually had two men fight a full-blown ghost fire duel over her."

"Yes, well —"

"Come on, you have to admit it's just like something out of one of those old films in which the hunky hunter hero goes down into the catacombs to fry the bad guys and save the lady."

"Not quite," Elly said.

"What do you mean?"

"I'm going to tell you something I haven't told anyone else," Elly said. "Call me shallow, but I admit that when I first heard the rumor that Cooper had fought a duel because of me, I got a little thrill."

"Hah." Lydia smiled widely. "I knew it. You wouldn't be a real woman if you didn't get a thrill from something like that."

"It was reassuring in a way." Elly clasped her hands and concentrated on the view. "You see, up until that point Cooper hadn't been what you would call demonstrative."

Lydia pursed her lips. "Hmm. From the way he was watching you tonight, I got the impression that the two of you had definitely been *demonstrative*."

Elly felt herself turn hot. "There was one incident, but it doesn't count because it was, uh, fueled by the aftereffects of Cooper's big psychic burn last night."

"Ah, yes, that sort of incident," Lydia nodded sagely. "I know what you're talking about. Such incidents may be fun, but they are, shall we say, inconclusive."

"Exactly. Anyhow, as I was saying, when Cooper and I were officially dating back in Aurora Springs, I had begun to wonder if maybe he didn't find me physically attractive, if you know what I mean."

"I know."

"His lack of interest in that department reinforced my fear that maybe he only wanted to marry me because of my qualifications for the position of Guild boss wife."

Lydia made a tut-tutting sound. "And then you discover that he fought a duel over you. Woohoo. Talk about injecting some real passion into the equation."

"I told myself that, although there was no getting around the fact that dueling was totally unacceptable behavior, in this case there were mitigating circumstances."

"Guild traditions," Lydia said solemnly.

"Yes. They are still very strong back in Aurora Springs."

"Still way too powerful here in Cadence, too, if you ask me."

"The thing is," Elly continued, "I thought that maybe the duel indicated that Cooper did have some intense feelings for me, after all."

"I can certainly see how you could leap to such a conclusion."

"I felt I could work with that." Elly cleared her throat. "I was going to insist that he get counseling, of course."

"Of course."

"And even though I thought there might

be a bright side to the dueling incident, I was absolutely furious."

"Rightfully so," Lydia said.

"They say that hunter duels don't usually result in a death, but I've heard enough stories to know that there can be disastrous psychic trauma to both of the people involved, especially if one of them loses control."

Lydia shuddered. "So I've heard."

"In addition, being the subject of a duel made me the talk of the campus. I knew the tabloids were going to have a field day. I was afraid I might lose my job at the college before it was all over."

"Serious stuff. You did, indeed, have every right to be mad as green hell."

"I was. Still, I kept telling myself that the incident offered some indication that our personal relationship was not doomed. I confronted Cooper in his office and demanded to know why he had fought the duel."

"And?"

Elly heaved a deep sigh. "He made it clear that he hadn't fought the duel for reasons of passion or love or my feminine honor."

Lydia frowned. "Why did he fight it?"

"Are you ready for this? To protect the balance of power on the Aurora Springs Guild Council."

Lydia's mouth opened in horror. "Oh, no."

"It's true. He told me so, himself. He was afraid Palmer Frazier might lure me into marriage and that, in turn, would lead to a family alliance between Frazier and my father, which would affect the Council."

Lydia groaned. "He fought the duel because of Guild politics?"

"Yes."

"Not because of you?"

Elly shook her head sadly. "You see now why I had to give him back his ring?"

"Of course I do." Impulsively, Lydia put her arms around Elly and gave her a quick hug. "Under the circumstances, it was the only thing you could do. Coming on top of all your other concerns about the relationship, you had no choice."

Before Elly could thank her for her understanding, she noticed movement in the doorway. Two dark shadows loomed in the opening. Cooper and Emmett stood silhouetted against the light behind them, their faces unreadable in the darkness.

"I believe I may have mentioned earlier that I stepped into some serious quicksand a while back," Cooper said neutrally.

"Yes, you did," Emmett said. "Hell of a sucking sound."

Chapter 16

"Just so I have this clear," Cooper said, snapping the Spectrum's gearshifter, "you ended our engagement not because I fought a duel but because I fought it for the *wrong reason?*"

Elly was very still and very tense in the seat beside him.

"I don't think we should talk about this anymore," she said. "There's no point."

"You sure as hell didn't have any problem talking to Lydia London about it."

"I like her. There was a sort of instant bond between us. She was very understanding."

"You just met her tonight and already you've got a bond thing going? What about me? You've known me for months. We were engaged. What about our bond?"

"What bond?" she asked politely.

"I think I've got a right to be pissed off."

"I knew you wouldn't understand."

"You're damn right, I don't understand." He was not going to lose his temper, he told himself. Damned if he would let her make him lose it. "Your logic is about as water-tight as a sieve."

"My logic doesn't have to hold water, it just has to make sense to me. And it does. By the way, in case you didn't eavesdrop long enough to hear every little detail, I'd like to point out that Lydia certainly got my logic."

"Sure she's on your side. She's a woman. You women all stick together when it comes to this kind of stuff."

"Please keep your voice down. You're upsetting Rose."

He glanced at Rose, who was sitting on the back of the seat, watching the night through the window. The jeweled bracelet glittered around her furry neck. She didn't look upset, he thought. Then again, she was a dust bunny. What the hell did he know about what was going through her brain? He couldn't even figure out what was going on in the brain of the human female sitting next to him.

He drove a couple of blocks without speaking, calling on years of training and habit to control the frustration and anger simmering deep inside him.

When that did not prove to be stunningly effective, he went with the positive thinking approach.

"Does it strike you that we sound like a typical married couple quarreling on the way home from a party?" he asked.

"No," she said. "It doesn't. For one thing, we're not married."

So much for positive thinking.

"No, but we're sleeping together."

She flashed him a look that could have scorched a ghost. "We are not sleeping together."

He should stop right now. This was a dangerous road. Even he could see that. But he couldn't seem to stop himself.

"What about last night?" he asked.

She gripped her purse very tightly. "Last night doesn't count. You were in the grip of a bad burn."

"You can use that line of reasoning to excuse my actions, but how do you explain the fact that you were just as hot as I was?"

"You hunters aren't the only ones who get hit with certain aftereffects from an extreme adrenaline rush," she said coolly. "The experience may be more intense for you after you've worked ghost light to the point of melting amber, but, trust me, the rest of us are susceptible, too. What with the encounter with that mugger in the alley and rescuing Bertha, I assure you, I was very highly rezzed myself last night. Let's just leave it at that, shall we?"

Not a chance, lady, he thought. But it was finally dawning on him that this was probably not a good time to pursue the subject.

"All right, if you don't want to talk about our past history," he said aloud, "we might as well talk business."

She gave him a wary, sidelong glance. "Guild business?"

"As far as you're concerned that's the only kind I care about, isn't it?"

She leaned her head against the back of the seat and closed her eyes.

"I may not approve of some of the things the Guilds do, and I've got problems with a lot of the outdated traditions," she said, "but I would remind you that I am a direct descendent on my father's side of John Sander St. Clair, a founder and first chief of the Aurora Springs Guild. Furthermore, I count a number of heroes of the Era of Discord and several former Guild chiefs and Council members on both branches of my family tree. My father is one of the most distinguished men in the Guild, and my brothers are all top-ranked hunters."

"I'm aware of your family history," he said quietly.

"Of course you are." She opened her eyes and turned her head on the seat to look at him. "It's one of the reasons you wanted to marry me."

He concentrated on the narrow street. "What's your point?"

"Regardless of my personal issues with the archaic traditions of the Guilds, I do have a strong sense of loyalty to them and a respect for their role in history. I also have an appreciation of their ongoing importance as emergency militias. I am not stupid. I realize that catching the blue freak is extremely important. You'll have my full cooperation in your investigation."

He paused at a stoplight.

"Thank you," he said quietly.

"You're welcome."

"By the way, I would never, ever call you stupid. One of the things I admired and respected about you from the beginning was your intelligence. I think you know that."

"Yes, I do," she said. "I apologize for implying otherwise."

"Damn. If this conversation gets any chillier we're both going to freeze our frickin' asses off inside this car."

Her mouth twitched. "I agree." She straightened in the seat. "So, on to business. When do you want to go to The Road to the Ruins?"

"Can you really get us inside tonight?"

"I think so, yes." She looked at her watch. "It's almost midnight. The place will just be starting to come alive." She reached into her purse. "I'll phone Garrick and Phillip. I'm sure they'll still be awake. They're late-night types. We can stop by their place on the way to the club and pick up the pass."

"What about Rose?"

She reached up and patted the dust bunny. "I think she's had enough excitement for one evening. We'll drop her off at my apartment."

Garrick Lattimer slipped his well-manicured hands into the pockets of his intricately embroidered black silk dressing gown and rocked gently on his silk-slippered feet. He surveyed Cooper with grave interest.

"So you're a friend of Elly's, and you're visiting from out of town," he said.

Cooper walked across the white carpet to take in the view of the Dead City. The interrogation had begun, he thought.

From the moment Garrick and his companion, Phillip Manchester, had opened the door of the apartment a few minutes ago, he had known he was under close scrutiny by the pair.

This was going to be almost as bad as the

day he invited Elly's father into his office and informed him that he would like to discuss the possibility of a Covenant Marriage with his daughter, he thought.

Garrick and Phillip were both urbane, middle-aged, and physically fit in a way that suggested regular spa and gym maintenance work. It had been clear from the start that they were very fond of Elly.

Their elegant white-on-white apartment was punctuated with valuable-looking Colonial-era antiques, the occasional elegantly lit alien artifact, and a judicious amount of pre–Era of Discord art. One large bookcase was filled with rare books.

The expensive, tasteful surroundings and the pair's polished veneer hadn't fooled Cooper for a second. He knew a couple of tough specter-cats when he saw them. Garrick and Phillip might be living a comfortable, sophisticated lifestyle these days, but he was willing to bet that somewhere in their pasts they had both spent time doing things that were a lot more dangerous and demanding than operating a fashionable antique shop.

Immediately following the introductions and a few pleasantries, Phillip had whisked Elly into the study to collect the magic nightclub pass, leaving Garrick alone with

Cooper. Not an accident, Cooper knew. More like a setup.

"I'm from Aurora Springs," Cooper said, choosing his words carefully. Elly's description of him as a friend had rankled.

Garrick nodded, as though some inner suspicions had been confirmed. "You're the ex-fiancé, then, I take it."

Cooper swung around, concealing his surprise with an act of will.

"She told you about me?" he asked.

"Elly mentioned that she'd been engaged for a time back in Aurora Springs." Garrick sank gracefully into a wing chair, twitching the fabric of the silk pajama trousers beneath the dressing gown. "She did not tell us much more than that. Never even gave us a name. Phillip and I were made to understand that the experience had been painful and that she wished to put it behind her and start anew."

"Painful."

"Yes. And now, after all these months, you show up out of nowhere." Garrick smiled coolly. "Forgive me, but we can't help but be curious and somewhat concerned. Elly has no family here in Cadence City, so those of us who consider ourselves her friends feel rather protective of her."

"I appreciate that," Cooper said. "Probably more than you know. I've been worried about her."

"She's doing quite nicely with her little business. Got a growing clientele. She has made a number of friends, but I think she gets a little lonely at times."

Cooper looked at him from across the room. "Meaning?"

"Meaning that, after all these months away from her hometown and her family, she is probably somewhat vulnerable emotionally." Garrick put his fingertips together and stopped smiling. "Phillip and I would be most unhappy if it transpired that you were here to take advantage of her or hurt her a second time."

Cooper whistled softly. "You guys play rez-ball with solid quartz, don't you?"

Garrick inclined his head. "We do play hardball, yes. I would advise you not to be deceived by appearances. Phillip and I have gone upmarket in recent years, but I assure you, we have not forgotten the lessons we learned when we were in a, shall we say, less savory end of the business."

Cooper nodded slightly. "I believe you."

"Good." Garrick looked satisfied. "I'm glad that we understand each other, Cooper. Enjoy yourself at The Road tonight."

Chapter 17

Twenty minutes later, feeling very much in control again because she was the one with the coveted amber pass and knew where to park, Elly guided Cooper to a side street near the nightclub.

"The car should be reasonably safe here," she said when he opened her door. "But you might want to do the license plate ghost trick, just in case. This was once an old warehouse district. Most of these buildings are deserted now, and that means there are a lot of transients."

He gave the poorly illuminated neighborhood and its seedy, run-down buildings a quick survey.

"Yeah, I think I'll do that," he said.

When he had a tiny little ghost going near the license, he took her arm.

The streets, parking lots, and lanes around The Road to the Ruins were crowded with expensive vehicles. Cabs and limos prowled the scene, disgorging their well-dressed passengers. Women in glittery little dresses the size and weight of handkerchiefs mingled with men who were attired in everything from tailored dinner jackets and trousers to designer leather coats and jeans.

The club occupied one of the Colonial-era warehouses. Elly had driven past it during the day and noticed that it was virtually unnoticeable, just one more aging Old Quarter building. The only thing that marked it as unusual was the black-and-amber-trimmed door. There was no number on the door. Part of the allure of The Road was that you had to know the address or know someone who did know it.

Elly assessed the crowd and concluded that she and Cooper blended in quite well. Neither of them had changed since dinner with the Londons. The deep violet sheath and high-heeled sandals that she had on fit in with the other trendy evening dresses.

Cooper wore a sophisticated, slouchy black jacket over a sleek, gray silk shirt and black trousers. He glided through the flashy crowd like a shark through a school of rainbow eels.

"There's the VIP entrance," Elly whispered, pointing to a second, unobtrusive doorway marked off with velvet ropes.

Two squat, massive men, who appeared to be twins, guarded the VIP door. They were dressed in silver-studded leather. Each wore a single gold earring. Their shaved heads gleamed in the flaring torchlight that lit the front of the club.

One of the twins glanced briefly at the pass that Elly showed him. With a crisp, sharp movement of his chin, he indicated that she and Cooper could enter.

"Ever been to Earth World?" Elly asked as they walked through a doorway that opened as if by magic.

"The big theme park in Resonance?" Cooper asked.

"Yes."

He looked thoughtful. "Not that I recall."

"Trust me, you would have remembered. They've got all these rides and exhibits designed to show you how things worked back on Earth before the time of the Curtain. There are clunky little cars that you drive without using amber to rez the engines and miniature houses where you can't even turn on the dishwasher with psi energy. Really weird."

"Doesn't sound familiar."

"Sheesh. Do you mean to tell me that your folks didn't take you there on vacation when you were a kid?"

"We usually spent our vacations at one of my mom's excavation sites."

"That is pathetic."

"I thought it was sort of interesting at the time." He shrugged. "But maybe you had to be there."

"Right. Well, the reason I mentioned it is because this club is what you might call an adult version of Earth World. Over the top."

"Thanks for the heads-up. I'll try not to walk around with my mouth hanging open."

He was very cool about it, she thought, watching him out of the corner of her eye, but he had to be at least somewhat impressed by the lobby. Sure, he had been around. That didn't change the fact that there was nothing like The Road to the Ruins back home in Aurora Springs.

The black-and-amber theme had been expanded upon in the lobby where the ebony walls and floor gleamed in the natural green glow of a number of large alien artifacts. The relics were museum quality and emitted a faint tingle of psi energy. The collection included a massive quartz sarcophagus, a couple of elaborately worked columns, and an assortment of urns and vases. The pieces had been placed at random around the shadowy space in a way that suggested the viewer had just walked into a mysterious, heretofore undiscovered archaeological site.

A wide, shimmering waterfall lit with green lights formed a curtain across one entire wall. The cascade of chartreuse water splashed into a pool to the accompaniment of the sultry beat of a rez-jazz number. An amber-colored pathway snaked around the rim of the pool and vanished behind the waterfall.

A hostess dressed in a diaphanous gown decorated with three strategically placed fabric triangles appeared.

"Please allow me to show you to your table," she said softly. She gave Cooper an intimate smile before she turned to lead the way along the waterfall path.

The back of the hostess's gown plunged so low that it revealed an inch or two of the cleavage that divided her buttocks.

Elly glanced at Cooper and saw that he was watching the woman's swaying hips. There was an expression of amused interest on his face.

"If you start drooling," Elly warned, "I swear, we're leaving."

"Sorry. It's just that you don't see a lot of dresses like that one back in Aurora Springs." He turned his attention to the waterfall. "You know, I don't want to be a poor sport or look like I'm from out of town, but I just had this jacket cleaned."

"Don't worry, you won't get wet," Elly assured him. "It's actually a series of water-falls, and they're all very carefully placed to give an illusion of a solid wall of water."

The path wound through the tiers of cas-cading emerald waters. When they emerged on the opposite side, Cooper checked his coat and seemed satisfied that it had not sustained any water damage.

The hostess led them to a curved booth upholstered in black velvet. The table was inlaid with glass and amber and lit from un-derneath.

When they were seated and the hostess had departed, Elly leaned back and watched Cooper take in his surroundings.

The lobby décor only hinted at the atmo-sphere of exotic, alien mystery that the dec-orators had obviously sought to achieve. Here in the main room and in the casino, a portion of which was visible from where she and Cooper sat, the theme had been pushed to the max.

The entire back wall of the old warehouse had been removed to expose the section of the glowing Dead City Wall behind it. The expanse of luminous quartz provided the ul-timate in mood lighting for the interior of the club, bathing the scene in an other-worldly glow.

Several more massive artifacts were strewn about the scene. The effect of so many relics massed together combined with the wall, itself, infused the intimate darkness with the gently intoxicating aura of psi energy.

A singer dressed in a long, green, skintight gown breathed the words of a lush, sensual song of doomed passion into the microphone. On the glowing dance floor, couples drifted in the shadows.

Elly smiled, feeling a little smug. "Pretty amazing, isn't it?"

"Well, it sure isn't the Rendezvous Room back in Aurora Springs," Cooper said.

"Certainly struck me that way the first time Phillip and Garrick brought me here. Okay, I got you inside. Now what happens, Mr. Enforcer?"

"The first rule of investigation is to avoid attracting attention. We're going to act like we're a real couple out to enjoy each other's company tonight."

"How do you suggest we do that?"

"We order drinks, and then we dance."

She stiffened, her mind flashing back to the few times they had danced together. On those occasions she had tended to melt like over-rezzed amber in his arms. Dancing with Cooper was dangerous.

"What's the matter?" Cooper watched a waiter glide toward them through the shadows. "Afraid to dance with me?"

"Don't be ridiculous." She needed to fortify herself for the ordeal, she thought.

"What can I bring you?" the waiter asked, setting a bowl of nuts on the glass-and-amber table.

"I'll have an Emerald Ghost," she said.

"A fun drink," the waiter said approvingly. He gave Cooper an inquiring look. "And for you, sir?"

"Whiskey," Cooper said. "Straight up. First Generation, if you have it."

"Of course, sir. The Road prides itself on a well-stocked backbar. I'll return in a few minutes."

When he returned he carried a small tray that held the whiskey and a tall glass filled with a frothy concoction adorned with a familiar-looking swizzle stick. He set the violently green drink and the whiskey on the table and left.

Cooper watched Elly sip the drink through a straw. "So that's an Emerald Ghost."

"Uh-huh." She drank some more very quickly.

"Looks like something that oozed out of the catacombs."

"It's very tasty." She was feeling better already, she decided. She could handle a dance with Cooper.

He drank a little whiskey and sat quietly, absorbing his surroundings.

"Ready to dance?" he asked after a few minutes.

She slid out of the booth and allowed him to escort her onto the dance floor. *Think of this as going undercover for the sake of helping the Guild catch a bad guy,* she told herself. *You're just playing a part.*

Cooper drew her into his arms, enveloping her in his heat and masculinity. She waged a brief but valiant struggle with her willpower, but the sensual rhythms of the music were her undoing.

Dancing with Cooper was one of the good memories of their time together in Aurora Springs.

Last night's bout of passion had been all fireworks and hot lust. Tonight was a different proposition altogether. Dancing with Cooper was all about a slow, seductive heat that built steadily deep inside, intoxicating her senses.

"Did I ever tell you that I like the way you smell?" he said, his mouth very close to her ear.

"Uh, no. No, I don't think you ever said

anything like that."

"Drives me crazy."

"Really?" She tipped her head back to get a better look at his face. "The way I smell drives you crazy?"

"Is that so hard to believe?"

"Well, yes, frankly. I mean, I certainly never noticed you going crazy when we were dating back in Aurora Springs."

His big hand pressed a little more firmly against the place where her spine curved into her rear.

"In hindsight," he said, "I think it's fair to say that there were some serious communication problems between us back in Aurora Springs."

"I'll go along with that."

"But I assume that at least one of those miscommunications was clarified last night," he said quietly. "You now know that I like the idea of having sex with you. I like it a lot."

She knew she was blushing and was grateful for the alien light. "You're absolutely sure that what happened last night wasn't just the result of the afterburn?"

"I've been burned before," he said moving his mouth closer to hers. "Trust me, last night was different."

And then he kissed her, right there in the

middle of the shadowy dance floor. Not just a brief, fleeting little brush of the lips, either. This was a deep, heavy, straight to the pit of the stomach kind of kiss. Slower and more deliberate than the kind of kisses he had given her last night, but just as intense.

She couldn't believe it. Cooper had *never* kissed her in public, let alone in the middle of a dance floor. Granted, it was highly unlikely that any of the other couples noticed, let alone cared. But, still, it wasn't the kind of thing that Guild bosses did. They were usually too concerned about their images.

Public displays of affection presented a twofold problem for a man in Cooper's position. On the one hand, a Guild exec did not want to appear to be a lecherous womanizer. Historically, the heads of the Guilds had a long-standing PR issue in that area. In addition, a Guild boss also had to make sure that he didn't give the members of the organization — always an overly macho lot — the idea that their boss was the kind of weak-kneed guy who allowed himself to be dangled on a string by a woman.

But Cooper was kissing her as if he didn't give a damn about his image. Of course, no one here knew who he was, but still. This kiss felt like he meant it.

She was crushed tightly against him, and she was very aware of his erection. He was fully aroused, she thought, dazzled by the knowledge that she'd had this effect on him.

Somehow Cooper managed to slide one of his legs between hers, easing his thigh intimately against her in a way that caused her short skirt to ride up even higher. He moved one hand down to her hip and squeezed gently.

She was torn between shock and an incredible thrill. Heat pooled inside her. The crotch of her panties was suddenly, devastatingly damp.

The couples around them spun away into another dimension, leaving her alone with Cooper, the dark, green-hued night, and the sultry music.

She moved one arm higher along Cooper's shoulder so that she could touch the nape of his neck. She was almost certain that he shuddered when she stroked her fingertips through his hair.

He really was responding to her, she thought, without the influence of a post-ghost buzz and with an extremely satisfying degree of passion. He was acting as though it was all he could do not to pull her down onto the glowing floor of the nightclub and make love to her right then and there. And she wasn't at all sure that she would have put up much of a protest if he had tried to do just that.

When he finally raised his head, she was breathless. She tried to think of a good reason for both of them to leave immediately and climb into the front seat of the Spectrum.

"Have we got the question of whether or not I am physically attracted to you when I am not in afterburn settled?" he asked.

"I . . . I think so, yes," she managed.

"Good," he said. He stopped dancing, took her arm, and steered her purposefully back toward their booth. "In that case, you'll have to excuse me."

"I beg your pardon?"

"I need to go to the men's room."

"Oh."

Good grief, had she actually made Cooper Boone come in his pants right there on the dance floor? A wondrous sense of her own female power swept over her.

She gave him her most inviting, most intimate smile and tried not to let her gaze drop below his belt.

"Sorry about that," she said lightly. "But you were the one who started that fire."

"What fire?" he asked absently, his gaze going toward the far wall where a hallway led to the men's room.

"You know." She leaned in close to him and lowered her voice. "I realize that a situation like this must be a little embarrassing for a man like you. Well, for any man, I suppose. But for you, especially. I mean, you're always so in control and all."

"Embarrassing?"

She laughed airily. "I hope you didn't ruin your nice trousers. They look expensive. But that will teach you to get all hot and bothered on the dance floor."

He brought her to a halt at the booth. "What," he asked, polite but blank, "are you talking about?"

It dawned on her that she might have leaped to a very awkward conclusion.

"Never mind," she mumbled, mortified.

"Damn it, Elly, I thought we were supposed to be practicing our communication skills here."

She cleared her throat. "It's just that when you said you had to rush off to the men's room, I assumed that perhaps you'd had a little accident out there on the dance floor. Because of that steamy kiss and . . . you know." She waved a hand to finish the sentence.

He gave her a slow, wicked smile. "Honey, if anyone could make me lose control in the middle of a dance floor, it's you. But as it happens, I didn't. Not this time at any rate. The reason I'm headed for the men's room is that I want to get a quick look at the back of the house."

"Back of the house?"

"I want to see how this place is laid out behind the scenes. Offices, kitchens, that kind of thing. I also want to locate the executive suite, if possible. Don't worry, I'll be right back."

So much for her stunning sexual powers.

"I could help you," she said quickly. "I'll check out the back of the house in the vicinity of the ladies' room. It's on the opposite side of the club."

"Like hell you will. You will stay right here and wait for me."

"We're supposed to be partners in this thing, if you will recall."

"No one said anything about a partnership."

"Hey, you wouldn't even be here tonight if I hadn't helped you."

"Elly, be reasonable," he said in a very low voice. "This is a casino. That means there's a lot of security everywhere, even if it isn't obvious. You don't know the first thing about evading cameras and guards."

"And you do, I suppose?" she demanded,

aware that she was starting to sound belligerent.

"Before I got this Guild boss gig, I spent years working undercover, remember?"

"Oh, yeah, right. I keep forgetting that you used to be an enforcer."

"Investigator."

"Whatever. Okay, okay, go do your thing." She was about to slide into the booth, but the thought of her damp underwear made her pause. "I still need to go to the ladies' room, though, even if you won't let me do any spying."

"Run along." He gave her a pat on her derriere that was both affectionate and possessive. "Probably not a good idea to sit down until your panties dry out, anyway."

He was gone, melting into the shadows and the crowd before she could take aim at his shin with the toe of her high-heeled shoe.

A short time later she emerged from an ornately carved and gilded green stall inside the small palace labeled Ladies. She washed her hands at one of the black-and-gold sinks and checked her appearance in the massive, elaborately framed mirror.

Her cheeks were still a little flushed, and she had to make some adjustments to her hair, but otherwise she did not look too much the worse for wear, she decided. Not at all like a woman who had just been making out like a hormone-crazed teenager on the dance floor.

She walked back out of the restroom into the elegantly furnished hall and started to turn toward the opening that would take her back into the main room of the club.

The swinging doors marked Employees Only at the opposite end of the hall caught her eye. She looked at the ceiling and saw no sign of a camera. *Doesn't mean there isn't one around somewhere,* she thought. Cooper was right, this was a casino, and in a casino someone was always watching.

Still, what harm could there be in just walking along the hall toward the swinging doors? If anyone questioned her, she could always pretend to be a little inebriated and say that she had gotten turned around coming out of the restroom.

She started forward, tipping her chin down and angling it to the side. If there was a camera somewhere, hopefully it would only catch the crown of her head. She pretended to rummage around in her small, glittery evening bag as though searching for a lipstick.

The doors opened abruptly just as she arrived in front of them. She had to step back quickly to avoid getting run down by a man dressed in the green-and-black livery worn by the male cocktail waiters.

"Excuse me, ma'am," the man said, letting the doors swing shut behind him. "Didn't see you. Can I help you?"

"I'm looking for the drinking fountain." She gave him her best high-rez smile. "Someone told me it was just past the ladies' room."

"Other direction. I'll show you."

"Thanks."

She kept her smile firmly in place as she allowed the waiter to guide her toward the black-and-green fountain at the opposite end of the hall. But it wasn't easy to maintain the facade of the happy, slightly drunk guest. Her heart was pounding.

That brief view of what Cooper had called the back of the house had been a revelation. She had felt as though she were standing on an elaborately decorated stage set, gazing into the wings behind the velvet curtains. The swinging doors were gates that divided the fantasy realm of the club from the real world on the other side.

The walls on the other side of the doors were not covered in gleaming black and amber tiles. Instead, they were painted drab beige. There was no carpet on the floor back there, and the lighting was the bright, cold kind that came from fluo-rez tubes installed in the ceiling.

In those few seconds she had glimpsed a number of people garbed in the various uniforms of their jobs — janitors, restaurant staff, croupiers, waiters — all moving about in a busy, purposeful manner.

She had noticed something else, too, something she was pretty sure would interest Cooper.

Harmony Drew, girl detective, eat your heart out.

Chapter 18

She was sipping her new Emerald Ghost when Cooper finally reappeared.

"It's about time you got back," she said when he slid into the booth beside her. "I was starting to think that something had gone wrong on your little tour of the back of the house."

"Nothing went wrong. I had to borrow a few things, and then I had to return them. Took a little more time than I had planned." He looked at the magnificent cocktail in front of her. "I see you ordered another one of those froufrou drinks."

"Actually, this is my third. I had to do something. The waiter was starting to feel sorry for me. He thought my date for the evening had ditched me."

"Yeah? What did you tell him?"

"That you'd had too much to drink, started feeling ill, and had gone to the men's room to throw up."

"A colorful story."

"I thought so." She jiggled the swizzle stick in the Emerald Ghost. "What things did you borrow and return?"

"A janitor's uniform and set of keys."

"Where did you get the clothes and the keys?"

"Out of a janitorial closet, where else?" he said.

She choked on a swallow of the Emerald Ghost and hastily patted her mouth with a napkin. "You stole a janitor's uniform and keys?"

"No," he said patiently. "I told you, I borrowed them."

"Good grief, Cooper, what if security had caught you? You could have been arrested."

"I wasn't." He patted one of the pockets of his jacket. "Got lucky and came across a little photocopied map of the club attached to one of the janitorial carts. Looks like the janitor used it to keep track of the rooms he'd cleaned."

"What are you going to do with it?" she asked, seriously alarmed now.

"I don't know yet. But it's always nice to have a good map."

A deep suspicion unfurled inside her. "You had fun, didn't you?"

"Fun?"

She took the swizzle stick out of the glass and aimed it at him. "I can tell you enjoyed yourself slipping around the back of the house, stealing stuff. You've got a real adrenaline buzz going, Cooper Boone."

His mouth curved faintly. "You can tell that, huh?"

"Yes, I can." She took another swallow of her drink. "What if I told you that three guys tried to hit on me while you were out playing detective?"

"Point 'em out to me, and I'll fry their brains."

"Hah. I don't believe that for a second. You only conduct duels when there's Guild business involved, remember?"

"We're back to the duel thing?"

"Sorry. Couldn't help it. Didn't mean to bring up that subject, honest." She examined her drink a little more closely. "You know, these things may be a bit sneaky. They taste good going down, but I seem to have become rather chatty in the past few minutes."

He looked amused. "I think it's time we went home. Been a long night."

"Yes, it has, hasn't it? Can't waste this, though. It was a very expensive drink." She picked up the glass and downed the last of the Emerald Ghost. When she was finished she smiled brightly at Cooper. "We can go now."

He helped her out of the booth and

steered her toward the green waterfall. "I do believe that this is the first time I've ever seen you tipsy."

"Probably because I always had to be very careful about that kind of thing back in Aurora Springs."

"I see."

"Other issues, like hangovers, aside, Mom always made it clear that having the daughter of a Guild Council member get drunk in public would be very embarrassing for Dad." She winked. "Guild image thing, you know."

"Belonging to a high-ranking Guild family has put a lot of pressure on you over the years, hasn't it?"

"Yep. Want to hear a little secret?"

"Sure."

"Before I met you, I had made up my mind that I was going to marry outside the Guild, no matter what everyone thought."

"Is that so?"

"Yep." She noticed that they were on the path that meandered through the waterfalls. She held out a hand to let water splash on her palm. "I'd been plotting my escape ever since I was a teenager. That's why you never had to worry about me running off with Palmer Frazier or anyone else on your dumb Council."

"But you changed your mind when you met me?"

"Thought you were different."

"What do you think about me now?" he asked.

"You're definitely different," she said. "But in a different way than I first thought. If you see what I mean."

"Not sure that I do," he said.

"Me, either," she confessed.

Outside the nightclub, the streets were still busy. The lights of the cars and taxis were reflected in the veil of fog. Elly took several deep breaths in an attempt to clear her head. After a while she abandoned the effort as futile.

When Cooper bundled her into the front seat of the Spectrum, she collapsed with a small sigh of relief and closed her eyes.

"So," Cooper said, climbing in beside her on the driver's side. "I've been wondering about something."

"What's that?" she mumbled, half-asleep.

"Did your panties ever dry out?"

"Don't know. Haven't checked."

He gave a low, sexy laugh and pulled away from the curb. "What do you mean? Can't you feel them?"

"Nope."

"Too far gone on those Emerald Ghosts

to figure out whether or not your underwear is still damp?"

"Nope. Can't tell if my panties ever got dry because they're in my purse."

"Your *purse*. What the hell are they doing there?"

"Took 'em off when I went to the ladies' room because they were sort of uncomfortable, and I was afraid that if I sat down in them, they might create a potentially embarrassing spot on the back of my skirt, which happens to be rather expensive."

"You were sitting there in that little scrap of a skirt without any panties on while you downed those Emerald Ghosts?" he demanded.

He sounded outraged to the depths of his Guild boss soul, she thought.

She smiled and snuggled into a more comfortable position in the seat. "Not exactly the sort of behavior you expect from a proper Guild boss wife, is it? Told you I did you a favor when I canceled our engagement."

Fifteen minutes later Cooper parked in the fog-bound alley behind St. Clair's Herbal Emporium. He was still waging a private internal struggle between hot lust and masculine outrage. He couldn't get the vision of Elly sitting in the booth without any panties on out of his head.

He went around to the passenger side and opened the door. She was sound asleep. She did not stir when he hauled her out and settled her over one shoulder.

He secured her with a hand high up on her thighs and immediately regretted the move. In her present position, the hem of her minuscule skirt was all the way up to the bottom of her sweetly rounded buttocks. His fingers were only inches away from the cleft between her legs. *And she wasn't wearing any panties.*

He managed to get the door of the shop open and carried Elly inside without banging her head.

When he rezzed the light he saw Rose watching him from one of the workbenches. The dust bunny blinked her blue eyes a couple of times and bounced up and down in agitation.

"She's okay," Cooper said. "One too many Emerald Ghosts."

He extended his arm. Rose scampered up his sleeve to his free shoulder.

He walked to the stairs. Pausing there, he adjusted Elly's weight, and assessed the climb.

"A Guild boss has gotta do what a Guild

boss has gotta do," he announced to Rose.

He started up the stairs.

At the top he stopped to take a couple of deep breaths.

"She's heavier than she looks," he informed Rose. "Probably all muscle."

He got his burden into the darkened bedroom and dumped her carefully onto the quilts. Rose hopped down beside Elly and nuzzled her chin.

Elly opened her eyes and patted Rose reassuringly. Then she gave Cooper a dreamy smile.

"Thanks for carrying me up the stairs," she said. "Not sure I could have made it on my own tonight."

"You're welcome," he said. "I needed the exercise."

He leaned down and removed first one flashy little high heel and then the other.

Elly yawned. "No need to undress me. Just throw a quilt over me."

"It's no trouble," he said, letting one palm glide up the curve of her leg.

"Go away," she ordered. "I don't think you could handle the shock of seeing me without my panties."

"Guild bosses are sturdier than you might expect," he said hopefully.

She reached for the edge of the quilt and

tugged it over herself. "Good night, Cooper."

He smiled and reluctantly went to the doorway. "Good night, Elly."

"By the way, remind me to tell you what I noticed when I went to the ladies' room tonight."

"Does it involve underwear?"

"No," she murmured, nestling deeper into the pillow. "Psi energy. The kind given off by those psi-bright herbs that Bertha found down in the catacombs. But real intense."

What?" He started back toward the bed. "Are you telling me you can pick up psi from *plants?*"

"I know, it's weird."

"Elly —"

She wagged a finger at him. "Big, dark family secret. The amber in my earrings is tuned. Promise me you won't tell anyone."

"Wait a second, Elly. Stay with me here. What were you saying about sensing herbs like those that Bertha found?"

"Bunch of 'em, I think. Enough to give off quite a buzz." She yawned. "Stored somewhere in that hallway just beyond the ladies' room at the club."

She closed her eyes and went to sleep.

Cooper watched her for a long moment,

aware of the deep, restless need that prowled through him.

After a while he went back out into the alley to retrieve his duffel bag from the trunk of his car.

On the way back up the stairs it occurred to him that he had neglected to tell Elly that he had checked out of his hotel earlier that day.

"Have to remember to mention it to her in the morning," he said to Rose.

Chapter 19

She awoke to a nagging headache and a familiar little psi buzz. A small paw gently patted her cheek.

Elly opened her eyes and looked at Rose, huddled beside her on the pillow. The dust bunny had a fresh green flower clutched in one paw.

"You went out last night after we brought you home, didn't you?" Elly asked, taking the flower.

Rose bounced up and down.

"Thanks. It's beautiful. But I gotta tell you, every time you show up with one of these, I get very nervous. Promise me you're not stealing them?"

Rose chortled happily, pleased that the gift had been accepted with proper appreciation.

Out in the kitchen a cupboard door closed.

Elly jackknifed into a sitting position. The movement allowed the quilt to fall to her waist. She looked down and saw that she was still wearing the dress she had put on to go out for the evening. A deep sense of unease gripped her.

Cautiously she peeked beneath the edge of the quilt. The skirt of the expensive cocktail dress was sadly crumpled. The hem had been pushed up almost to her waist. She noticed that she was not wearing any underwear.

Probably not a good sign, she thought.

Cooper appeared in the bedroom doorway. He was wearing his black-and-amber framed glasses, a black crew-neck pullover, and khaki trousers. He had a copy of the newspaper in his hand.

Instinctively, she yanked the quilt protectively up to her chin.

"What are you doing here?" she demanded.

"I'm your friend from out of town, remember? You're letting me stay with you."

"That was just a story. I didn't mean it literally."

"Unfortunately, I'm a literal kind of guy. At any rate, I checked out of my hotel. I don't have anywhere else to go."

"Now hold on here just a minute, Cooper. I never said —"

"How's the head?"

"Terrible." She massaged her temples with her fingertips. "I don't feel very good.

Maybe I'm coming down with the flu."

"Don't think so. What you have is a classic hangover. Remember those Emerald Ghosts last night?"

She concentrated. "I've got a vague recollection of a large glass filled with some sort of green stuff. It was delicious. Sweet and tart at the same time."

"There were three large glasses, and they were obviously pretty potent."

"Oh." A few more memories floated back. A dark, intimate dance floor, sultry music, a kiss that had made her insides melt. She winced. "Right. I remember now."

His smile was slow and knowing. "Yeah, I can see that. Got anything downstairs in your shop for that headache, or do you want something from the medicine cabinet?"

She marshaled her thoughts. "Downstairs. First cabinet. Bottom shelf. There's a packet labeled Harmonic balm. Put a spoonful into a mug and add boiling water."

He unfolded his arms and straightened. "I'll get right on it."

"On second thought, make that two spoonfuls."

"Check."

An uneasy thought intruded. "Wait a second," she said when he turned to leave. "Where did you sleep last night?"

"On your sofa."

"If that's true, what happened to my underpants?"

He smiled slowly. "You know, I think I'm going to let you work that one out all by yourself. See you at breakfast."

She heard him whistling in the hall.

She was standing under an invigorating spray of hot water, trying in vain not to think about the night that had just passed, when the bathroom door opened.

"What in the world?" She grabbed a fistful of the shower curtain and peered around the edge.

Cooper stood in the small space, enveloped in steam. He had a mug in his hand. Rose was perched on his shoulder, nibbling on a piece of toast.

"You, again," she said, beetling her brows at him. "Now what? I'm in the shower, for heaven's sake."

"Sorry," Cooper said. "Didn't mean to scare you. Thought you might want to get going on your special tonic."

She sniffed, inhaling the soothing aroma of the Harmonic balm. The promise of headache relief seemed a lot more important at the moment than trying to make Cooper aware of the fact that they were not on the sort of intimate terms that allowed him to wander in and out of her bathroom at will.

She took the mug from him. "Thanks."

"You're welcome. When you come out, we'll talk about what you said you sensed when you made your trip to the ladies' room last night.

He departed, taking Rose with him.

She stood there for a while, sipping the tisane and forcing herself to relive the night.

She finally remembered what had happened to her panties.

"When did you figure out you could sense psi energy from plants?" Cooper asked, scraping eggs out of the pan onto Elly's plate.

She shrugged, her attention riveted on the eggs. The tisane had done its job, and now she was ravenous. "At about the same age that my brothers came into their dissonance-energy para-rez abilities. Shortly after puberty."

He put the plate in front of her. "The usual time when strong paranormal senses develop."

"Yes." She forked up a large helping of the eggs. "The thing is, my kind of talent isn't supposed to exist."

"Neither is mine," he reminded her dryly.

"Correction. Yours may be a big Guild secret, but at least there are those who acknowledge that it exists. Heck, they've even gone to great lengths to conceal the information. But in my case, the experts would be strongly inclined to say that I was delusional. That kind of diagnosis would have killed my chances of leading a normal life. That's why Mom and Dad were so serious about keeping it a secret."

"Humans have only been living on Harmony for two hundred years," Cooper said mildly. "That's not very long in evolutionary development terms. We've only identified a narrow range of paranormal talents. Who's to say that there aren't a whole bunch more just waiting to be stimulated in the population?"

She aimed the fork at him. "The problem at the present time, as you and I both know, is that people tend to be very uneasy about parapsych talents that don't fit the normal profiles."

"Can't argue that. Who figured out that your para-senses weren't coming in at the usual points on the spectrum?"

"Mom. She noticed that I seemed unusually fascinated with plants and flowers and herbs of all kinds. I spent hours hiking through the woods hunting for them, and when I found the ones I wanted, I brought them home and ran experiments with them. Started blending my own herbal concoctions. Somehow I could tell which herbs would do what for a particular person."

He looked at her. "That's what you mean when you say you custom blend the tisanes for your customers?"

She nodded and took another bite of eggs. "I can sense what herbs will resonate best with an individual's parapsych profile. Take moonseed, for example. It's an old folk remedy for insomnia. But there are several different species and a dozen different preparations. Taking the stuff as a sleeping aid has always been hit or miss in terms of effectiveness."

"Probably why it has always been relegated to the status of a folk remedy instead of a real medication."

"True. But if I do a proper consult using tuned amber, I can match the right species, preparation, and dose to the customer. The dose, by the way, is critical with moonseed. The stuff is practically tasteless in liquids, so people are inclined to take way too much of it. If it does work, it can wipe you out for a full day."

He looked amused.

"What's so funny?" she asked.

"I'm thinking about the lecture I got from your father."

"What lecture?"

"The one in which he advised me that you were a delicate, gentle creature who had to be treated with great care."

She glowered. "Dad said that?"

"Uh-huh."

"Is that the reason why you never tried to do anything more than kiss me good night when you took me home from a date back in Aurora Springs?"

"Hell, no. Regardless of what your family believed, I knew that you were no fragile piece of spun amber the first time I met you."

"Really? Do you mean you sensed that I had a fairly strong degree of psi power? I've heard some people can pick up on that kind of thing in others."

"No." He looked at her over the rim of the mug. "The strength I felt in you was another kind of power."

"Like what?"

He hunted for the words to express what he had known that very first day when she had walked into the Department of Archives. "You're the kind of person your friends know they can trust and count on no matter what. You're loyal, but your loyalty can't be bought. You've got a soul-deep notion of what's right and what's wrong, and you'd go down fighting for what you thought was right, every time, regardless of the obstacles. And you're kind."

"Good grief, you make me sound as dull as untuned amber."

He frowned. "Just the opposite. You're the most interesting woman I've ever met."

She got a little tingly feeling in the pit of her stomach. "Really?"

He held up one finger. "What's more, just so you know, you possess one special quality that puts you way out of the boring category."

"What?"

"You're sexy as hell."

"Hah." She narrowed her eyes. "If I'm so gosh-darned sexy, why did you keep us at arm's length back in Aurora Springs?"

He leaned back in his chair, stretched his legs out under the table, and cupped the mug in both hands. "At the start it was because I knew I was cruising under what you would consider false colors."

"Oh, yeah, right. The fact that I actually believed you were a librarian."

"I was a librarian." He shrugged. "But I wasn't sure how you would react when I became a Guild boss. When it happened, I could tell that you were very uneasy about the situation. I rushed to get the ring on your finger, but once I had it there, I told myself I should take things slowly and give you a chance to get used to the idea of marrying the head of the Guild. I knew you were not real keen on the idea."

She put down her fork. "Who says Guild bosses aren't insightful and perceptive?"

"Not me. Being a shrewd, farsighted, perceptive kind of guy, I assumed that hot sex would complicate the situation."

"How?"

He rubbed the back of his neck. "I was afraid that if we went to bed together, you might convince yourself that the only thing we had going for us was sexual attraction. I had a vision of you trying to reduce our relationship to the status of an affair and eventually calling it off entirely. Figured if I courted you in the old-fashioned Guild tradition, you would see that we were a good match in other ways."

She surprised him with a quick, amused smile. "Talk about overthinking a problem. Guess it was that scholarly upbringing your parents gave you. Too much history, logic, and philosophy."

"Guess so."

"Is there any more toast?"

And they said it was men who tried to avoid relationship discussions, he thought.

"I'll make some more." He got to his feet and went back to the kitchen counter to pop another slice of bread into the toaster. "Maybe we'd better get back to the subject of what happened last night at the club. You said you picked up traces of the same psi energy that you sensed when you handled those herbs that Bertha brought out of the tunnels?"

"Psi-bright. Yes."

He glanced at her over his shoulder. "But you didn't actually see any of the stuff?"

"No, but as I told you, for me to pick it up at a distance means there must have been a large amount of the herbs in the vicinity or else a highly refined form of them."

"Enchantment dust."

"Probably."

He turned around slowly and lounged back against the counter. "No doubt about it, there's a strong connection to The Road."

"What are you thinking?"

"That there are a couple of possibilities. The first is that Ormond Ripley, the owner of the club, is running a drug operation."

"Why do you look doubtful about that possibility?"

"London told me that Ripley has always been careful to stay on the right side of the legal line."

She raised her brows. "Greed has no limits."

"Can't rule it out," he agreed. "But it's also possible that someone in his organization is running a little drug business on the side and that Ripley isn't aware of it."

She got an uneasy expression. "You're going to go back to The Road, aren't you?"

"I don't have much of a choice." He took the map out of his pocket, unfolded it on the table, and pointed to one of the rooms. "That's the women's restroom. Show me exactly where you were when you picked up the psi buzz from the herbs."

She examined the map closely. "I came out that door and turned right." She moved her finger along the hallway. "There are swinging doors here. I was standing right about there when a waiter came through the doors. That was when I caught the trace of psi."

He studied the markings on the map. "Looks like all the rooms on the other side of the doors are allocated to catering and food storage. There's also one marked Janitorial Supply. Can't see anyone storing dope in any of those places. Too likely to be discovered."

She tapped the map with one finger. "I'm sure I felt something, and it had to be coming from somewhere in the vicinity of the swinging doors."

He looked up. "Any chance the energy was coming from underneath the hall or from the ceiling above?"

"Not the ceiling," she said, very sure of herself. "But down below the floor is a real possibility. Most of the buildings in the Old Quarter have basements, cellars, and underground storage rooms of one sort or another. Wouldn't be surprised if there's a hole-in-the-wall somewhere beneath the club, too. Like I told you, this part of town is riddled with them."

He flattened both hands on the table on either side of the map. "I'm going to take a look today."

"How will you get in?"

"Same way I did last night, as a club employee. Shouldn't be too difficult. There are several hundred people working there. Even during the day a business like that will have a lot of staff running around."

"I don't know, Cooper, it sounds awfully dangerous."

The phone on the wall bonged loudly. Cooper reached for it, relieved to have a convenient interruption to a discussion he did not wish to continue.

"No." Elly shot up out of her chair, something akin to panic widening her eyes. She waved her hands madly. "Don't answer that," she mouthed.

But it was too late.

"Hello," Cooper said automatically.

"Cooper? Is that you?" The familiar female voice rose on a questioning note. "This is Evelyn St. Clair."

"It's me," he said. He gave Elly an apologetic look. "Good morning, Mrs. St. Clair."

Elly bounded around the edge of the table, hand outstretched. "Give me that phone."

"It's a bit early in the day," Evelyn observed bluntly. "What are you doing there at Elly's apartment at this hour?"

"Having breakfast," Cooper said, holding the phone out of Elly's reach. "Elly took me out on the town last night. Showed me some of the sights of the big city after dark. Got to say, I was amazed."

Evelyn laughed. "Cooper, you're teasing me. We both know you've spent plenty of time in places other than Aurora Springs in recent years. In fact, you didn't even move back here until you took the job in the Department of Archives."

"I'm serious, Mrs. St. Clair. Cadence

City has been a real eye-opener."

Elly managed to get a grip on the phone. He let her have it and went to see how the toast was doing.

"Mom?" Elly scowled ferociously at Cooper. "Yes, I know. He slept on the sofa, Mom. Not that it's anyone's business."

The toast had popped up. Cooper removed the slice, put it on a plate, and carried it back to the table. Rose hopped down off the windowsill to join him.

"He's just a houseguest as far as the neighbors are concerned, Mom," Elly said. "Also, I might add, as far as I'm concerned."

There was another pause in the conversation. Elly listened with an air of grim patience.

"Yes, Mom, I know how it would look back home in Aurora Springs, but, see, that's the beauty of living in Cadence. Here in the big city, no one worries about what you do or with whom you do it. Everybody minds their own business. It's an interesting concept. Well, got to run. Almost time to open up the shop. Give my love to Dad. Bye."

She hung up the phone, crossed her arms, and glared at Cooper. "Henceforth, you do not, under any circumstances, answer my phone. Is that clear?"

Cooper gave Rose one half of a slice of toast and ate the other.

"Your house, your rules," he said. "But just out of curiosity, are you sure no one around here is interested in your love life?"

"For Pete's sake, I don't have a love life."

"You've got a sex life now, though. In my experience, a lot of folks, even your big-city, sophisticated, wine-snob types, are interested in other people's sex lives."

"Isn't it time you got busy with your so-called investigation?"

"Well, if you're going to be that way about it —"

"I am."

Chapter 20

Shortly before three o'clock that afternoon, a familiar figure materialized out of the heavy fog that still filled Ruin Lane. The door of St. Clair's Herbal Emporium opened, setting off the overhead chimes.

Elly cringed. She was developing a phobia to the stupid little doorbells, she thought. They had been ringing almost constantly all day. Ever since she had turned the Closed sign to Open she'd had an abnormal number of visitors. Very few had been interested in purchasing her tisanes.

Beatrice Kim, the owner of Dead City Rarities located two doors down, bustled into the room. Her face glowed with anticipation.

"Good afternoon, Elly," Beatrice said cheerfully.

"Hello, Mrs. Kim. Come to pick up your week's supply of rez-root tisane?"

"Yes, indeed, dear." Beatrice beamed at her. "Can't go through the week without my rez-root. And how's little Rose?"

Rose left off sorting through her box of

bracelets and scampered along the top of the counter to greet Beatrice, mumbling happily.

"My, don't you look lovely today." Beatrice admired the beads of the bracelet-necklace that peeked through Rose's tatty fur. "The blue matches your eyes. Definitely your color, sweetie."

Rose batted her lashes with blatantly false modesty and looked hopeful.

"Gracious, did you think I'd forgotten?" Beatrice removed a clear plastic bag bulging with cookies from the pocket of her coat. She opened it and took out one cookie. "There you go. Peanut butter and chocolate chip. Baked them fresh just last night."

Rose accepted the snack with a polite air and fell to nibbling daintily but with great efficiency.

"Here's your rez-root, Mrs. Kim." Elly put a small white sack on the counter and stepped briskly to the cash register. "That'll be fifteen dollars, please."

"Thank you, dear." Beatrice put the plastic bag full of cookies on the counter and gave Elly a conspiratorial wink. "I made some extra for you and your houseguest."

"Thank you," Elly said, determined to be polite. "That was very thoughtful of you."

Beatrice raised her eyes to the floor above

with a politely inquiring expression. "The two of you got home quite late last night. Expect you were out having a wonderful time on the town, hmmm?"

"How do you know that we got home late?"

Beatrice waved one hand in a casual manner. "Saw your lights come on for a few minutes around three in the morning." She chuckled. "Not your usual bedtime, is it, dear?"

Elly leaned both elbows on the counter. "Were you spying on me, Mrs. Kim?"

"Heavens no." Beatrice's eyes widened. "I wasn't sleeping very well. Got up to fix myself some of your excellent moonseed tonic and couldn't help but notice the lights over at your place."

Elly's jaw tightened. "You and everyone else on the block, apparently."

"I beg your pardon?"

Elly sighed. "Sorry, Mrs. Kim. The thing is, I've had a nonstop stream of people in here today, all from around the neighborhood. Everyone seems to be extremely curious about my houseguest."

"Well, you can't blame us, dear."

Elly raised her brows. "I can't?"

"With the exception of Griggs, the florist, this is a very friendly neighborhood," Beatrice reminded her. "We take an interest in each other. By the way, I saw Phillip and Garrick a short time ago, and they told me that they let you borrow their pass to The Road to the Ruins. I'll bet you and your friend danced the night away."

"We did dance, yes."

"How romantic. Phillip mentioned that he thought he saw your friend's car pull out of the alley earlier this morning. Did he go home?"

"No. He went out to take in some of the local sights."

"Which ones?"

"I believe he said something about going to the zoo."

"Oh, I see. Then he'll be returning soon?"

Elly drummed her fingers on the counter. "Yes, Mrs. Kim."

"I'll come back later, in that case."

"Why?" Elly asked bluntly. "Your rezroot is ready now."

Beatrice peered into her pocketbook with an air of vague dismay. "I seem to have forgotten my wallet."

"Don't worry, I'll put it on your account, Mrs. Kim."

"No, no, dear, that's quite all right. I prefer to pay cash."

"I wouldn't want you to make an extra trip."

"I'm just down the street." Beatrice smiled benignly and went to the door. "The exercise will do me good."

She let herself out onto the narrow sidewalk and vanished into the fog.

Elly looked at Rose, who had finished her cookie and was showing a marked interest in the bulging plastic bag that Beatrice had left behind.

"So much for my theory that here in the big city people aren't interested in their neighbors' private affairs," Elly said. "Looks like Mr. Guild Boss was right about folks being entertained by the goings-on in other peoples' sex lives."

Rose made a sympathetic sound and began to fiddle with the little plastic slider that sealed the bag.

Elly tried to shake off the restless anxiety that had been growing steadily within her. She glanced at the clock. "He's been gone for hours. What do you suppose is keeping him?"

There was a soft whisper of plastic on plastic. Rose had gotten the bag open. Gleefully, she reached inside to pluck out a cookie.

Elly thought about the new quartz-green flower in the vase on the kitchen windowsill.

"Speaking of wild nights and fast living,

just where did you go last night, missy?" she whispered.

Rose chomped down on a cookie.

The doorbells chimed again. Elly watched another familiar local, Herschel Lafayette, take one last, nervous look over his shoulder before he ducked inside the shop.

"Afternoon, Elly."

She groaned. "Not you, too, Herschel."

"Huh? Huh?" Herschel scuttled toward the counter. "Not me, too, what? What?"

"Are you here to ask about my private life? Because if so, you can turn around and go straight back outside."

Herschel stopped in front of her, pinched features screwed into an impatient scowl. "Why in green friggin' hell would I give a fried ghost ass what you did in private?"

A heretofore undiscovered sense of fondness and affection for the little ruin rat rose within Elly. She gave him a warm smile.

"I always knew there was something unique and special about you, Herschel."

"Yeah, yeah, I'm special, all right." He checked the misty view through the windows again. "Came by to see if you've heard from Bertha Newell lately."

Elly stiffened before she could help herself. Fortunately, Herschel didn't seem to notice. He was still watching the sidewalk.

"No, I haven't, now that you mention it," she said, injecting what she hoped was a suitably unconcerned note into her voice. "Why? Is there a problem?"

"Dunno." He turned back, jiggling a little. "Been by her shop a couple of times since yesterday. She's not there. Wanted to show her something I found in my sector. Get her opinion, y'know? When it comes to identifying the valuable stuff, she's as good as any of those fancy para-archaeologists up there at the university."

"She's probably working underground."

"Don't think so." He pulled the grease-stained collar of his jacket up around his neck, compulsively attempting to shield his features from passersby on the street. "She never stays underground overnight. Sleeping down in the catacombs spooks her."

"Maybe she went to see her daughter and grandchildren," Elly offered helpfully.

"Nope. She told me she was there a couple of weeks ago for one of the kid's birthdays. No reason she'd go back so soon."

"Well, I wouldn't worry if I were you," Elly said, trying for a soothing approach. The last thing they needed was to have Herschel start asking questions about Bertha's extended absence. "I'm sure she'll turn up. Meanwhile, why don't I fix you a nice cup of Harmonic balm tea?"

Herschel's eyes darted to the table that held the hot water pot and plastic cups. "Yeah, sure, that'd be great. Thanks."

Elly crossed to the tea table and selected a canister from the shelf while she tried to think of a way to distract Herschel from Bertha's closed shop.

"You say you've come across a particularly valuable relic?" she asked casually.

"Maybe. Don't know yet." He shoved his hands into his pockets and bounced on his toes a couple of times, peering out at the street. "That's why I want Bertha to look at it before I sell it. If it's as special as I think it is, I may go straight to the folks at the Cadence Museum with it, instead of my usual cheap-ass dealers."

"Good plan." She put the herbs into a cup, poured hot water over them, and stirred gently.

"Can't figure out why she'd up and disappear like this." Herschel began to pace. "Thought maybe the guy who runs the flower shop next door to her place, Griggs, or whatever his name is, might have seen her or at least know where she went. But he was closed, too."

She carried the cup of tea to the counter and set it down together with a small paper napkin. "Here you go, Herschel. Be careful, it's hot."

"Yeah, yeah, sure." He picked up the cup and inhaled the steamy aroma. Some of the nervous tension in him eased. "Thanks."

"You're welcome."

Herschel took a cautious sip and went toward the door. "I ran into Benny and Joe. They hadn't seen her either."

"Who are Benny and Joe?"

"Freelance hunter-tangler team. Some of the ruin rats hire 'em to go underground as protection. Griggs uses them a lot because he doesn't have any para-rez talent of his own."

"Stuart Griggs, the florist?" she asked, startled. "He goes into the catacombs to search for relics? I didn't know he was in that line."

"He's not." Herschel made a face. "Benny and Joe don't know why he likes to go down into the catacombs, but he hires them on a regular basis. They don't give a damn what he's looking for as long as he's willing to pay for their services."

"I see."

"Well, thanks for the tea. See ya."

"Bye, Herschel."

Elly leaned on the counter and watched Herschel hurry away into the gray mist.

"Guess the state of my sex life isn't of great interest to everyone in the neighborhood after all, Rose."

Rose crouched over her hoard of jewelry like some tiny, fluffy dragon gloating over a pile of gold, and munched her second cookie.

"You know, it occurs to me that other people may start to notice that Bertha isn't around," Elly said. "We don't want folks to get too curious about her absence. Maybe I should trot on down to her shop and put up a little sign saying she's out of town for a few days."

The more she thought about it, the more it seemed like a good idea. She had a key, she reminded herself. She could slip down the alley, enter the shop through the back door, put the sign in the window, and depart very discreetly.

Given the rapidly thickening fog, it was unlikely that anyone would notice her coming and going via the alley. But even if someone did see her, no one would think it odd. Everyone knew that she and Bertha were friends. She could always say that she'd had a call from Bertha. Something about a family emergency.

She used a felt pen to hand-letter the sign on a sheet of paper. When she was satisfied with the results, she turned over the Back in Ten Minutes sign in her own shop window.

She yanked her coat down off the hook, put it on, and opened her tote for Rose.

"Let's ride, sister."

Mumbling cheerfully, Rose dashed along the top of the counter and hopped down into the tote. She hooked her front paws over the top and poked her head up, blue eyes open wide, so as not to miss anything.

Chapter 21

The small, individually wrapped packets were packed neatly inside the three cardboard boxes stacked inside the old storage closet. The boxes were labeled Toilet Tissue, which struck Cooper as oddly appropriate under the circumstances.

He let himself out of the closet. The two-hundred-year-old basement was walled and floored with stone, but water had seeped in, as water always did in such places, creating a damp, moldy atmosphere.

Water was not the only thing that trickled into the large, dark space, he noticed. A lot of stray psi energy permeated the atmosphere down here, too. Not surprising, given the proximity of the Dead City Wall. Probably a hole-in-the-wall somewhere in the vicinity, just as Elly had suggested.

He used the flashlight to make his way back to a heavy wooden door that looked as if it had been there since the building was constructed.

Opening the door, he went up the old, cramped staircase. At the top of the staircase, he paused to listen intently for a moment before opening another door and moving into the janitorial storage room.

The shelves were crowded with cleaning supplies, cartons of industrial-sized rolls of toilet tissue, and paper towels.

He crossed the room, selected a few rolls of paper towels, and let himself out into the hall.

The janitorial cart was waiting right where he had left it. He grabbed the handle and went down the corridor and around the corner to a private elevator marked Executive Offices.

Finding the stash of drugs had been easy, he thought. Maybe too easy.

Chapter 22

The alley was choked with damp, gray mist. An uneasy chill flashed down Elly's spine and raised the hair on the nape of her neck. The close, looming walls of the buildings that lined the narrow service lane cut off much of what little light the fog allowed to filter through. She could barely make out the shape of the trash container across from her. The thick vapor acted like an otherworldly sound absorber, muffling the engines of the cautiously moving cars on the surrounding streets.

"Perfect cover," she whispered to Rose. "No one will see us."

She went forward, unable to suppress an icy prickle of tension.

The fog *was* a good thing under the circumstances, she thought. So why was it making her so nervous?

She found herself listening intently for the familiar clatter of a garbage can lid or the soft thud of footsteps behind her.

From time to time she glanced down at Rose, watching for signs of the dust bunny's second set of eyes.

Rose appeared alert but showed no indication of alarm.

When they arrived at the opening at the end of the alley, Elly felt a sharp sense of relief. The sensation vanished quickly when she discovered that the cramped street in front of her was disconcertingly empty of traffic and pedestrians. The entire neighborhood seemed to be suddenly deserted.

Hurrying across the pavement, she entered the alley that serviced the next block of shops. Maybe it was just her imagination, she thought, but the fog seemed denser and more ominous now. It had a disorienting effect on her sense of sight and direction. Rose rumbled softly in what seemed a reassuring manner.

She paused at the rear entrance of a shop to check the sign, afraid that she might overshoot her goal.

"Stuart Griggs, Florist," she read aloud to Rose. "Almost there. Bertha's shop is next."

She looked down at the dust bunny and froze when she saw that Rose was staring very hard at the closed door of the florist's shop. All four eyes were wide open, but there was no sign of any razor-sharp teeth.

Rose rumbled softly.

"What is it?" Elly asked. She looked from

Rose to the door and back again. "I know you don't like Mr. Griggs, but I wish you wouldn't growl at his door. It's embarrassing."

Rose's attention remained riveted on the door. Something was wrong; Elly felt it, but Rose was not acting as if she sensed a threat.

Herschel's comment about the floral shop being closed, too, went through her head.

Tentatively, she tried the doorknob. It twisted easily in her hand. Rose rumbled again, but there was still no sign of her teeth. She had not gone all sleek and dangerous, either, Elly thought. So far, so good.

She opened the door of the florist's back room. The faint hum of a refrigeration unit vibrated in the darkness. Her psi senses tingled gently. The rich, lush scents of cut flowers and greenery wafted toward her.

There was something heavy and unpleasant blended into the mix of floral smells, something that did not belong.

Probably dead and decaying flowers, she thought. Whatever it was, it made her feel queasy. She had to fight the impulse to turn and run.

The only thing that held her there, poised on the step, was the realization that Rose was still not displaying any indication that she sensed an imminent threat.

"Mr. Griggs?"

There was no answer. She knew then, deep down, that she had not expected a response.

The smell intermingled with the floral fragrances was that of death.

Chapter 23

Ormond Ripley checked his amber-faced watch as he went past his executive assistant's desk. "Please tell Maitland I want to see him in my office in half an hour to go over the new set of financials."

"Yes, Mr. Ripley." The assistant reached for the phone. "Mr. Dugan called while you were out. He said to tell you that he's found a new, very hot act for the club. The group will be auditioning at four this afternoon if you want to check it out for yourself."

"Thanks, I'll be there." He went to the door of his office. "Send Maitland in as soon as he arrives."

"Yes, sir."

He opened the door and walked into his office, savoring as he always did the hushed atmosphere. In his considered opinion, the room exuded an aura of power and luxury that was infinitely more intoxicating than any drug and more compelling than any woman he had ever met.

The walls were paneled in wave-wood that had been cut and shipped from the jungles of remote islands. The intricately inlaid stone flooring had been quarried in the mountains of the Northern Continent.

The artwork on the walls had once belonged to the private collection of one of the founders of the Cadence Museum. The paintings had been destined for the museum's galleries, but Ormond had made certain that they ended up here, instead. He was no great fan of the softly hued works of post–Era of Discord modernism, but that was not important. What mattered was that the art of that period was considered by connoisseurs to be brilliant and extremely valuable; in short, the province of the most elite collectors.

He had come a long way from the dusty, backwater mining town where he had been born and raised, he thought, and every time he walked into this office he took a moment to reflect on that journey.

His dissonance-energy para-rez talents had been his ticket to a good-paying job as a Guild man. He'd had no family connections to lean on, but an aptitude for internal politics and an intuitive ability to choose the winning side had helped him rise within the Guild to the status of Council member.

But he had known from the start of his career as a hunter that he wanted to do more with his life than chase ghosts through the catacombs. His driving goal had been to establish his own empire. The Road to the Ruins was the culmination of his ambitions, and he gloried in the most minute details of the day-to-day operations of his kingdom.

He started toward the heavily carved wooden desk at the far end of the room.

The door of his private bathroom opened almost but not quite soundlessly. Startled, he turned on one heel.

He scowled at the janitor lounging in the opening.

"What are you doing here?" he asked. "That bathroom is never cleaned at this time of day unless I request it."

"We need to talk," the janitor said, leaning on his mop. "Better have your assistant hold your calls for a while."

"Who are you?"

"At the moment I'm the only thing standing between you and an extended stay in prison."

"Not my vacation destination of choice. What's going on here?"

The janitor took a small packet out of one pocket. "I think you've been set up to take the fall for dealing the crap they call enchantment dust."

"What in the name of green hell?"

Ormond held out his hand. "Let me see that."

The janitor tossed it to him without comment.

He caught the plastic bag and unsealed it cautiously. There was no need to taste or sniff the powder inside. His parapsych senses were very acute. This close to the drug, he could feel the faint tingle on the paranormal wavelengths to which he was attuned.

So much for the possibility that the janitor was bluffing.

"Where did you get this?" he asked, buying some time to think while he resealed the bag. Visions of his hard-won personal empire crumbling before his eyes flashed through his head. He had not come this far only to lose it all now.

"Found it down in the old basement. Place leaks like a sieve, by the way, water and psi energy. Got a rat hole down there?"

Ormond ignored that. "I don't sell drugs."

"Going to be tough to prove if the cops raid this place and find the stash that I just found."

"There's more of this junk down there?"

"Three large cardboard boxes filled with little packets like that one."

Ormond went to stand behind his desk, trying to collect his thoughts.

"You really think someone is trying to frame me?" he asked finally.

"That's how it looks."

"Why not assume that I've gone into the drug-dealing business?"

"I did a little research before I came here today." The janitor's smile was cryptic and cold. "If you did decide to deal drugs, I don't think you'd pack them in nonwaterproof boxes and then stash them in an empty closet in a damp basement. You're smart, and you're a strong para-rez. You'd be far more likely to conceal them in the catacombs where the odds would be against anyone finding the stuff."

"You sure about that?" Ormond asked. "Maybe I was going with the hide-it-in-plain-sight theory."

"A possibility. But there's something else that makes me think you're not involved in this."

"What's that?"

"Like I said, I checked around." The janitor gave the expensive room an assessing look. "You've worked hard to build this place, and you've been damn careful to stay inside the legal zone. You're a risk-taker, but I don't think you're the type to put all this on the line for the sake of some short-term drug profits. Not just my opinion, by the way. There's someone else who agrees with me."

"Who?"

"Mercer Wyatt."

Ormond went very still. "This is Guild business?"

"Yes. Wyatt said you served on the Council here in Cadence for a few years."

"What of it?"

"It means you're cleared to discuss blue freaks."

"There's one involved in this thing?"

"Yes." The janitor indicated the mop in his hand. "Wyatt asked me to clean up the mess before it becomes a major PR problem for him."

"Well, hell." Ormond exhaled and lowered himself slowly into his chair. "You're not the janitor. You're the librarian."

Chapter 24

Elly put one hand just inside the opening, groped for and found the lights.

Two overhead fluo-rez tubes came on, illuminating the scene in a cold blue light. Masses of flowers and bunches of decorative greenery filled the room. Arrangements in vases of various shapes and sizes lined the shelves behind the glass doors of the cooler. The effect was funereal.

The body of Stuart Griggs, sprawled facedown on the floor, provided the finishing touch.

There was no sign of blood, she noticed, no indication that the florist had been attacked. Perhaps he'd had a stroke or a heart attack.

She reached into the tote for her phone and punched in the emergency number.

Instinctively she started to turn away from the body on the floor. But the sight of a strip of white bandage sticking out from under Griggs's rolled-up sleeve made her hesitate.

She forced herself to move closer to the

body, ignoring Rose's warning grumble.

Holding her breath and fighting her roiling stomach, she leaned over, caught hold of the sleeve with the thumb and forefinger of her right hand, and twitched the fabric back a couple of inches.

There was a wide, white bandage wrapped snugly around Stuart Griggs's lower left arm.

"Oh, damn," Elly whispered.

Chapter 25

Cooper saw the flashing amber and red lights of the ambulance when he turned the corner onto Ruin Lane. They created an eerie, strobelike effect in the fog.

An uneasy sensation gripped his insides. The emergency vehicle was almost directly in front of Bertha Newell's shop. There was a police cruiser in front of it.

He had been driving slowly because of the fog, but now he lowered the Spectrum's speed to a crawl. When he got closer he could make out the small group of figures gathered on the sidewalk. His tension eased slightly when he realized that they were watching the open door of the floral shop.

He spotted Elly immediately. She stood with Garrick Lattimer and Phillip Manchester.

He brought the Spectrum to a halt at the curb, got out, and walked back down the sidewalk to join Elly and her friends.

Rose was perched inside Elly's tote, watching the action. Her head swiveled around abruptly. She rumbled a greeting when she noticed Cooper approaching.

Elly and the two men turned to look at him, too.

"There you are," Elly said. She had a strained, shadowed expression on her face. "I was getting worried."

He nodded at the two men. "What's going on?"

Garrick angled his chin toward the front door of the floral shop. "Stuart Griggs, the owner of that business, died sometime this afternoon. Elly found him a short while ago."

Cooper looked at Elly's withdrawn, un-readable face. "How did you come to find the body?"

"I was taking a note to Bertha's shop to hang in her window." She gave him a mean-ingful look. "People have been wondering where she is."

"Got it," he said quietly.

"When I went past Griggs's back door, Rose started making odd little noises. I think she sensed that something was wrong. So I tried the door. It was unlocked. When I opened it, I saw the body on the floor."

Two medics emerged from the front of the shop. They carried a stretcher with a draped figure on top.

"I heard someone say they think it was a

heart attack," Phillip volunteered.

"The cop came over here to talk to us for a few minutes," Garrick added. "Actually, it was Elly he wanted to speak with, because she was the one who found Griggs. He said there were no obvious signs of violence except for a bad cut on the florist's arm that was mostly healed."

Cooper frowned. "A cut?"

"The cop figured Griggs had probably injured himself sometime in the past couple of weeks with one of the tools he used to trim flowers," Phillip explained.

Elly turned back to watch the stretcher being loaded into the back of the ambulance. She did not speak.

He touched her arm. "Let's go home."

"Yes. Good idea." She spun toward him, clearly relieved to have an excuse to leave.

He bundled her into the car. As soon as she was settled Rose elevated out of the tote and drifted up onto her favored perch on the back of the seat.

Cooper got in on the driver's side, rezzed the engine, and pulled away from the curb.

"You okay?" he asked.

"Yes. What about you? Did you find the drugs? I've been worried sick all afternoon."

"I found the stash. I also had a conversation with Ormond Ripley."

"The owner of the casino?"

"He's a former member of the local Guild Council. I can't rule out the possibility that he's the dealer, but I'm inclined to agree with Wyatt that it's very unlikely. I'll tell you all about it later. What exactly happened back there? I'm getting the feeling I haven't heard the whole story yet."

"Very perceptive of you." She cleared her throat. "It's a little more complicated than it appears."

"How much more complicated?"

"Do you remember me telling you that there had been an attempted burglary in the neighborhood about ten days ago?"

He found a parking place in front of St. Clair's Herbal Emporium. "I remember."

"Yes, well, I left out one tiny little detail."

He de-rezzed the engine and turned in the seat. "*What* tiny little detail?"

"The shop that was broken into was mine."

His insides clenched. "You never said anything about a break-in to your folks. Your dad would have mentioned it to me."

"I'm sure he would have," she said dryly. "And he and Mom would have gone bonkers. I could just see my father picking up the phone and calling Mercer Wyatt, himself, to demand a full-time bodyguard for me. Mom would have started in again, pressuring me to return to Aurora Springs. I'd be getting lectures from my brothers on the dangers of the big city."

He closed his eyes and scrubbed his face with one hand. "Okay, I get the picture. You didn't tell your family because you didn't want to deal with the fallout."

"Do you blame me?"

"Hell, yes. But that's another issue. Much as I hate to say it, I think we'd better stay focused here."

"Cooper —"

"Tell me why you're bringing up the subject now."

She drew a deep breath. "You're not going to like this."

"I already don't like it."

"Brace yourself. Rose and I were home when the burglar broke into my shop."

He felt as if he'd been kicked in the gut.

"Neither of us was hurt," she added hastily. "Rose scared the guy off."

"How?"

"She sensed him the instant he was inside the shop, of course. I woke up when she did, realized something was wrong, and jumped out of bed to lock my bedroom door. But before I could stop her, Rose went flying out of the bedroom, teeth and eyes blazing. She shot down the hall to the top of the stairs. The next thing I know, the burglar's screaming green murder. He sounded panic-stricken. He ran back down the stairs and out into the alley."

"What about the cops?"

"I called them, of course. But by the time they got there, he was long gone."

"Naturally," Cooper muttered.

"I filled out a report, but they made it clear that in cases of that sort there wasn't much hope of turning up a suspect."

"So you went out and bought new locks."

"I also alerted my neighbors, and we set up the block watch program."

"Nothing like a good block watch program, I always say." He ran his fingers through his hair. "Damn. All right, let's keep on track. You're bringing this up now because . . . ?"

She cleared her throat. "When the burglar ran out, I caught a glimpse of him from the top of the stairs. I couldn't see his face. He was all wrapped up in a heavy, dark coat and some sort of stocking cap pulled down very low. But when he ran through a shaft of moonlight, I could see one thing very plainly."

"What?"

She reached up to touch Rose. "He was

clutching his left arm. Later, when I turned on the lights, I found blood on the stairs. I'm sure Rose bit him quite badly."

Comprehension settled on him like an icy mist.

"On the left arm?"

She looked at him with big, serious eyes. "Right about where Stuart Griggs had a wide bandage covering a recently healed wound."

Chapter 26

"Let's take this from the top," Cooper said, halting in front of the kitchen window. "Why would Stuart Griggs have tried to break into your shop? What was he looking for?"

Seated at the table, Elly watched him across the top of her mug. The first thing she had done when they had returned to her apartment was brew up a pot of Balance Tea to soothe her edgy nerves.

"I suppose," she said slowly, "that he might have been looking for money, but somehow, it doesn't seem likely, does it?"

"Given the really big coincidence we're dealing with here, no."

"Coincidence?"

"He's the owner of the shop next door to Bertha Newell's business, and he turns up dead only a couple of days after someone tries to murder Bertha."

She shuddered. "I see what you mean. I hadn't thought about that connection."

"When did Griggs open his shop on Ruin Lane?"

"I'm not sure. My friend, Doreen, across the street, mentioned that the floral shop has been around forever. But Griggs was a dour sort and very much a loner. None of us knew him well. He never got involved in any of the neighborhood activities."

"Looks like he may have had his reasons." Cooper shifted his attention back to the foggy alley below the window. "Did he buy herbal products from you?"

"He came in a few times and bought some moonseed tisane. But the only time I had what you might call an extended conversation with him was the day I took one of Rose's flowers to his shop to ask him if he recognized it."

She looked at the green flower on the windowsill.

Cooper followed her gaze. "When was that?"

"Just a couple of weeks ago," she said quietly. "As I told you, I'd had no luck researching the blossoms in my herbals. I'd hesitated to ask anyone else about the flowers because I was afraid that Rose was snatching them out of some local gardener's hothouse. But I finally got so curious I decided to take one to Griggs."

"You told him that Rose had brought it to you?"

"Yes." She winced. "And immediately regretted it."

"Why?"

"Just a feeling. I had Rose in my tote that day and I didn't like the way Griggs looked at her. I could tell that Rose didn't like him very much, either."

Cooper picked up the green vase and held the flower closer to the light to examine it. "Did you and Griggs ever meet again?"

"He came into the shop a few days ago and made a show of buying another tisane. While I was preparing it, he asked me if Rose had brought me any more flowers. Rose growled at him. It was embarrassing."

"What did you tell Griggs?"

"I lied through my teeth and said that there hadn't been any more flowers. But I don't know if he believed me." She gripped the mug a little more tightly. "Do you think Griggs came here that night to steal the flower? Why?"

Cooper shrugged. "He was a florist. Obviously he had a special interest in flowers, and you say this one is very unusual. You said orchid growers can be obsessive. Maybe Griggs became fixated on your flower."

A thought struck her. "Or maybe he was like me, sensitive to plant psi. The energy buzz off that flower is very strong. There's no reason to think that I'm the only one in the world who can sense it."

"No." Cooper looked at Rose, who was hunched over her food dish, munching on cheese and crackers. "But if he was obsessed with the green flowers, it's possible that he came here to get the one character in this mystery who knows where to find them."

"Oh, my lord." Elly sat up very straight, shoulders stiffening in alarm. "Do you think he came here to steal Rose?"

Rose batted her eyelashes at the sound of her name.

"What I think," Cooper said quietly, "is that I need to have a look around his shop. The sooner the better."

"Tonight?"

"Yes, but not until after your neighbors have gone to bed." He went back to the window to study the fog-shrouded buildings. "Folks around here seem to be just as nosy as the ones you had back home."

She got to her feet. "I'll come with you."

"No," he said, flat and final.

"You'll need Rose. She's an excellent watch bunny."

He gave Rose a thoughtful look. "You've got a point."

"Where Rose goes, I go," she said, closing the deal.

"Damn it, Elly, I said no."

She went to the refrigerator. "We'll need to fortify ourselves. I'm going to make some pasta with pesto sauce. Why don't you whip up a nice salad to go with it?"

"Not sure whipping up nice salads is in the Guild boss job description."

She opened the refrigerator and reached into the vegetable drawer for the lettuce. "A good Guild boss should be able to handle any challenge that comes along, I always say."

"That's strange. I don't recall ever hearing you say that."

"The lettuce is already washed. Olive oil and vinegar are on the counter. Don't worry, I'll talk you through this, big guy."

He smiled faintly. "Promise?"

"Yep." She opened a cupboard door and took out a package of pasta. "And while you're at it, you can tell me what would make an intelligent, extremely well-educated young boy from a respectable family of distinguished academics decide to pursue a career as boss of the Aurora Springs Guild."

For a few seconds she thought he was going to change the subject. Then, to her surprise, he went to the sink to wash his hands and started to talk.

"Growing up as a dissonance-energy para-rez predisposed me to want to become a hunter." He dried his hands on a towel and removed the lettuce from the plastic bag. "My parents were not keen on the idea."

"Of course not. Joining the Guild is not exactly at the top of the list of great careers as far as most well-educated, mainstream parents are concerned."

"I think they'd had a few hints," Cooper said, eyeing the lettuce. "Once the full range of my parapsych abilities came in, they realized there was something different about me, even for a dissonance-energy para-rez. I started sneaking out of the house and going down into the catacombs alone to experiment with blue energy. My father followed me one night and saw what I was doing."

"How did he react?"

"There had been a few hunters in the family over the years. Although he was a college professor, Dad knew enough Guild lore to recognize that I was working blue ghost light." Cooper paused. "Do I need a knife to cut this stuff?"

"No, you tear lettuce, you don't use a knife." She pushed a large salad bowl toward him. "Go on with your story."

"Dad did what any parent would do when he realized he had a dissonance-energy para-rez freak in the family. His first instinct was to hide me from the Guild."

She glowered. "You aren't a freak."

"Well, let's put it this way. Regardless of how you describe it, my variation of dissonance-energy talent is definitely not normal. My folks were pretty sure that if they consulted the local Guild authorities, things would get complicated in a hurry. At the very least there would have been a tremendous amount of pressure to let the Guild oversee my para-rez training."

She filled a pan with water from the faucet. "No doubt about it."

"Dad and I had a very long talk that day. He explained the facts of life concerning what little he knew about the risks of working blue energy. Mostly he tried to make it clear that it had to be kept secret, even from my best friends."

She smiled wryly. "Sounds like the same talk I got when my folks realized I could pick up plant psi."

"See? I knew we had a lot in common."

She decided to let that go. "Okay, so you kept your talent a secret while you were growing up. I can understand why you might have wanted to try being a ghost hunter. Every kid with para-rez talent wants to find out what it's like to use it down in the catacombs, at least for a while. But what made you so determined to become a Guild boss, instead of, say, a history professor?"

He tore some lettuce very neatly and dropped it into the bowl. "That decision was probably due to another little-known Boone family secret."

"This is getting interesting." She folded her arms and leaned against the counter. "Are you going to tell me that secret?"

"I think the time has come," he said. "Remember the legend of Wild Watson Whittaker?"

"Of course." She plucked a tomato out of the bowl on the counter and gave it to him. "Every kid in Aurora Springs knows the story of Watson Whittaker. He was the hunter who saved the town almost single-handedly during the Era of Discord. The big cities were too busy fighting Vance's legions to be able to spare any dissonance-energy para-rezzes to guard the outlying villages and communities. Small towns like Aurora Springs were left on their own."

He examined the tomato as though it were a strange alien artifact. "What do I do with this?"

"You slice it." She handed him a paring knife. "With this."

"Knew there would be a knife involved in this thing sooner or later."

"I want to hear the rest of your story about Watson Whittaker."

Cooper positioned the tomato on the counter. "You said you knew the legend?"

"Sure. Vincent Lee Vance assumed that Aurora Springs had sent what few hunters it had to the main battle sites at Resonance and Cadence. He figured he could use the tunnels under our town as a staging point. He sent a contingent of his followers to take control of the catacombs beneath Aurora Springs. But Watson Whittaker, who had been left in charge of the town's defense, set a trap."

"Vance's followers walked right into it."

"Most of the rebels wound up brain-fried," she concluded on a note of triumph. "The rest fled in disarray. To this day, no one knows exactly how Whittaker managed to pull off the victory."

Cooper cut cautiously into the tomato. "After the Era of Discord, Aurora Springs founded its own Guild, just as the big cities did. They selected a Council and chose the town's first Guild boss."

"My ever-so-great-grandfather, John

Sander St. Clair," she said proudly. "May he rest in peace."

"At the time," Cooper said, continuing his deliberate slicing, "there were some who expected that Watson Whittaker would get the job."

"Hah. Not a chance." She chuckled, thinking of the books and films she had seen over the years. "They didn't call him *Wild* Watson Whittaker for nothing. He was one of those larger-than-life heroic types who comes through in a crisis, but he certainly wasn't management material. The founders of the Aurora Springs Guild recognized that."

"They pinned a lot of medals on Whittaker, held a parade in his honor, and put up a statue in the park." Cooper sliced boldly into the tomato. "Then they gave the Guild boss job to John Sander St. Clair."

"They sure did." She opened a box of croutons for him. "And Whittaker went right out and proved beyond a shadow of a doubt that the founders had been absolutely right to pass him over. He vowed revenge on the Guild and the town. Went from being a legendary hero to being the most notorious catacomb raider in the history of the colonies."

"Yeah, Whittaker was pretty pissed,"

Cooper said, looking thoughtful.

"And the rest, as they say, is history. In the six months following the establishment of the Aurora Springs Guild, a fortune in alien artifacts was stolen from excavation teams working in the sectors that the Aurora Springs hunters were responsible for protecting. The raids were all daring and brilliantly executed. The raider was never caught, but everyone knew it was Watson Whittaker. Then, one day, he did what all great legends do, he vanished into the realm of myth."

Cooper reached into the box and helped himself to a crouton. "Over the years, the official version of the legend has lost a few details in the telling."

She frowned. "You're not supposed to eat those straight out of the box. You sprinkle them on the salad."

"Yeah?" He fed one to Rose, who was drifting around the floor at his feet. "Thought maybe they were an hors d'oeuvre or something."

"Forget the croutons," she said. "You know, sometimes I forget that you really do have a background in history and archival research. Tell me what's missing from the official version of the Watson Whittaker story."

He scooped up the sliced tomatoes and arranged them in neat rows on top of the lettuce. "Among other things, there was a woman involved."

"Really?" She got some cheese out of the refrigerator. "I never heard that."

"Probably because the lady ended up marrying your ever-so-great-grandfather, John Sander St. Clair."

"What?" Dumbfounded, she straightened abruptly, packet of cheese in her hand. "Watson Whittaker and St. Clair were rivals for my multi-great-grandmother's hand?"

"Yes. When Whittaker realized he wasn't going to be given control of the Aurora Springs Guild, he tried to convince your ancestor to run off with him. She declined and married St. Clair, instead." He took the cheese from her. "That was when Whittaker went rogue and became a blue freak."

She whistled softly. "Watson Whittaker could work blue ghost energy?"

"Yes."

"That certainly explains a few things, like how he managed to save Aurora Springs pretty much all on his own during the Era of Discord."

Cooper unwrapped the cheese. "Right. The Guild knew that if the truth about the blue ghost light got out, it would make folks nervous. So they hushed up the facts."

"That wouldn't have been hard to do, seeing as how it was primarily Guild historians who wrote the official accounts concerning the Era of Discord."

"You know what they say, history is written by the winners."

"This is fascinating." She watched him study the hunk of cheese he had uncovered. "You've done some serious research on Wild Watson Whittaker, haven't you?"

"Oh, yeah." He crunched another crouton and dropped one into Rose's waiting paws. "You might say I had a personal interest in him."

She nodded. "Because he had a rare parapsych talent like yours. Makes sense. So what actually happened to Whittaker? Did he die alone somewhere underground, or did he live to enjoy his ill-gotten gains?"

"He changed his name, built a new identity for himself in one of the big cities, got married, and started a family."

"Sounds a trifle boring after all his adventures in Aurora Springs."

"Even guys like Watson Whittaker have to settle down sometime." He examined the cheese closely. "Now what?"

"Cut off a chunk and crumble it," she said absently, her thoughts on what he had just told her. "What about the fortune in artifacts that Watson Whittaker stole? What happened to the relics?"

"Let's just say that Watson Whittaker showed more business acumen than the members of the Aurora Springs Guild credited him with having."

"Aha. He invested well?"

"Very well. Unfortunately, few of his descendents displayed the same gifts for finances. Over the years, Whittaker's offspring managed to fritter away the empire that he built." He dropped a piece of cheese to Rose. "But, hey, easy come, easy go."

"What about Whittaker's descendents? What happened to them?"

"A few became hunters, but for the most part they were fairly standard para-rez talents. The majority of his offspring showed no dissonance-energy para-rez talents at all. They chose other careers."

"Were there any more who could work blue ghost light?"

"Eventually there was one." Cooper crumbled cheese into the bowl. "But he didn't come along for quite a while."

"Did he turn out to be notorious like Watson Whittaker?"

"Depends on your point of view." Cooper crumbled cheese onto the salad. "He recently became the boss of the Aurora Springs Guild."

She had been so wrapped up in the story that it took a second or two before she got it.

"You?" She dropped her arms in shock. "Watson Whittaker was your direct ancestor?"

"Yeah." He studied the bottles of oil and vinegar. "What do I do with these?"

She stared at him, openmouthed, and then she felt the ironic humor of the situation strike her full force.

"Oh, my," she said. "Oh, my goodness."

She was suddenly laughing so hard, she had to grab the edge of the counter to steady herself. "This is priceless. The funniest thing I've heard in ages."

"I live to amuse. Part of the Guild boss job description."

She reeled against the kitchen counter, slapping a palm across her mouth in a vain attempt to stifle the giggles. "If only the Council members back home knew about this." She flapped a hand. "Wait. *Do* any of them know? Or is this still a deep, dark family secret?"

He watched her with an unreadable expression. "It's still a deep, dark family secret."

"Not anymore. Now I know it. Oh, wow.

This is so cool. I know your deepest, darkest family secret. I know that you are the descendent of the most notorious man in Aurora Springs history. I have you in my power, Cooper Boone."

"The way I figure it, you're going to be family one of these days, so it's okay for you to know the secret."

That stopped her laughter as effectively as if he had suddenly pumped all of the oxygen out of the air.

"You figured what?" she sputtered.

"You heard me."

She put up both hands, palms out. "Oh, no you don't. There has been no change in the status of our relationship regarding marriage."

"That hurts. We've been living under the same roof for a couple of days. We've dined together, we've danced together, and we've had some great sex."

"Once. We had great sex one time. That's all."

"Whatever. My point here is, can you blame me for thinking we were making progress?"

"Having sex one time is not progress."

"What do you call it?" he asked.

"*Sex,*" she yelped.

"What about the fact that I've just told

you my deepest, darkest family secret? As far as I'm concerned, that's the kind of secret only a wife should know."

"Relax, Guild Boss. You have my word of honor that I won't tell a soul about your connection to Watson Whittaker." She winked. "Frankly, though, I doubt if the story would do you any real damage if it did get out. Might even give you a major boost in the popularity ratings back home. People love legends."

"I'm not really into popularity ratings," he said in a musing tone. "But I do take secrets seriously. The way I look at it, if you don't marry me, you've got only one other option."

"Oh, yeah?" She gave him a challenging smile. "What would that be?"

"You'd better run like hell."

She blinked. "You're teasing me."

"I'm a Guild boss, remember? I have no sense of humor."

Chapter 27

He had been teasing her, she assured herself several hours later when they went out into the alley. The problem with handling Cooper was that he was so good at concealing his reactions and emotions, it was almost impossible to read him.

"Stay close," Cooper said. He was definitely all business now as he glided forward into the heavily shadowed alley. "I don't want to use the flashlight unless it's absolutely necessary. Keep an eye on Rose. She's our trouble indicator."

"I'll watch for the teeth," Elly promised.

Perched on her shoulder, Rose appeared eager for the adventure. She did not seem the least bit tense or alarmed.

The fog was not as heavy as it had been that afternoon, but it was still thick enough to hamper visibility. The lights over the rear doors of the shops glowed weakly in the mist.

Cooper chose a path that kept them out of the small circles of illumination that surrounded each door. When they arrived at the end of the alley, Elly saw that the street was deserted. The fog here was infused with the subtle green light created by the Dead City Wall a few blocks away.

It seemed to Elly that the service lane that ran behind the row of shops in the next block was darker than the one they had just traversed. It took her a few seconds to understand why.

"There are no lights over the back door of Griggs's shop," she said in a low voice. "Must have burned out."

"Maybe," was all Cooper said.

He gave Rose another look. Evidently satisfied that their trouble indicator was still untroubled, he led the way into the shadows of the second alley.

They arrived at the back door of the floral shop without incident. Rose muttered irritably when Cooper took out a pair of thin gloves, pulled them on, and tried the knob.

"I told you, she never liked Griggs," Elly explained softly.

"The lady has excellent taste." Cooper paused. "Door's open."

"Probably because there was no one around to lock up after they took the body away," Elly said.

"Maybe," Cooper repeated.

She was getting the impression that he

said *maybe* in that particular tone of voice whenever he had some serious doubts about the exact answer to a question.

"It was open when I found Griggs this afternoon," she added.

He said nothing this time, just motioned her to stand to the side. She obeyed. Cooper eased the door inward.

The heavy scent of wilting flowers wafted out. Plant psi whispered across her senses.

Rose snorted softly in disgust, but she didn't show any teeth.

Cooper flicked on the flashlight and moved through the doorway. Elly followed.

"Looks like someone got here before us," Cooper said quietly.

Elly stopped abruptly, shocked by the scene of chaos. Buckets of flowers and greenery had been overturned, spilling water and decorative foliage across the workbenches. An assortment of vases, decorative pots, and small planters had been yanked off the shelves and carelessly smashed on the floor.

"This place was very neat and tidy when I found the body," Elly said. "Do you think maybe some opportunistic thieves saw Griggs's remains being carried out earlier and decided to see if there was anything worth stealing?"

"Maybe." Cooper took another look at an unconcerned Rose and then walked through the mess, careful not to step in the wet spots. "But I think whoever did this was searching for something in particular." He speared the light around the room. "Wonder if he found it."

"It's going to be hard to tell, because we don't know what he was looking for."

Cooper methodically checked the drawers in the workbenches. Most had been emptied. Elly dug her own small light out of her pocket and aimed it into the nearest drawer. A handful of ready-made ribbon bows, thin wires, and an assortment of other small, fanciful items designed to decorate floral arrangements lay inside.

Rose chattered excitedly and scampered down her arm.

Cooper frowned. "What's up with her?"

Elly watched Rose hop into the drawer and start sorting through the bows and small ornaments. "I'm not sure, but I think she may be shopping for a new addition to her jewelry collection."

"Figures," he said, sounding resigned. "Other Guild bosses have loyal minions to guard their backs. I get a dust bunny who's into glitz."

He went to a door and opened it carefully.

Elly looked past him and saw the shadowed front room of the shop. The shades had been pulled tightly closed, keeping out the streetlights, but in the glow of the flashlight she could see that room, too, had been thoroughly ransacked.

"Let's take a look upstairs before we check out the basement," Cooper said.

Elly reached into the drawer for Rose. "Let's go. The boss is giving orders again. He's in charge tonight."

Rose squeaked once in protest, but she allowed herself to be picked up. Elly put her back on her shoulder.

They went up the stairs. At the top of the landing Elly saw a small, one-bedroom apartment almost identical to her own.

The kitchen and living area had been torn apart. Cooper prowled through the space, saying nothing.

When they went into the bedroom, Elly was surprised to see three leather-bound volumes on the floor where the intruder had dumped them.

Cooper picked up one of the books and leafed through it with the aid of the flashlight. "This is old. I mean, really old. It's a private journal written before the Era of Discord."

Elly examined one of the other tomes.

"So is this one. Doesn't look like the sort of light reading I'd have expected Griggs to use to put himself to sleep at night."

"No."

She scooped up another volume. The leather binding was burnished and smooth in her hands. She opened it carefully and aimed the narrow beam of the flashlight at the title page.

A thrill of disbelief flashed through her.

"Good grief," she managed.

"What?"

"*Medicinal Herbs and Flowers of Harmony* by Dr. Mary Tyler Jordan," she read aloud. She could hear the shock and wonderment vibrating in her own voice. "This is amazing."

"It's an herbal?"

"Not just any herbal." She looked up from the title page. "Unless this is a forgery, and I can't see why anyone would go to the trouble of creating one, this is Jordan's record of her personal observations and experiments."

"Who was Mary Tyler Jordan?"

"An eccentric botanist. She died about fifty years ago and was consigned to the dust heap of history in her own time. Her work was never recognized as legitimate. Her peers considered her an outsider, a real crackpot."

"Eccentric being a polite term for crazy?"

"Not in my opinion. Jordan devoted her life to studying the therapeutic uses of herbs and plants. I use several of her old tisane recipes. In my opinion, she was a genius. But the mainstream medical community dismissed her work because she was not able to do the kind of controlled studies that scientific researchers demand."

"Why no controlled studies if she was so good?"

"Because she was dismissed as a quack and couldn't get funding from the government or any reputable research firm." Elly looked at the herbal in her hands. "That's how it works, you know."

"Can't argue with that."

"And there's no getting around the fact that she contributed to her own downfall when she declared that she had discovered what came to be known in the field as Jordan's Jungle."

"Never heard of it."

"Jordan wrote that she had discovered a vast underground jungle in the catacombs," she explained.

"No wonder everyone wrote her off as eccentric. In the whole history of catacomb exploration no one has ever discovered any signs of plant or animal life growing in the tunnels."

"True," Elly said. "The assumption is that Jordan may have experimented on herself with some of her own psychoactive herbal concoctions and experienced a few major hallucinations. In any event, her work was ignored and later forgotten except, of course, by Jordan's Jungle fanatics."

"Those would be folks who believe that the jungle exists?"

"Right. They are a small but sturdy lot of diehards who have been known to spend years searching for the jungle." Elly hefted the heavy volume, unable to believe that she was holding it in her hand. "Do you realize how rare this book is? There are only three known copies still in existence, and all of them are in the libraries of private collectors who have refused to allow access to them."

"You tried?"

"Oh, yes. I've always been interested in Jordan because of her early work with medicinal herbs. After I started coming across obscure references to this herbal, I couldn't rest until I tracked down every extant copy of her book. I contacted each of the three collectors and asked for permission to examine their copies. They all turned me down flat."

"Did they give any reason?"

She smiled wryly. "They're all book collectors. They didn't need reasons. In fairness, two of the three are elderly and quite reclusive. I think they were simply afraid to allow strangers inside their homes, let alone into their private libraries."

"What about the third?"

She cleared her throat. "Dr. Frances Higginbottom informed me that she only allowed those with what she termed 'proper academic qualifications' access to her private library."

"You've got plenty of academic qualifications."

"Not in Dr. Higginbottom's view. She went on to make it clear that she didn't think anyone from a *Guild* family could possibly have the right degrees or a suitably serious, scholarly mind."

"A trifle biased against the Guild, huh?"

"As we all know, the Guilds do have some image issues. And, to be honest, although I've got a couple of degrees, the highest post I held at Aurora Springs College was that of a lowly instructor. In addition, I can't claim any significant publications. I really didn't have the proper academic qualifications to be allowed into her library."

"Three extant copies," Cooper repeated thoughtfully. "So, we ask ourselves, how did a third-rate florist like Stuart Griggs come by an extremely rare, presumably expensive herbal and a couple of highly collectible pre–Era of Discord journals?"

"Excellent question." She looked around at the spare, shabby furnishings. "I don't know the answer to it, but I'll tell you one thing about Mr. Griggs that I hadn't realized until this very moment."

"What's that?"

"I think it's safe to say that he chose to set up his shop here in Ruin Lane for the same reason I did."

"Which was?"

"Mary Tyler Jordan once lived on this street," she said. "In fact, if the old records are correct, she lived at this exact address. I remember talking about it with the Realtor when I was searching for a suitable location for my herb shop."

"Let's check out the basement."

"You know, this is kind of exciting." Clutching the precious Jordan herbal, Elly hurried after him. "I'm starting to feel just like Harmony Drew."

"Who's Harmony Drew?" he asked, halfway down the stairs.

"You never read the Harmony Drew, Girl Detective stories when you were growing up?" she asked.

"Doesn't rez any bells."

"Well, you're a guy. You probably read The Amber Boys series instead. My brothers loved those. All about a couple of brothers with strong dissonance-energy para-rez talents who solved crimes."

"That must have been the year I was reading Espindoza's *A History of the Era of Discord.*"

"Oh, sure. Every kid reads Espindoza's *History* when they're ten years old. How many volumes in that set? Two? Three?"

"Four, not counting the index."

"Gosh, how could I forget the index? Yes, indeed, fun, youthful reading, all right."

"You're mocking me, aren't you?" he asked.

"You have to admit, your childhood reading program was a little unusual."

"My parents assumed that I would follow in their footsteps. When they discovered that I had a strong appetite for history, they fed it, figuring I would become a history professor like Dad."

"Little did they know," Elly murmured darkly.

Cooper did not respond to that comment. He reached the floor of the back room and went behind the staircase.

Elly felt the wave of strong psi energy the

instant he opened the cellar door.

"There's a hole-in-the-wall down there," she said.

"Sure is."

Cooper descended first into the darkness. Elly followed, keeping a close watch on Rose, who showed interest but no alarm.

At the foot of the old staircase Elly saw the thin arc of green light. It emanated from a narrow, jagged opening that was partially obscured by several large boulders.

"It's not far from the hole next door in Bertha Newell's cellar," Cooper said, crossing the space to examine the opening on the other side of the rocks. "I wonder if she knows that Griggs had an entrance into the catacombs only a few yards away from the one she uses."

"I don't think so. She never mentioned it. You know how it is in the catacombs. You can have two bolt-holes separated by only a few feet on the outside, but once you go inside, you're back in the labyrinth. You might never find the second entrance from the interior unless you stumble into it accidentally."

Beyond the narrow tear in the quartz wall she could see a short corridor that ended in a rotunda. Five other hallways branched off the circular space.

A small utility sled was parked just inside the jagged opening.

"If we're lucky, Griggs left the amber-rez locator set to his last destination," Cooper said.

He slipped sideways through the opening, walked to the vehicle, and leaned into the driver's compartment. Elly watched him fiddle with the instruments.

"Well?" she asked.

"Got it." He straightened, looking coolly satisfied. "Care to take a spin?"

"You bet."

She squeezed through the opening with Rose on her shoulder and hopped up onto the passenger seat of the sled.

Plant psi shivered across her senses. Turning in the seat, she surveyed the cargo bed of the sled.

"Sense something?" Cooper asked, getting in beside her.

"Yes. Psi-bright or some form of it. Very faint, but I recognize the buzz."

"I think we're on a roll here," Cooper said.

He hit Retrace Route on the locator and rezzed the small motor.

The trip was a short one. The sled hummed through a couple of turns and stopped in front of a vaulted chamber.

Cooper got out and walked to the door of the room. "Nothing in here."

She went to join him. The chamber was empty, as he had said, but the tingle of psi-bright was stronger.

"The herbs were here," she said. "And probably quite recently."

"There's another room off of this one."

Cooper started across the space. He paused halfway and abruptly changed direction.

Elly saw something glitter in the corner. She watched Cooper pick it up.

"Looks like broken glass," she said.

"It is. I think it's the bottom half of a beaker, the kind you use to run chemical experiments. There's still some white residue in the bottom."

"Let me see." She hurried to join him.

There was no need to touch the shattered glass. Her psi senses flared wildly.

"Enchantment dust," she said.

Chapter 28

"The son of a bitch had a lab going in that chamber." Cooper eased open the rear door of Griggs's shop and stepped out into the alley. "The question is, what in green hell happened to it?"

He listened with all of his senses. Fog still swirled in the alley, limiting visibility. A glance at Rose, perched on Elly's shoulder, assured him that there was no immediate threat.

"I can't get over the notion of Stuart Griggs as a big-time drug dealer," Elly whispered. "It boggles the mind. He must have made a fortune. Wonder what he did with the cash."

Cooper thought about the two journals he was carrying and the herbal that Elly clutched as though it were a box of amber diamonds.

"Looks like he may have used some of it to buy these books," he said. "But a few rare volumes wouldn't have put much of a dent in the kind of profits Griggs must have been pulling in with the chant. Looks like I'm going to have to do some follow-the-money research on him tomorrow."

"Maybe that's what the intruder was looking for tonight, Griggs's drug money."

"Or a stash of chant."

"Well, we know where a lot of that wound up," she reminded him. "In the basement of The Road to the Ruins."

"Yes."

"I'll bet he dismantled the lab and moved the drugs after he realized that Bertha had escaped his vortex."

"That theory assumes that Griggs was the blue freak I'm chasing," he said.

"You've got doubts about that?"

"It occurs to me that the odds of Griggs just happening to collapse and die from a heart attack shortly after Bertha Newell discovered his underground lab seem a little long."

She turned her head quickly to look at him in the shadows. "Are you saying that you think there's someone else involved in this?"

"It crossed my mind. Death by a strong blast of intense blue ghost energy can look a lot like death by heart attack. But if someone murdered Griggs that way, he would have had to do it underground. I told you, blue energy is very weak outside the tunnels, too weak to kill."

"I suppose the killer could have murdered Griggs down in the catacombs and then dragged his body up the stairs into the back room of the shop," she said slowly. "It would probably require an autopsy to determine the truth. I doubt if one will be ordered in this case. Neither the medics nor the cop had any reason to think they were dealing with a crime scene today."

"I'll call Mercer Wyatt first thing in the morning," Cooper said. "This is his town. He shouldn't have any problem pulling whatever strings it takes to get an autopsy performed."

She cleared her throat. "Generally speaking, the mainstream media here in Cadence takes a dim view of the quaint practice of referring to the city as a particular Guild boss's *town*. It invites unfortunate comparisons to mob boss rule."

"Damn. Done in by semantics again."

They were almost back to the mouth of the alley. The green-tinged mist roiled in the empty street. On the other side of the pavement he could just barely make out the haloed lamps over the back doors of the next row of shops.

Rose rumbled softly. A warning this time.

"Cooper," Elly said, voice tight with urgency.

He felt the spectral fingers of awareness on the nape of his neck and reacted instinctively. He pushed Elly into the dense, dark shadow cast by a large metal trash container.

Rose, nearly invisible except for her four glowing eyes, started to tumble toward the ground.

"No, Rose," Elly whispered. "You mustn't." She caught the dust bunny in one hand and tucked her safely into the crook of her arm.

Two figures moved into the alley opening, silhouetted against the acid-hued fog light. The features of both men were covered by stocking masks. Flickers of green ghost-energy snapped and crackled in the mist around them.

At least one of them was a hunter, Cooper thought. When the adrenaline started flowing, a lot of them unconsciously summoned bits of whatever stray ghost light happened to be in the vicinity.

Unlike a lot of dissonance-energy pararezzes who generally chose to stick with UDEM energy as the weapon of choice when they went into this kind of work, these two were armed. One carried a gun. Light glinted on the edge of the wicked-looking blade in the other man's hand.

The man on the right rezzed a pocket flash. He was the one with the gun. His stocking cap had a tassel on top.

"Don't move," Tassel Top ordered. "Either one of you even breathes hard, and you're both dead. You," he said to Cooper. "You're dressed like a hunter. You the real thing or just a wannabe?"

"It's a fashion statement," Cooper said.

The other man snickered. "Hey, Joe, the guy thinks he's a stand-up comic."

"Skip the jokes," Joe snarled. "Unless you want to feel what it's like to take a bullet."

"Anyone who knows me well knows I never joke," Cooper said quietly. "What do you want?"

"Whatever you found back there in Griggs's shop," Joe said.

"You went in ahead of us, didn't you?" Cooper asked. "That means you know there wasn't anything of value left inside. Unless you count the books." He held up the one he carried. "But somehow I don't see either of you as big readers."

"Why'd you take those old books?" the other one demanded. His mask was trimmed with two white circles around the eyes, giving him a rather startling resemblance to a moon-rat. "Somethin' special about 'em?"

"My friend, here, is a librarian," Elly offered helpfully. "He likes books."

"Shut up," Joe snapped. "I don't like mouthy babes."

"Elly," Cooper said without inflection.

She went silent, but he could have sworn he heard the simmering. He could almost feel the steam.

He did a quick survey of his options. Neither of the two thugs had noticed Rose. Elly was holding her just out of sight behind the corner of the big trash container. The position blocked the men's view of the dust bunny's four eyes.

Rose, too, had gone quiet, he noticed. He didn't know much about dust bunnies, but he knew a lot about hunting strategy. Some things remained the same across species lines. When a predator, large or small, stopped growling a warning and went very quiet, it was time for the prey to start worrying.

"We grabbed the books because they looked valuable," he said aloud, putting a shrug into the words. "Didn't seem to be anything else left that was worth taking. What were you guys looking for? Drugs? Cash?"

"There wasn't any," Moon-Rat blurted. "We know he must have had plenty of both around somewhere. He always paid us with the chant."

"Shit, Benny, keep your dumb mouth shut," his companion rasped.

"Okay, take it easy." Cooper slowly unfastened his jacket. "I'll show you what we found."

The small section of the glowing fog in the street behind Benny and Joe started to change color, shifting subtly from green to blue. Neither of the two men noticed.

Cooper probed hard for the blue psi energy he needed. Fortunately, this close to the Dead City there was enough of it around to serve his purpose.

"Hurry up," Joe said hoarsely. "We ain't got all night."

Blue flames leaped out of the open trash container.

"What the hell?" Benny jolted backward a couple of startled steps and swung around to stare at the blaze. "There's a fire in the garbage."

"Shit." Joe retreated a couple of paces. "We've got to get out of here. Someone is going to see the flames and call the fire department."

Cooper moved.

"Stay where you are," Joe snapped. He whipped back around to face the spot where

Cooper had been standing a couple of seconds earlier.

But Cooper was already on him, using the momentum of his body to slam him into the side of the heavy metal container. The gun clattered on the stones.

"What the hell?" Belatedly realizing that things were getting out of control, Benny swung around, knife in hand.

Cooper kicked out with one booted foot, catching him high on the thigh.

Benny staggered backward, trying to keep his balance.

Elly came out of the shadows, swinging the heavy herbal. The weighty tome slammed against the side of Benny's skull.

Benny shrieked in pain and sank to his knees. He lost his grip on the blade.

There was a sudden scampering noise on the ground. Four eyes glowed in the night, rushing toward Benny's leg.

Benny screamed. "Get it away from me. Get it away."

"Rose, no," Elly said quickly. "You mustn't bite anyone else, sweetie. Someone may call the pound."

To Cooper's surprise, the dust bunny halted, albeit reluctantly, and dashed back to Elly, who grabbed her with both hands and tucked her close.

"Are you all right?" Cooper said, bending down to scoop up the gun.

"Yes." Elly took a deep breath. "I'm okay."

Joe was on the ground, moaning. Cooper yanked off Benny's ski mask and discovered that the disguise had been an apt one. The guy actually did resemble a moon-rat.

"Now, why don't you tell me exactly how you came to be acquainted with the deceased," Cooper said.

Benny's faced scrunched up in confusion. "Huh?"

"What was your connection to the florist?"

"I'm not tellin' you nothin'," Benny stated.

"Let me put it this way," Cooper said. "You can talk to me, or you can talk to Mercer Wyatt."

Benny looked horrified. "Hey, all we did was a little off-the-books work for Griggs. This isn't Guild business."

"It is now," Cooper said quietly. "Talk to me, Benny."

"Me and Joe are a team," Benny whined. "Freelance. The florist hired us to take him down into the catacombs. Paid us with chant. We knew he was making the stuff, but we never found his stash, y'know?

351

Anyhow, it was a good deal. We resold the chant and turned a nice profit. But this afternoon, word went around that Griggs was dead."

"So you and Joe conducted another search in hopes of finding his supply of the drug?"

"Figured it was worth a shot," Benny muttered. "But we couldn't find the drugs or the money. There's a rumor going around that the florist had started working with someone else to sell the chant. We decided to hang around and keep watch tonight to see if anyone showed up. When you went inside, we thought maybe you were the new partner. That's all, man, you gotta believe me."

"Oddly enough, I do, Benny."

The small green ghost Cooper had summoned floated up behind Benny and touched him lightly on the back of his head.

Benny crumpled to the ground, unconscious.

Cooper maneuvered the ghost toward Joe. Joe moaned one last time and passed out.

"Now what?" Elly asked.

"This is Mercer Wyatt's town. We'll turn these two over to his people for questioning."

Elly cleared her throat. "I think I mentioned that it is not considered appropriate to refer to Cadence as Mercer Wyatt's town."

"I'll try to remember that the next time the subject arises."

Chapter 29

They waited in the alley until the long, dark car arrived. Two hunters dressed in khaki and leather got out and loaded Benny and Joe into the backseat.

One of the pair nodded respectfully toward Cooper.

"Mr. Wyatt says to keep in touch," he said.

"I'll do that," Cooper said.

Elly was still feeling shaky from the after-effects of adrenaline when she unlocked the back door of her shop a short time later.

Cooper followed her into the fragrant back room and turned to rez the lock. "You sure you're okay?"

"Yes." She headed toward the stairs with Rose and the Jordan herbal. "But I could use a nice hot cup of Harmonic balm tea."

"I was thinking of something a little stronger, personally."

"All I've got is some leftover white wine."

"Not exactly a real Guild boss drink, but a Guild boss is nothing if not adaptable. I'll take it. Remind me to pick up a bottle of

First Generation whiskey tomorrow, though."

He was certainly making himself at home, she mused. She paused halfway up the stairs and turned to study him over her shoulder. "Are you sure *you're* all right?"

He looked grimly amused. "Don't worry, I'm not going to lose control and climb all over you. I just summoned a little stray blue and green energy tonight. Didn't even melt amber."

She glowered. "I wasn't thinking about sex."

"Huh. I must have been the one thinking about it, then."

"Enough with the teasing, Boone." She went on up the stairs and into the kitchen, put Rose on the floor, and reached for the kettle. "This isn't the time."

"Whatever." He opened the refrigerator and took out the half-empty bottle of white.

"Herschel, one of the local neighborhood ruin rats, mentioned that Griggs occasionally hired a freelance team to take him down into the catacombs," she added. "Now I know why. Griggs was looking for Jordan's Jungle."

"Tomorrow I'm going to chase down more information on the florist. He's the key to this thing."

She spooned the tea into a mug. "A dead key, unfortunately."

"Okay, I admit that's a problem." Cooper grabbed a glass out of a cupboard and sat down at the kitchen table. "But we've got a couple of other angles to work here."

"Such as?"

"I'm still waiting for another shoe to drop at The Road to the Ruins. Now that Griggs is dead, I don't think it will be too much longer before we find out what our blue freak had planned for that stash of dope he hid in the club's basement."

The kettle whistled. She picked it up and was not surprised to see it tremble a little in her hand. She poured the hot water quickly into the mug.

Rose hopped up onto the windowsill and hunkered down beside the green flower. Cooper took a long swallow of the wine and watched the dust bunny.

"I guess things haven't gone quite the way you planned since you arrived in Cadence, have they?" Elly asked, carrying her mug back to the table.

"No." He drank more wine and lowered the glass with a reflective air. "They haven't."

He did not offer anything more.

"What about your other business?" she

pressed cautiously.

He looked at her. "Other business?"

"The business that brought you here in the first place." She motioned with one hand. "You know, the *private* business you said you had here in Cadence."

"Oh, that." He exhaled slowly. "Well, I hope to get around to that eventually."

She blew on her hot tea. "Cooper?"

"Yeah?"

"Mind if I ask you a personal question?"

"Depends on the question."

"I just wondered if the reason you haven't had a relationship with anyone else in the past six months is because you were too busy."

He raised his brows. "Here's a flash for you, Elly. Men who like sex are never too busy to have it. Where there's a will, there's always a way."

"I see. You like sex."

"Oh, yeah."

"So, why haven't you had any for the past six months?" she asked.

"Eight months, five days," he corrected. "And the answer is that I didn't consider our engagement terminated."

"I don't understand. I gave you back your ring. What was your interpretation of that move?"

"Figured we'd just put things on hold for a while. I thought if you had some time away from Aurora Springs and all the pressures of your situation there, you might change your mind about marrying me."

"I see."

No "I love you desperately and I can't live without you," or "Please come back to me; I'll do anything including give up my job as a Guild boss for you," she thought.

Cooper was still locked into his fully focused executive mode. At the age of nine he had set out to become the chief of the Aurora Springs Guild, and he had stayed on track until he had achieved his objective. Eight months and five days ago, he had concluded that she would make the perfect wife for the head of the Aurora Springs Guild, and he was still pursuing his objective.

"I've got a question for you," he said.

"What is it?"

"I get the feeling that *you* haven't gone to bed with anyone else during the time we've been apart."

"I've been awfully busy," she said quickly. "Running a small business is extremely time-consuming."

"Try again."

She put her mug down, got to her feet, and went to stand at the window. Maybe it was all they had been through together in the past few days. Or maybe it was late and she was weary and her guard was down.

Or maybe it was because he hadn't slept with anyone else since she had left Aurora Springs.

Whatever the reason, she decided to tell him the truth.

"Ever since the day I met you, I haven't wanted to go to bed with anyone else," she said quietly. "But in Aurora Springs you didn't seem all that interested. And lately, well, you haven't been around."

There was no sound, but suddenly he was behind her, his hands resting on her shoulders.

"I'm here now," he said.

She caught her breath and turned to face him, her hands flattening on his shoulders.

"Cooper."

He kissed her, taking his time about it. She closed her eyes beneath the waves of emotion that swept through her.

She was vaguely aware of him reaching around her to pull down the window shade. The next thing she knew he had picked her up in his arms and was carrying her out of the kitchen.

She heard him de-rez the light switches as they went down the hall, allowing the small apartment to fill with intimate shadows.

The drapes were open in the bedroom. The reflected glow of the green-tinged fog illuminated the bed in an otherworldly aura.

Cooper stood her on her feet and used his powerful hands to angle her face so that he could kiss her again. There was no mistaking the force of his desire. It thrilled her senses. Maybe he didn't love her, but without a doubt, he wanted her.

All the midnight dreams and fantasies that she had tried so hard to ignore, resist, and suppress were springing to life with a vengeance.

He caught the hem of her pullover and eased the garment up over her head. The instant her arms were free, she wrapped them around his neck.

"Cooper," she repeated very urgently.

"No," he whispered. "Not so fast. Not this time. Don't get me wrong, the car sex was terrific, but it wasn't what I'd had planned for our first night together. I'd like to get it right tonight."

She tilted her head back so that she could see his face. "Wait a second. You *planned* our first time?"

"Sure." He found the fastening of her small, satiny bra and slipped the straps off her shoulders. "Until the day you gave me back my ring I had every move in our relationship planned down to the smallest detail."

"Good grief." She gripped his shoulders, holding him inches away from her. "And just when did you do all this detailed planning?"

He kissed her ear. "Started that first day when you came into the Guild Archives to see if your father was there. I had started working there the week before. It was the first time I'd met you."

He was cupping her breasts in his warm palms now. She shivered when his thumbs glided across her nipples.

"Wait," she gasped. It was getting hard to talk, but she needed some answers. "What made you think you had to *plan* things?"

"It's the way I work," he said simply. "It was a good plan, too. There was only one problem with it."

"What?"

"You." He brushed his mouth deliberately across hers. "You didn't respond according to plan."

"Maybe you should have discussed your scheme with me before you tried to implement it."

He traced the line of her jaw with his forefinger. In the emerald shadows she could see his faint, wry smile.

"I'm not used to talking about my plans with anyone else," he said. "I've always worked alone."

"Got news for you, Boone." She started unfastening the buttons of his shirt. "You're not alone anymore. You're working with me, at least for now."

"Elly."

He picked her up and fell across the bed with her in his arms. She landed on top, feeling shaky and excited. He tugged off her running shoes, and then he unzipped her pants.

She fought a sensual battle to undress him. It was not an easy task. In the end, Cooper had to sit up to yank off his boots and get rid of his trousers.

For a moment he stood looking down at her, drinking in the sight of her lying there in the light that angled across the bed. Under his intense, hungry eyes, she felt incredibly sexy and powerful in her femininity.

When he moved to come back down onto the bed, she reached up to draw him close.

He made love to her with a slow, ghost-hot passion that rezzed all of her senses. Taking his time, he found the most intimate places on her body with his mouth. His fingers explored parts of her that she had never before considered erogenous zones.

Sweet heat and a greedy need built within her. The same delicious tension that she had experienced when they had made love in the front seat of the Spectrum was back, gripping her insides in honeyed talons.

She braced her hands against his chest and tried to push him onto his back so that she could settle herself astride him.

"Not yet," he whispered, anchoring her beneath him with one heavy leg across her thighs.

"Can't wait," she panted, twisting impatiently.

"You were in charge last time. Ruined all my plans. This is my night. This time we do it my way."

"Okay, okay, as long as you hurry up about it."

He laughed softly and reached across her and down over the side of the bed. She realized that he had picked up an object, but she could not see what it was.

He loomed over her again, reaching back toward the elaborate headboard. She heard a faint click and then the soft slide of leather being fed through a belt buckle.

She opened her eyes very wide. "What are you doing?"

He caught one of her wrists and then the other. He put the end of the leather belt into her hands.

"Giving you something to hold on to when the going gets interesting," he said against her mouth.

"Uh, Cooper?"

"Just hang on tight and don't let go, no matter what happens."

"I'm not sure —"

He started working his way down her body, dropping kisses as he went. When his tongue touched her nipple she gasped, instinctively tightening her grip on the belt.

"That's it," he whispered.

He slid lower on her body, separating her thighs. When he found the excruciatingly sensitive spot between her legs she nearly screamed.

And then his mouth was on her *there* and he was doing something incredible with his fingers just inside her and she could see little flickers of ghost light dancing in the air around the bed and she knew that he was closer to the limits of his self-control than he would ever admit.

Energy pulsed through all of her senses. Her need was fierce and hot and compelling.

"Hold on," he ordered in a low, husky

voice. "Melt amber for me."

And she did.

As the last of the shattering release rippled through her, she was vaguely aware of Cooper changing position. His broad shoulders blocked the exotic green light coming through the window.

He entered her, pushing deep.

She let go of the belt, sank her nails into his shoulders, and wrapped her legs around his waist.

"The belt thing is okay," she whispered. "But I'd rather hold on to you."

She bit him very gently on the shoulder.

He muttered something dangerously explicit and incredibly erotic.

She laughed at the sexy threat and clung harder to his powerful frame.

His release roared through both of them with the force of ghost fire.

Dancing waves of energy lit up the night.

Chapter 30

His phone rang a little after three in the morning. Cooper stirred against the warm, comfortable softness of Elly's curved backside and stretched an arm out from under the quilt to answer.

"Yeah?" he said.

"Ormond Ripley, here. Thought you'd like to know that my evening was very nearly ruined a short time ago by a glory-hunting detective named Grayson DeWitt of the Cadence Police Department's Drug Task Force. Maybe you've heard of him?"

Cooper felt the adrenaline splash through him. He sat up against the pillows. "Saw the name in the papers."

"DeWitt does like the media," Ripley said. "And the media loves him. He showed up here tonight with a warrant and what looked to be about half the available manpower of the department. He also had a bunch of intrepid reporters from the *Cadence Star* and the tabloids."

"What did he want?"

"Evidently he had received an anonymous tip from a reliable informant to the effect that there was a large stash of drugs on the premises."

Elly rose on one elbow. In the reflected glow of the fog Cooper could see the concern on her face.

"I assume Detective DeWitt did not find any drugs," Cooper said.

"Of course not." Ripley sounded quietly satisfied. "The Road to the Ruins is a legitimate business that pays its taxes and operates strictly within the laws."

"Right."

"Pursuant to our earlier conversation, I found it interesting that Detective DeWitt did not feel the need to conduct a full-scale top-to-bottom search of my club and casino. He headed straight down to the basement. Evidently, the anonymous tipster gave him very explicit directions."

"What happened when he failed to turn up a drug stash?"

"He did not look very cheerful," Ripley said, sounding quite cheerful, himself. "I do believe that he was counting on another headline in tomorrow's papers. He's going to get it, but I doubt if it's the one he wanted."

"Are the headlines going to be a problem for you?"

"Haven't you heard the old saying that there is no such thing as bad publicity? There will be lines around the block tomorrow night."

"Any luck with that other matter we discussed?" Cooper asked.

"Nothing yet, but I'm still going through the video recordings from the security cameras. I'll be in touch tomorrow."

"Thanks."

"By the way, anytime you and your lady friend want to stop by for a drink on me, let me know. I'll give the VIP door staff your names."

Cooper looked at Elly, who was watching him intently. "Might take you up on that. Got to say, the nightlife here in Cadence is a whole lot different than it is back home."

"Wouldn't be much point in coming to the big city if everything was just the same as it was back home."

Ripley cut the connection.

Cooper put the phone down on the table beside the bed.

"Well?" Elly demanded. "What happened?"

"Detective DeWitt raided The Road tonight. Knew right where to look for a stash of drugs. Didn't find any, though, and evidently went away unhappy."

She searched his face. "That would appear to prove your theory that someone wanted Ormond Ripley to take a very public fall for drug dealing."

"Yes," he said. "It would. And it also suggests the name of at least one person who had a lot to gain from what would have been a very high-profile arrest."

"Detective Grayson DeWitt?"

"Yes."

"Do you think it's possible that DeWitt is the blue freak?"

"I don't know the answer to that yet, but I sure as green hell need to find out more about him. Wyatt should be able to get some background for me."

"Because this is his town?" she asked dryly.

He caught a tendril of her hair and wound it around his finger. "Because in every town the Guilds make it a policy to maintain a good working relationship with the local police."

"Spoken like a diplomatic Guild boss."

"Thanks. I do try."

She did not smile. He could feel her anxiety.

"This is getting very complicated, isn't it?" she asked.

"Some aspects of it certainly are." He slid

down on the pillows and pulled her across his chest. "But not this part."

A long time later she was still awake, watching the glowing fog-scape outside the window. After making love to her the second time that night, Cooper had fallen into a deep, totally relaxed slumber.

She was learning that having a man in one's bed all night took some getting used to. Cooper's sleek, muscled body was curved around her own, generating so much heat that she'd had to kick off the blankets on her side. The weight of his arm was heavy around her midsection. In addition, he had somehow managed to take up more than his share of the available mattress space.

She looked down at the foot of the bed and saw two bright eyes staring at her. Rose was also wide awake.

Very carefully she eased herself out from under Cooper's arm and slid from the bed. She took her robe down off the bedpost and slipped into her slippers.

Rose drifted silently across the quilt. Elly scooped her up and went out into the hall, pausing briefly in the doorway to marvel once more at the strange and exotic sight of Cooper in her bed. Even in sleep, he dominated the space he occupied. In the strange, eerie light, he was the embodiment of every dark, erotic fantasy she had ever had about him.

She plopped Rose on her shoulder, went down the hall to the kitchen, and rezzed the light. At the counter she selected a cookie from the jar and gave it to Rose. Then she washed her hands very carefully and went to sit at the table. Rose fluttered up to the windowsill and settled down next to the quartz vase to munch.

Elly reached for Jordan's *Medicinal Herbs and Flowers of Harmony* and opened it carefully. She used a clean cloth napkin to turn the pages so as not to risk marring them.

The volume was in excellent condition, she noticed. Evidently it had been little used during the years it had resided in the libraries of various collectors. The paper was of good quality and had lasted well. There were no marks or tears on the pages.

She leafed through the herbal slowly, admiring the beautifully rendered illustrations of familiar and not-so-familiar herbs and plants. Mary Tyler Jordan had, indeed, been a true artist, she thought. There were photographs, but it was the superb botanical drawings that compelled and transfixed. Each was fine enough to hang in a museum. Each showed details in a way that no camera could ever capture.

She found the thin slip of paper when she turned to the last chapter. It had obviously been placed there to mark a page that contained a drawing. Shock sizzled through her when she saw the elegantly rendered flower on the page.

"What is it?" Cooper asked.

Startled, she raised her head and saw him lounging, arms crossed over his bare chest, in the doorway. He had put on his trousers. His feet were bare, and his hair was tousled.

"I think I know now why Griggs tried to steal my flower and possibly Rose, too," she said softly.

She turned the herbal around so that he could see the drawing.

Cooper dropped his arms and padded across the room to the table. He picked up the small case he had left there earlier, removed his glasses, and put them on.

He studied the picture closely. After a few seconds, he looked at the green bloom in the vase on the windowsill.

"It's a drawing of your flower," he said quietly.

"Correction, it's a drawing of Rose's flower." She turned the book back around so that she could read it. "And just listen to what Jordan wrote in the text."

. . . When I awoke, I found this aston-ishing flower still clutched in my hand. I am convinced that, in some way that I cannot explain, I was able to use it to navigate through the catacombs and return to the surface.

My memories of the time that I was lost in the alien underworld are, at best, shards and fragments devoid of meaning or context. I have been told not to trust any of the images in my head as they are likely all delusions and false recollections forged by a troubled mind. The experts say that I show symptoms of the type of severe parapsych trauma typically induced by an encounter with either a UDEM or an illusion trap.

But I have this drawing and my dreams to remind me that I once jour-neyed through a strange and won-drous rain forest, a realm lit by an em-erald sun and a jade moon, an under-ground world of vibrant green where every shadow conceals mysteries waiting to be discovered.

Chapter 31

Cooper spent the morning in Elly's cozy kitchen, a cup of amber-root tea within easy reach, his computer at hand, and his notes spread out across the table. With the exception of occasional visits from Rose, who came upstairs periodically to check in and grab a snack, he had the place to himself.

Ormond Ripley had been right about the headlines in the morning papers. The *Cadence Star* led with "False Tip Leads to Raid on Casino." The accompanying photo showed a shot of Ripley standing in the middle of his crowded club looking politely amused. The caption underneath said, "Ormond Ripley accepts apology from police department spokesperson. Claims he will not sue."

The tabloids used more colorful language. "Has Wonder Boy Lost His Touch?" screamed the *Cadence Tattler.* Beneath the main headline was: "Cadence PD Humiliated by DeWitt's Big Mistake."

All of the papers featured large photos of a tight-mouthed, grim-faced DeWitt, dressed in a really sharp, hand-tailored suit, getting into an unmarked car outside The Road.

The detective had to be squirming this morning, Cooper thought. That was a good thing. People who started to squirm usually tended to start screwing up.

"I'll be waiting," Cooper promised the photos. "I'm good at that."

Elly had opened her shop punctually at nine. Judging by the frequent muffled tinkling of the doorbells, he assumed that she was either doing a brisk business or else her neighbors were making excuses to stop in to get updates on her personal affairs.

In the interest of saving time he had contacted Emmett London first thing. The job of researching DeWitt's background had been turned over to Wyatt's assistant, a man named Perkins.

The business of finding the former owner of Mary Tyler Jordan's *Medicinal Herbs and Flowers of Harmony* was a little trickier. Cooper had reserved that task for himself.

Thanks to Elly, he had the names of the three collectors known to have copies of the rare volume in their collections.

It took patience and some serious name-dropping to get the first two on the phone. They had informed him that their copies of the Jordan herbal were still in their libraries.

He got lucky with number three. Edwin Sheridan was a retired member of the Cadence Guild.

"Thank you for speaking with me, Mr. Sheridan," Cooper said in his most polite tone.

"My housekeeper said you told her this was Guild business." The voice on the other end of the line quivered with age. "Used to be a Guild man, myself, back in the days when this was Connor Hyland's town."

"That was a little before my time, sir." *Say, about fifty years before,* Cooper added silently. He rubbed the bridge of his nose. It had been a long morning.

Edwin snorted. "Let me tell you, son, when Hyland was in charge, things were different in this town. The Cadence Guild upheld tradition. There wasn't any of this modern nonsense about going mainstream, that's for damn sure."

"I understand, sir."

"Every time I pick up a newspaper these days there's some damn article about how the Cadence Guild is trying to modernize, trying to become a respectable social institution. Ridiculous."

Cooper cleared his throat. "As a matter of fact, sir, I'm from the Aurora Springs Guild."

"Aurora Springs, eh? Now, there's a good, solidly run, old-fashioned outfit. I hear they've got a proper respect for tradition over there in Aurora Springs."

"We like to think so, sir."

"Heard the new Guild boss there was all set to marry a nice young woman from a good Guild clan a few months back but that the wedding got called off."

"It was postponed, sir, not canceled."

"Is that right? What happened?"

How in green hell had he ended up discussing his love life with Edwin Sheridan? Cooper wondered.

"There were some complications," he said evenly, "but the new boss is working to straighten them out. Sir, I'd like to ask you about your copy of Jordan's herbal."

"How the heck did that book become Guild business?"

Cooper looked at the herbal in front of him. "It came up in the course of an internal Guild investigation."

"Ah, one of those," Edwin said wisely. "The Guilds police their own."

"Yes, sir. Could you tell me if —"

"That's one damn good reason why the organizations shouldn't get involved in this mainstreaming stuff. First thing you know, they'd have to open up their files to every police detective or attorney or politician who comes along thinking he can build a reputation by going after some high-ranking Guild man."

"You make a very good point, sir. Now, about the herbal. Is it still in your collection?"

"Nope, sold it a few months back. To tell you the truth, I didn't even know it was in the library. You see, it was my wife who was the collector in the family, not me. She passed on a few months ago."

"My condolences, sir," Cooper said.

"Thank you. Well, the long and the short of it is that neither my sons nor my grandkids are interested in the books, so I'm selling them off here and there whenever I get a good offer."

Cooper sat forward and reached for a pen. "Who was the buyer of the herbal?"

"Don't know. Buyer insisted on remaining anonymous."

"How was the transaction conducted?"

"It was handled by a dealer named Bodkin who specializes in private sales between clients who don't like publicity."

"I'd like Bodkin's address, if that's not too much trouble."

"No trouble, but I doubt if he'll tell you the name of his buyer. Bodkin evidently has a reputation for confidentiality."

"I'm sure he won't mind doing a favor for the local Guild boss," Cooper said.

Five minutes later he hung up the phone, folded his glasses into the case, and headed downstairs, keys in hand.

Elly was at the counter, measuring out a small amount of dried purple flowers from an herb jar. Her client was a middle-aged woman who beamed when she spotted him in the doorway.

"Oh, hello, there," the woman said. "You must be Elly's friend from Aurora Springs. I'm Sally Martin. I work in Butler's Relics just down the street."

"Nice to meet you, Mrs. Martin."

"I have a cousin over in Aurora Springs," Sally said brightly. "Maybe you know her. Laura Meehan?"

"I don't think I've had the pleasure," Cooper said in a tone he hoped would cut off that line of inquiry. He looked at Elly.

"I'll be back later this afternoon," he said.

She frowned a little. "Everything okay?"

"Got a lead on the sale of the herbal."

"Good luck," she said. "And please be careful," she added, lowering her voice slightly.

It occurred to him that he had been living alone a long time, long enough to forget how it felt to have someone tell him to be careful when he went out the door.

He walked to where she stood with her measuring scoop and jar and kissed her. It felt good to be able to kiss her like this; good to know that he would be returning here later; good to know that she would be waiting for him.

"I'll do that," he said.

He was halfway across the back room, reaching for the knob of the alley door, when he heard Sally Martin's low-voiced comment to Elly.

"My goodness, I can certainly understand the attraction, dear. There was a time when I had a thing for khaki and leather, too. I suppose every woman does at one time or another. Best to get it out of your system while you're still young and single, though."

Business slacked off rapidly after lunch. Elly went upstairs to make herself a sandwich and fresh tea. She ate at the table, sharing bites with Rose, and listened for the sound of the door chimes.

When she finished, she picked up the Jordan herbal and took it back down to the shop so that she could leaf through it in her spare moments.

She was alone with Rose, who was busily rearranging the contents of the jewelry box, when she looked up from the herbal and saw the curtain twitch in Doreen's kitchen window.

She closed the herbal, dove for the phone, and rezzed Doreen's number. She had already called several times. Each time she had gotten the shop's after-hours message. ". . . We are closed for the day. Please call back during regular business hours or leave a message at the beep . . ."

"Doreen, this is Elly. I know you're there. Pick up your phone, or I'm coming over there with my key."

There was a long pause. For a time she thought Doreen was going to ignore her. But finally there was a click.

"Hello, Elly." Doreen's voice was weary and oddly thick. "What do you want?"

"What do you think I want? I want to know if you're all right."

"I put a sign in the window."

"Yes, I know. I went across the street and read it a couple of hours ago when I realized you hadn't opened up for the day. It says Closed Because of Illness. What kind of illness?"

"Flu."

"Are you running a fever?"

There was another pause. "Probably. I don't know."

"I'll bring over some fever-light. It works wonders on a temperature."

"*No.* You can't come over here. Not today. The last thing you want to do is catch this stupid flu, trust me."

"Doreen? Is there something else wrong? You don't sound like yourself."

"I told you, I'm sick. I don't even feel like talking. I just got up to get a glass of water. I'm going straight back to bed. I'll call you when I'm better. *Don't come over here.*"

There was a click and a sudden silence.

Elly looked at the phone in her hand for a long moment, thinking about the strange raspy quality in Doreen's voice.

"She didn't sound sick," she said to Rose. "She sounded like she'd been crying."

She went around behind the counter, grabbed her keys, and held out her arm. "Something is very wrong. Let's ride, sister."

Rose abandoned her jewelry hoard and tumbled down the countertop until she could scamper up to Elly's shoulder.

On her way out the front door, Elly flipped the Back in Ten Minutes sign.

The fog had finally lifted, but the day was overcast and damp. There was very little traffic in Ruin Lane. She cut across the street, moving between a Float that was searching for a parking space and a sleek Coaster.

When she reached the front door of Doreen's shop she de-rezzed the lock with the spare key that Doreen had given her and went inside.

She made her way to the staircase in the back room and started up the steps.

"Doreen?"

The floorboards creaked upstairs.

"I told you not to come here," Doreen called down from the landing.

"I know there's something wrong." She went swiftly up the stairs. "You can't expect me to just ignore a situation like this."

"Please, go," Doreen said from the vicinity of the bedroom.

Elly reached the landing and looked down the short hall. Doreen stood, or rather sagged, in the doorway of the bedroom, propping herself up with one hand braced against the frame.

She was swathed in a bathrobe. Her amber pendant, which she never removed, gleamed against the dark skin of her throat.

She held an ice pack to the side of her face.

"Doreen?" Elly started toward her.

"What in the world?" Then she saw Doreen's swollen lip and the bruises under her eyes. "Dear heaven, what happened to you?"

Doreen started to weep. "I feel so incredibly stupid."

Elly reached her and put an arm carefully around her. Rose chattered anxiously.

"Did you fall down the stairs?" Elly asked. "We need to get you to an emergency room."

"No." Doreen's eyes widened in panic. "I can't do that."

"I don't understand. You've been injured. Why don't you want to see a doctor?"

"He hurt me." Doreen pressed her face against Elly's shoulder. The tears turned into sobs. "I thought . . . I thought he was going to kill me."

"Someone attacked you? Did you call the police?"

Doreen shook her head. "I can't."

A terrible chill of premonition shot through Elly. "Don't tell me it was your new boyfriend, the undercover cop?"

Doreen sobbed harder.

"Let's get you into the kitchen. I'll make a cup of tea. You can tell me all about it."

Five minutes later she had Doreen ensconced at the kitchen table with a box of tissues nearby. Rose hovered near Doreen making anxious little noises.

Elly filled the kettle at the faucet. "All right, tell me the whole story."

Doreen sniffed and reached for a tissue. "You already know most of it. I met him at a club a couple of weeks ago. We danced. He was hot. He was also a great dresser. We started dating. He told me that he was a police detective working undercover to take down a major drug lord. He said that until the case was completed, we had to keep a very low profile. He didn't want to be seen with me because it might put my life or the case or both in jeopardy."

"You entertained him here in your apartment?"

"Sure." Doreen picked up the ice pack and reapplied it to her cheek. "He was here a lot. Usually showed up late at night. Always came through the alley door. What can I say? The sex was pretty intense. Very exciting. Until yesterday, that is."

"That's when he attacked you?"

Doreen closed her eyes in pain. "It was the first time he ever came here during the day. He showed up in the middle of the afternoon. I could tell right away that there was something different about him."

"Different?"

"It was obvious that something had happened." Doreen opened her eyes and gingerly adjusted the ice pack. "He was very rezzed, very aggressive. Told me to close up the shop. Then he demanded sex. I got scared. I wondered if he had been drinking, but I didn't smell any booze on him."

"Was he high on drugs? It wouldn't be the first time in the history of the world that a vice cop got involved with the vice he was supposed to be investigating."

"I don't know." Doreen grimaced and then sucked in a painful breath. "I swear it was as if he'd had a personality transplant. He had always been so smooth, so cool. But yesterday he was a sex-crazed thug. When I fought back, he started beating me. He's a lot bigger and stronger, and I'm sure he would have raped me, but for some reason, he suddenly seemed to get nervous. I got the impression he was scared of hanging around here, like something terrible would happen if he didn't leave right away."

"What did he say?"

"Among other things, he told me that if I breathed a word about what had happened to anyone, let alone went to the police, he would come back and slit my throat." Doreen shuddered. "I believed him."

A sex-crazed thug. Elly thought about that.

The medics had said that Stuart Griggs had likely been dead for a couple of hours by the time she found him. If he had been murdered with blue dissonance energy, as Cooper believed, the killer might well have melted amber to accomplish his goal. That meant that shortly afterward he would have been consumed by a very intense case of lust.

A killer in the grip of a serious amber meltdown might attempt rape. But he would be operating within a very narrow window of opportunity. It was only a matter of time before he started to sink into a heavy sleep, and he would not want to do that while he was near his victim.

"Doreen, please think carefully. Exactly when did the bastard come here?"

Doreen's face puckered up in close contemplation. "Somewhere around three. Right after the mail was delivered. Why?"

"Stuart Griggs died of a heart attack yesterday afternoon. I found the body at about four."

"The florist up the street?" Doreen frowned in surprise. "He's dead? I heard the sirens, but I was in such bad shape that I didn't even bother to look out the window."

"Which explains why you weren't in the crowd of onlookers with the rest of us when they brought the body out."

"I don't understand. What does Griggs's death have to do with what happened to me?"

"I'll tell you later. Did you see which way the bastard went when he left here?"

Doreen shook her head. "No. I really thought that he was going to kill me. I was amazed, frankly, when he didn't. If he hadn't gone into that panic mode, I think you'd have found my body today."

He couldn't have gone far after the attack on Doreen, not if he was plunging into a post–amber meltdown burn, Elly thought. He would have needed at least a few hours of deep sleep. Odds were, he had gone to ground somewhere in the Old Quarter.

"You should have called me," Elly said, opening another cupboard to look for the tea.

"I was too scared. All I could think of was that if I told anyone, he would find out somehow and come back to kill me. He's a cop, Elly. He could get away with it."

"He's not going to get away with anything."

Doreen wiped her eyes. "What do you mean?"

There was no canister of tea in the next cupboard either. Elly gave up in frustration. "Oh, the hell with making the tea. Let's go back to my apartment. I'll make some there. I need to call Cooper, anyway, and I'd rather do it on my own phone. Yours might be bugged or something."

"Bugged?"

"You said he was a cop."

"Yes, but why would he bug my phone?"

"How should I know? He's a cop. They do stuff like that."

Elly started to close the cupboard door, but the sight of the bottle on the top shelf stopped her cold. She looked at it, unable to tear her eyes away from the label.

"Doreen?" she said very quietly.

"Yes?"

"Since when did you start drinking Founders Reserve scotch?"

"What? Oh, the scotch." Doreen winced. "I don't drink it. Can't afford it, even if I did like the taste, which I don't. You know me, I'm a cheap wine spritzer kind of gal."

Elly swallowed hard. "So who gave you the Founders Reserve?"

"He brought it here. Said he wanted to have it on hand whenever he came to see me. He was very particular about it. Why?"

"Dear heaven."

Elly slammed the cupboard door and whirled around. "We've got to get out of here. Right now."

"Are you kidding? I can't go outside looking like this. I'm not even dressed."

"Put on an overcoat and a pair of shoes. You've got to hurry, Doreen."

Doreen got slowly to her feet. "You're serious, aren't you?"

"Yes."

Elly grabbed Rose and rushed into the hall. She opened the closet door and yanked a knee-length purple coat off a hanger. When she got back into the kitchen she saw that Doreen was starting to respond.

"Okay, I'm not arguing." Doreen took the coat and followed Elly down the stairs. "Guess I'm still too scared to be logical."

"Faster," Elly said. She led the way across the shadowed shop, fighting back a tide of panic.

She yanked open the front door and paused a few precious seconds to check the street.

Nothing moved that she could see. She glanced at Rose, who appeared unalarmed.

Heartened, she led the way across the street, fishing for her key.

"Why the sudden panic?" Doreen asked, watching anxiously as Elly rezzed the lock on the door of her shop.

"I used to date a man who drank only Founders Reserve scotch," Elly said. "He was very particular about it."

"What was his name?"

"Palmer Frazier."

"But the guy who did this to me was named Jake Monroe."

"That's the name he gave you." Elly shoved open the door, ushered Doreen inside, and whirled around to yank the shades down in the front windows. "No wonder he didn't want you to introduce him to me."

It dawned on her that Doreen had gone absolutely silent behind her and that Rose was growling softly in her ear.

With a sickening sense of dread, she turned around.

A man loomed in the shadow-filled doorway of the back room. He had a pistol in his hand.

"Eldora St. Clair, you are under arrest for the possession and sale of illegal parapsychoactive substances," Grayson DeWitt said.

Chapter 32

"Stuart Griggs was a Jordan's Jungle fanatic." Benjamin Bodkin peered at Cooper over the rims of a pair of old-fashioned reading glasses. "Did a bit of small-time business with him over the years, the occasional journal, that sort of thing. But he could never afford the expensive items. Not until fairly recently, that is."

Bodkin's Rare Books was a dimly lit space saturated with the unmistakable aroma of old volumes. The shelves went from floor to ceiling on every wall. They were crammed with books of all sizes, shapes, and descriptions. Under other circumstances, Cooper thought, he could have spent hours here browsing the collection.

Bodkin, himself, went very well with his bookshop. He was comfortably plump and rumpled, with a shrewd, scholarly air.

"When did the situation change?" Cooper asked.

"A couple of months ago Griggs called and said he knew that there were three copies of Jordan's herbal in private collections. He asked me to approach the three collectors and see if any of them would be willing to sell. One proved willing, and I handled the transaction."

"How much did he pay for the herbal?" Cooper asked.

"Far too much." Bodkin snorted, removed his glasses, and started to polish the lenses with his handkerchief. "What can I say? To most collectors the herbal is merely an expensive oddity, but to a true Jordan's Jungle buff, it is the Holy Grail of herbals and therefore no price is too high."

"Where do you think he got the money this time?" Cooper asked.

Bodkin was clearly amused. "That, sir, is a question that I never ask my clients. All I can tell you is that sometime during the past few months, Stuart Griggs must have come into an inheritance."

More likely Griggs had turned to dealing dope to pay for his lifelong search for Jordan's Jungle, Cooper thought on the way back to where he had parked the Spectrum. But it was unlikely that the sophisticated business techniques required to run a successful drug ring were taught in horticulture school.

According to the research he had done,

the history of chant on the streets of Cadence had altered significantly over time. It had been little more than a trickle in the Old Quarter for a couple of years, virtually ignored by the authorities, who had bigger problems on their hands. Then, sometime during the past few months, the drug had suddenly exploded into a headline-grabbing issue.

It seemed probable that the rumor Benny and Joe had heard was correct. Griggs had acquired a partner in recent months, an entrepreneur who had seen the full potential of the enchantment dust business and figured out how to take a small, one-man drug operation into the big time.

Cooper's phone rezzed just as he was getting into the Spectrum.

"This is Boone," he said.

"Ormond Ripley, here. I've got some surveillance tapes that I think you might want to look at."

"I'm on my way."

Chapter 33

Elly rattled the handcuff that chained her right wrist to the chair. "We want our lawyers."

"Yeah, we know our rights," Doreen said icily. Her wrist was fastened to the chair on the opposite side of the table.

Grayson DeWitt scowled at them. He had taken up a post at the kitchen window where he could keep watch on the alley. His elegant, silver-and-gray pin-striped jacket was draped neatly over the back of a chair. The sleeves of a white-on-white, hand-tailored shirt were rolled up high on his forearms, revealing an expensive looking wristwatch. The silvery metal grip of the gun tucked into the handmade shoulder holster matched the suit and looked like a custom design.

"You'll get your lawyers," Grayson said. "Right after Cooper Boone shows up. If it's any comfort to you ladies, he's the one I'm after."

Rose rumbled softly. Elly gripped her tightly with her free hand, trying to convey with voice and body language the idea that taking a bite out of the detective was probably not a good idea.

Rose seemed to have gotten the message. She was obviously seriously annoyed, but she had settled down to a semifluffed state with only her daylight eyes showing.

"What makes you think Cooper will return here any time soon?" Elly asked.

"If he doesn't come back, I guess you'll have to take the fall for him." Grayson's media-bright smile did not reach his eyes. "But I've got a hunch he'll show up. There's a fortune in chant down in the trunk of your car. Can't see him walking away from it."

Doreen made a disgusted little sound. "This is all about you making yourself even more famous by bringing down a Guild boss, isn't it?"

"The chiefs of the Guilds have gotten away with murder, literally in some cases, ever since the organizations were founded," Grayson said in righteous tones. "The bosses think they don't have to live by the same rules as everyone else. Slapping one in prison on dope charges will be a wake-up call to the others."

"Doreen's right," Elly said. "This isn't about bringing the Guild bosses in line. It's all about your image as a heroic crimefighter. I don't think Cooper was your initial target. First you went after Ormond Ripley. Arresting him would have given you some real splashy press. But you screwed that up, big-time, didn't you? So now you're going to try to take down a visiting small-town Guild boss."

"Not like he'd have the guts to go after the local Guild chief," Doreen sneered. "He knew he couldn't touch Mercer Wyatt in his own town."

"That's enough," Grayson snapped. "Boone may not be the most powerful Guild boss in the City-State Federation, but he's a boss, nevertheless. When he goes down, people are going to notice."

Elly changed position slightly in the chair, trying to ease the growing stiffness in her right shoulder. "Tell me, where does Palmer Frazier fit into this?"

To her surprise a faintly baffled frown crossed Grayson's square-jawed features. "Who in green hell is Palmer Frazier?"

"I'll give you a few clues," Elly said, watching him closely. "He's tall, good-looking, sandy-haired, and dresses as well if not better than you do. When I knew him he always wore an amber-and-black-steel watch made by Luchane. And he drinks only Founders Reserve scotch."

Doreen stiffened a little in her chair. Her eyes widened.

Grayson shook his head impatiently. "I don't know who you're talking about."

He was telling the truth, Elly thought. What was going on here?

"I can't help but notice that you're doing a great job of watching the alley," she said after a couple of minutes of silence. "Going to be a bit awkward if Cooper comes back in through the front door, isn't it?"

"I've got men on the rooftops on Ruin Lane and overlooking both ends of the alley," Grayson said, sounding coolly satisfied. "No way Boone can return without being seen."

So much for hoping that Grayson was working alone, Elly thought glumly.

Doreen studied Grayson. "How did you find out that Cooper Boone had stashed drugs here in Elly's car?"

Grayson shrugged. "The usual way. An informant tipped me off."

"Would that be the same helpful, reliable informant who sent you into The Road to the Ruins to search for a drug stash?" Elly asked brightly.

Grayson's excellently hewn jaw clenched. "My informant has been one hundred percent accurate all along. Something went wrong the other night at The Road."

"It sure did," Elly said. "Just like it's going to go wrong again today."

"I've been thinking about the raid," Grayson continued softly. "It's not beyond the realm of possibility that Boone and Ripley are partners in the drug distribution ring. Maybe you'd know something about that, Miss St. Clair?"

Elly raised her eyes to the ceiling. "Get real, DeWitt. Your problem is your informant, whoever he is. He's manipulating you. Can't you see that?"

Grayson's expression solidified. "If you had any sense, you'd start spilling whatever you know about Boone. Sure, you're sleeping with the guy but, trust me, he won't repay you by protecting you. Drug dealers only care about their own hides."

Elly opened her mouth to argue, but she closed it again very quickly when Doreen uttered an anguished groan and dropped her forehead down onto a bent arm.

"I think I'm going to be sick," Doreen said.

"My friend needs a doctor," Elly said. "You can see she's been badly hurt."

Grayson glanced absently at Doreen. "She'll live. Those bruises are a day old. If she wanted a doctor, she should have gone to the emergency room yesterday."

"Thank you for your sympathy," Doreen muttered without raising her head.

Grayson lounged against the window frame. "What happened to you, anyway? Looks like you got beat up by your boyfriend."

Doreen did lift her head at that. She glared at him wordlessly.

"So that's it." Grayson shook his head in disgust. "You two ladies run with some real bad company, don't you? One of you has a boyfriend who beats her, and the other," he switched his gaze to Elly, "has a guy who gets her involved in a major drug peddling operation."

"Cooper is not dealing drugs," Elly said fiercely.

"The thing you should know is that drug dealers don't appreciate loyalty in a woman. Hell, they don't appreciate anything except the profits they make off the crap that they sell." Grayson smiled a humorless smile. "Boone found a real winner in you, didn't he? I'll bet you're the one who cooked up the dope for him, aren't you? We knew there had to be an expert botanist or chemist involved in this thing. It isn't that easy to make chant out of the psi-bright herbs. Not the kind of thing you do on a kitchen stove, that's for sure."

"If you found dope in my car it's because someone put it there to implicate Cooper and me," she said icily.

Fury leaped in his eyes. "I don't plant fake evidence, Miss St. Clair."

She shrugged. "Then it must have been your informant."

He snorted. "Oddly enough, I hear lines like that a lot from people in your situation all the time. It's known as the SODDI defense."

"What's the SODDI defense?"

"Stands for 'some other dude did it,' " Grayson said dryly.

"If you don't believe that your informant is manipulating you, how do you explain the screwup at The Road the other night?" Elly asked. "Think maybe you've got a leak in your elite little band of intrepid detectives?"

"It's a possibility," he said. "When this is over, I'll find it."

"Maybe it's your tailor." Elly studied his elegantly draped trousers. "Next time you're in the dressing room getting fitted, you might want to watch what you say."

Doreen gave a choked cough that turned into a hoarse groan. She put her head back down onto her arm.

Grayson looked at her, irritated. "Now what?"

"I've got a bad headache, and it's getting worse. I think maybe I'm going to throw up."

Grayson's sculpted features tightened in an expression of deep unease. He was no doubt considering the potential damage to his beautifully shined shoes, Elly thought.

Doreen moaned.

Elly looked at Grayson. "I have some herbs downstairs that will ease her headache and calm her stomach."

Grayson hesitated.

Doreen put her hand on her stomach. "Oh, geez, I feel so bad."

"Please let me fix her a tisane," Elly said to Grayson. "We're going to be sitting here a very long time. Cooper isn't due back for hours."

"Yeah?" Grayson appeared interested. "Where did he go?"

"To talk to some people," she said vaguely.

"Someone else involved in the drug dealing?"

"No," she snapped. "I told you, he's got nothing to do with the drugs you claim you found in my car."

Doreen sat up quickly and clutched her stomach. She swallowed visibly.

Grayson backed farther away from her.

"Stop it. I'm warning you, if you get sick —"

Doreen wrapped one arm around her midsection and rocked back and forth in the chair, eyes squeezed tightly shut.

"Damn it." With an air of sudden decision, Grayson yanked a key out of his pocket and de-rezzed the handcuff that chained Elly to her chair.

"We're going downstairs to get those herbs you said would help her," he said roughly. "I swear, if you make any attempt to escape, you'll regret it."

"Okay, okay, I get the point." Elly stood cautiously and put Rose on her shoulder.

The dust bunny watched Grayson very intently as they went down the staircase and into the front room of the shop.

"Does your dust bunny bite?" Grayson asked.

"No, of course not," Elly said, opening an herb jar. "She's just a little thing, and she's very friendly. I'm not saying she wouldn't nip your finger if you provoked her, but she couldn't do much damage."

"I can see why they call them dust bunnies. Looks like something that rolled out from under the bed."

Elly ignored that and concentrated on measuring out the herbs.

When she had filled one packet, she

sealed the jar, opened another one, and scooped some of the contents into a second packet.

"That's all I need for the tisane," she announced, putting the lid back on the second jar.

"Let's go."

Doreen raised her head when Elly, Grayson behind her, walked back into the room.

"Hurry," Doreen said hoarsely. "I'm feeling worse by the minute."

"I'll brew these up as fast as I can." Elly set the herbs on the counter and reached for the kettle. "But first I have to make some rez-root tea."

Grayson suddenly looked interested. "Got any coffee?"

"No." She opened the canister of rez-root tea. "I don't drink coffee. I prefer this, instead. It has a similar effect, though. The herbs I'm preparing for Doreen work best when mixed with a stimulant-based beverage. It's an old trick with analgesics." She reached for a teapot. "Mind if I make some extra tea for myself?"

"No." He turned back to the window. "Make some for me, too, while you're at it. I'd rather have coffee, but I'll take what I can get. Looks like it's going to be a long wait."

"Is there a rule somewhere that says innocent prisoners have to make tea for the guys who arrest them?"

"Just make the damn tea, okay?"

"Whatever you say." She took three mugs down out of a cupboard and got busy spooning tea into the pot. "Although, I must say, if I were you, I'm not sure I'd want to drink any brew that had been made by a suspected drug dealer."

Grayson chuckled. "As long as you're drinking the same tea, it should be safe."

"I can't wait much longer," Doreen whispered in a tortured voice.

"Just a few more minutes," Elly promised, opening one of the packets.

The water came to a boil. She poured it quickly over the tea leaves, filling the glass pot.

While she waited for the tea to steep, she opened the cookie jar, took out one of Mrs. Kim's peanut butter and chocolate chip specials, and gave it to Rose.

"Are those chocolate chip?" Grayson asked, watching Rose nibble at the cookie.

"With peanut butter," Elly said. "One of my neighbors made them. They're Rose's favorite."

"Are they real cookies or some kind of special dust bunny food?"

"They're real cookies. Rose eats human food." She took another cookie out of the jar and bit into it.

"Ugh." Doreen turned her face away. "I can't watch."

"Tea's ready," Elly said brightly.

She poured the brew into two of the mugs, leaving the third mug empty.

She took a pinch of herbs out of one of the packets and dropped them into Doreen's mug. "I think I'll have some, too." She sprinkled herbs into her own mug, "I can feel a headache coming on. Must be the stress."

She carried the mugs to the table and set them down.

"Drink it slowly," she warned. "It's very hot."

"Thanks." Doreen pulled the mug toward her and inhaled the aroma. "Wonderful. Just what I needed."

To Elly's dismay, Grayson handcuffed her right wrist to the chair again.

Satisfied that she was secured, he crossed to the counter, picked up the teapot, and filled the third mug. Without asking permission, he helped himself to a cookie.

Rose muttered ominously.

"Take it easy, lint ball," Grayson said. Mug in hand, he went back to the window.

"Plenty left for you. I haven't had anything to eat since I got the call this morning. That would have been sometime around three a.m."

"Would that have been the call from Palmer Frazier informing you that he had another hot tip regarding the location of some illicit drugs?" Elly asked politely.

Grayson gave her an irritated look. "Why do you keep going on about this Palmer Frazier character?"

It was Doreen who responded. She touched her bruised face.

"For starters, it sounds like he's the bastard who did this to me," she said. "Although he used another name. By the way, he told me he was an undercover cop working on a big drug case. What a coincidence, huh?"

"I think he probably murdered Stuart Griggs, too," Elly offered helpfully.

Grayson shook his head. "You two can really spin the stories." He took a sip of his tea and smiled slightly. "But the tea isn't half bad, I'll give you that."

"We all have our talents," Elly said.

Chapter 34

Ormond Ripley froze the video frame. "Recognize him?"

"His name is Palmer Frazier." Cooper studied the image on the screen. "This just turned into an even bigger problem than I thought it was."

Ripley set the video in motion again.

The recording showed Frazier walking swiftly down a hallway in a back-of-the-house section of the nightclub. He was dressed in the black-and-white uniforms worn by the members of the food-and-beverage staff. One of his pockets was stuffed with what appeared to be small cocktail napkins. A cluster of plastic swizzle sticks stuck out of another pocket.

"I found one of those swizzle sticks at the scene," Cooper said. "He must have dropped it and never realized it."

"Probably got pretty excited when he started rezzing blue light," Ripley said.

Frazier was obviously in a hurry. When he reached the door of the janitorial storage room, he opened it quickly and disappeared inside.

"I've been through this video from start to finish," Ripley said. "At no point does Frazier come back out of that storage room. And there is no video of him leaving the casino through the front entrance that night. He just disappears."

Cooper rechecked the date stamp on the video. "That was the night he tried to kill Bertha Newell. He must have been here at the casino when he somehow learned that Newell had become a problem that had to be dealt with immediately. Maybe Griggs called him. In any event, he probably knew that he was going to have to kill someone."

"Realizing there was an outside chance that he might someday need an alibi, he slipped out through my little hole-in-the-wall down in the basement." Ripley lounged back in his executive chair and steepled his fingers. "He no doubt planned to return the same way. If anyone questioned him later, he could say he was here at work the whole time."

"But he wasn't able to return because he melted amber creating the massive blue ghost vortex that he used to trap Newell in the catacombs."

"He would have plunged into a bad afterburn," Ripley concluded. "There would have been no time to come back here and act normal for a couple of hours. He had to go somewhere to crash."

"But first he would have wanted a woman," Cooper said softly.

Ripley tapped his fingertips together. "He would have wanted one very, very badly."

"The hooker who was found dead three blocks from Ruin Lane the next morning." Cooper walked slowly across the room, thinking. "The papers said it was a chant overdose. But the woman's roommate told the reporters that it looked like her friend had been roughed up by her last client. She called it murder."

"She may have been right." Ripley leaned forward and checked a printout. "According to my human resources department, Palmer Frazier, aka Jake Monroe, was hired three months ago. Been a model employee."

"Got a hunch he'd been planning to set you up for that raid for a long time," Cooper said.

"Question is, why?"

"He's a hunter who can work blue ghost light." Cooper shrugged. "They tend to be long-range planners."

"Yeah, I've heard that. The plan seems to have gone along very smoothly until you arrived on the scene. You have screwed things up for him since you hit town."

"Not me." Cooper headed for the door. "I think he was setting me up, too, which is kind of embarrassing for a Guild boss to have to admit."

"If you weren't the one messing with his plan, who was?"

Cooper paused, his hand on the doorknob. "My fiancée." He smiled slightly. "He made the mistake of underestimating her right from the start."

"Fiancée? Didn't know you were still engaged. Thought the wedding had been called off."

"Just postponed."

"Yeah? Well, when you set a new date, be sure to send me an invitation."

"I'll do that."

Chapter 35

"He's not dead or anything, is he?" Doreen asked. She looked uneasily at Grayson DeWitt, who was stretched out flat on the kitchen floor, snoring gently. "Killing cops is generally considered a no-no."

"Don't worry." Elly finished de-rezzing the handcuff that bound Doreen to the kitchen chair. "Just asleep. But he won't wake up for a few hours. The dose of red moonseed that I put in the tea was pretty strong."

"I don't get it." Doreen stood, gently rubbing her chafed wrist. "I saw you make the tea. All three of us drank it. Why aren't you and I snoozing away on the kitchen floor?"

"It's true, we all drank the same tea, and I did slip a heavy dose of moonseed into it when DeWitt was busy checking the alley." Elly went to the window, put her back to the wall, and peered behind the shade. "But the additional herbs that I put into the tea that you and I drank were an antidote to moonseed. In fact, when you combine those two herbs you get a brew that is actually a high-energy stimulant."

"Huh. Guess that explains why I'm feeling like I could go to the gym and work out."

"My compliments on the great acting job, by the way. I thought you really were about to throw up all over DeWitt's nice shoes."

"Frankly, it wasn't too far a stretch for me. I wasn't feeling very good at the time. But I'm much better now." Doreen moved around the table. "See anything?"

"A couple of guys on the rooftop across the way. Looks like DeWitt wasn't kidding when he said he had men watching the street and the alley."

"Oh, jeez. That means we don't dare leave."

"Not via the alley or the street, that's for sure." Elly reached for the wall phone. "I've got to warn Cooper."

"Wait." Doreen's eyes widened. "Not that phone. It might be tapped. Remember what you said about cops and bugs."

Elly stared at the phone in her hand as though it had become a chroma-snake. "You're right." She slammed the instrument back into the receiver. "I'll use my personal phone. I left it in my tote."

"Do you think the cops can bug personal phones, too?"

Elly halted in the doorway, appalled. "I don't know."

They looked at each other for a long moment.

Doreen turned to stare at Grayson DeWitt. "Why not use his phone?"

"Good thinking." Elly rushed back to crouch beside Grayson. She patted his pockets and found a small phone inside one of them. It was a very attractive and expensive brand, she noticed.

She rezzed the phone and punched in Cooper's private number. He answered on the first ring.

"Cooper, where are you?"

"Just left The Road. What's wrong?"

He spoke in the flat, cold voice she had only heard him use when he dealt with emergencies or major Guild politics.

She gave him a quick rundown of events.

"And now DeWitt's passed out cold on the kitchen floor," she concluded. "You can't come back here, Cooper. There are men on the rooftops waiting to arrest you."

"Frazier is a bigger problem at the moment. I don't know where he is. You and Doreen have to get out of that apartment."

"There's only one way out that probably isn't being watched," she said, meeting Doreen's anxious eyes.

"Your little hole-in-the-wall?" Cooper asked.

"Yes." Elly scooped up Rose and signaled to Doreen to follow her toward the stairs. "We're on our way downstairs now."

"Any chance Frazier knows about it?"

Elly looked at Doreen. "Did you tell your ex-boyfriend about my private little bolt-hole?"

"No. Subject never came up." Doreen made a face. "And even if it had, I wouldn't have told him. Frazier and I had some fun together, but it wasn't like I was in love with the bastard."

"Spoken like a true ruin rat," Elly said wryly. "Okay, that answers that question," she said into the phone. "He probably doesn't know about my secret tunnel entrance."

"I still don't like the idea of you going down there," Cooper said.

Elly, with Doreen behind her, reached the bottom of the staircase and hurried across the space to open the cellar door.

"We'll be okay," she assured him. "Doreen is a very good tangler. She can handle any illusion traps we might come across. Rose will give the alarm if there are any stray ghosts drifting around that section of the tunnels. We'll steer clear of them."

"What about an exit strategy?"

"I've got the coordinates for Bertha's hole-in-the-wall. We'll head for it. There's no reason DeWitt's men would be watching her shop."

"You've got plenty of tuned amber?" Cooper asked.

She glanced at the amber locket around Doreen's neck. "Doreen has hers." She touched her earrings. "And I've got mine."

"Give me both frequencies."

She rattled off her own and then held the phone away from her mouth. "Doreen? What's your freq?"

Doreen gave it to her. Elly repeated it into the phone.

"Got 'em," Cooper said.

"We're heading into the cellar now." Elly led the way down the steps into the pool of darkness below. "We won't be able to keep this phone connection much longer."

"Be careful, both of you," he said. "I'll pick you up at the exit point in about twenty minutes. I want you and Doreen in safe-keeping at Guild headquarters before I go after Frazier."

Elly knelt down to open the concealed trapdoor in the floor of the cellar.

"Yes, sir, Mr. Guild Boss," she said. "See you soon."

A wave of psi power wafted up through the opening in the floor.

She cut the connection and dropped the phone into her pocket.

"I'm the tangler here," Doreen said. "Stand back; I'll go first."

"You know something?" Elly said, "When it comes to the catacombs, people have been saying that to me for my entire life. One of these days, I'm going to be the one who gets to say it."

Chapter 36

Something had gone wrong. Again.

Palmer hit redial on his phone for the third time. There was still no answer from Grayson DeWitt.

He went to the window and stood looking out across the rooftops of the Old Quarter.

What was going on over there on Ruin Lane? The scheme was cut and dried. Everything had been on schedule since he'd made the phone call to DeWitt early this morning.

In his last call, DeWitt had reported that he had found the dope in Elly's car and that his men were in position on the rooftops.

What could have gone wrong this time?

Frustration and rage threatened to choke Palmer. His left hand clenched and unclenched.

Boone had figured out the second setup, he thought. It was the only explanation. The son of a bitch was probably on his way back to the safety of his office at Guild headquarters in Aurora Springs right now, leaving Elly behind to take the fall for the drugs.

So much for his working hypothesis, Palmer thought. He had been so damn certain that Elly St. Clair was Boone's one weak spot. Now it looked as if he had miscalculated.

He knew that it was time to pull another disappearing act, but he hated to walk away from the plan at this stage. He had spent so much time and money on this project. Every detail had been so carefully thought out. He had killed twice to preserve the integrity of the plan.

If Boone was on his way back to Aurora Springs, it meant that everything had fallen apart.

"Bastard. Bastard. *Son of a bitch bastard blue freak.*"

He slammed his fist against the side of the window and then sucked in his breath when pain flashed across his knuckles. He looked down and saw blood dripping on the windowsill.

"Bastard," he whispered. "This is all your fault, Boone. Everything has gone wrong, and it's all your fault, you damned freak."

He went into the small bathroom and ran cold water over his bruised knuckles. The mask in the mirror stared back at him. Every day it looked less and less like him. He was falling apart.

Control. The key was control. If he didn't regain it, he would fall into the blue vortex.

He took some deep breaths. When he felt steadier he turned off the water.

Think like the Guild boss you were destined to be.

Deal with facts, he told himself. All right, something had gone wrong with the final stage of the revised plan. There was nothing to be done about the disaster. Escape and survival were his priorities now.

He had to get back underground as quickly as possible. In the catacombs he was the master of blue energy. Down there he was invincible.

He had made preparations for this contingency, he reminded himself.

He went back out into the unfurnished room and wiped down everything in sight with a damp cloth. It was doubtful that anyone would ever find this place, let alone connect him to it, but he was not going to take any more chances. There were rumors that some police detectives had a kind of psi talent that enabled them to detect whether a suspect had been in a room at some point in the recent past. The authorities claimed that was an urban legend, but he knew a little something about Guild legends, and he wasn't taking any chances. Courts required proof. He didn't plan to leave any.

When he was satisfied that he had erased all traces of his presence in the small, dilapidated apartment, he picked up the duffel bag that held his emergency supply of cash and some extra chant that he could sell if he ran short of money. He had a change of clothes and his journal in the bag, too.

He let himself out the door, not bothering to rez the antique lock. The old flophouse had been abandoned years ago. He'd been lucky that someone had neglected to shut off the water.

He went quickly along the empty hall and took the fire stairs down into the deep basement.

The psi energy pouring out of the hole-in-the-wall revived and calmed him. Down here he was in control.

He slipped through the jagged opening in the quartz, climbed into the sled, and paused to check the fix on the locator. He wished he could leave town right that instant. It made him nervous to hang around any longer than necessary now that he knew his plan had failed.

Unfortunately, there was one last detail that had to be taken care of before he could be assured of his personal safety. He had to get rid of the silly little bitch. Although she did not know his real name, Doreen Thornton could describe him.

Should have killed her yesterday, he thought, rezzing the sled's engine. But he hadn't wanted any more dead bodies showing up in Elly's neighborhood at that particular point. Another one would have raised too many questions with the authorities and, quite possibly, with Cooper Boone.

Don't worry, he thought. *Doreen isn't going anywhere. Not with that face you gave her. And she thinks you're a cop. She'll keep her mouth shut.*

But she was definitely a problem that he had to deal with as quickly as possible.

He checked her personal amber frequency. The stuff didn't work as a locating device aboveground, but it was as good as a homing beacon down here, provided you knew the number.

Doreen was a ruin rat. If she did decide to hide, she would head for the catacombs.

The frequency pinged, startling him so badly that he nearly drove into the nearest wall.

Doreen had, indeed, fled into the tunnels.

He braked to a stop and sat staring at the

directional device, not daring to believe his good fortune.

She wasn't too far away. According to the grid, the coordinates he was looking at corresponded to a section of the tunnels located close to Ruin Lane.

The coordinates shifted as he watched the screen.

His quarry was on the move.

Was she alone? That was the next question. If DeWitt had lost control of the situation back at Elly's apartment, as it appeared, it was very possible that the two women were on the run together.

With a sense of rising anticipation, he dialed in the second frequency number that he had recently memorized.

There was another loud, satisfying ping from the device. Elly was with Doreen.

Finally, it looked as though he was going to get a break.

He rezzed the sled's engine.

Chapter 37

Rose's teeth flashed. Simultaneously she growled a warning.

"Wait." Elly grabbed Doreen's arm, halting her. "Something's wrong. Look at Rose."

Doreen stopped and stared at Rose, who was crouched on Elly's shoulder.

"What's wrong with her?" Doreen took a step back in alarm. "I've never seen her like that. She's all teeth and eyes. I thought you said she didn't bite."

"I lied." Elly reached up carefully to take hold of Rose. "But she won't bite you."

"Are you sure?"

"Pretty sure. This is her way of telling us that there's trouble nearby. Maybe a stray ghost."

"Got it. Okay, we'll be careful." Doreen looked at Rose. "Don't worry, I'm your fashion friend, remember? I know what I'm doing down here. I've got pretty good psi senses. We won't walk into any ghosts."

Rose did not appear reassured. She scrabbled furiously in Elly's grip and made odd whimpering noises.

"All right, I'll put you down, sweetie." Elly set her on the floor. "But please don't run off."

Rose disobeyed immediately. She dashed away, full tilt, down a corridor. When she realized that Elly wasn't following, she stopped, sat up on her hind legs, and chittered loudly.

"I've never seen her like this," Elly said. "I think she wants us to follow her."

Doreen frowned. "We can't do that. We've got to get to Bertha's personal exit point as quickly as possible. Cooper will be waiting."

A faint, high-pitched hum echoed in the distance. Elly stilled.

"I think I hear a sled," she whispered.

Doreen cocked her head, listening.

The whine of the engine grew louder.

Doreen's bruised face went pale. "You're right. Sound gets distorted down here, but if we can hear him, we have to assume he isn't too far away. Probably another ruin rat. He might be able to help us."

Elly looked back over her shoulder. "Or not."

"What do you mean?"

"I'm convinced that dust bunnies have an animal version of parapsych senses. Rose's judgment when it comes to people has always been amazingly accurate. For whatever reason she doesn't think we should stick around to find out who is piloting that sled. I vote we go with her."

Rose scurried back toward Elly, made urgent, anxious noises, whipped around, and ran off again.

"That settles it," Elly said. She grabbed Doreen's arm and started forward at a run. "Follow that bunny."

Doreen did not argue.

Rose rounded a corner at top speed, claws clicking on the quartz floor.

Elly and Doreen ran faster.

"Little sucker sure can move when she wants to," Doreen panted.

The engine noise grew louder.

"Damn." Doreen glanced back over her shoulder. "He's getting closer, and I think I'm picking up some ghost energy. He must be following us. How can he be doing that?"

"Your amber," Elly said. "He must have your frequency."

"Oh, shit," Doreen said. "It must be Frazier or whatever his name is. He had plenty of opportunity to get my frequency."

"Toss your amber into one of the chambers."

"Are you nuts? We're underground. If we

lose this amber, we'll never find our way out."

Elly touched one earring. "I've got some."

Doreen looked at her earrings, startled. "That's *tuned* amber you're wearing?"

"Yes."

"I thought it was just a fashion statement. You never said anything about having strong para-rez senses."

"I'll explain later. Trust me, this amber is tuned. And the frequency is unique. There's no way Palmer could know it, because he doesn't know that I have a strong parapsych profile."

"What kind of profile? Hunter? Tangler?"

"Neither. Look, can we talk about this some other time? We've got a situation here."

"But I always work with my own amber," Doreen said uncertainly.

Elly felt a trickle of energy across the nape of her neck. She looked down the length of the tunnel. Blue light sparked in the distance.

"Oh, damn. Looks like a blue light special. It must be Frazier. You have to get rid of your amber, Doreen."

Doreen followed her gaze. "What is that thing? It looks like ghost light, but it's blue.

And it's whirling in a weird way."

"He's using your amber to guide that ghost."

"This is so weird." Doreen whipped off her pendant and hurled it back toward the advancing vortex.

The ghost swooped down on the necklace and locked on to its frequency.

"Okay, I believe you now," Doreen whispered.

"That bought us some time," Elly said. "Hurry. Rose is moving fast."

Up ahead Rose veered around another corner, paws scrabbling frantically on the glowing green stone. Elly followed her, Doreen close beside her.

But when they turned the corner, a massive wall of quartz blocked their path. The hallways on either side were solid. There were no branching corridors or vaulted chamber entrances.

Elly slammed to a halt. Doreen did the same. Together they stared in mute horror at the quartz wall.

"There's no way out except back the way we came," Doreen said flatly. "Maybe we can reach that last intersection before Frazier does and turn down another passageway."

Elly shivered beneath a gentle tide of

strong, pulsing energy. It was different from what she normally sensed underground. It had an eerily familiar feel.

"Do you sense anything unusual?" she asked.

Doreen frowned. "I'm scared to death, if that's what you mean."

"I'm talking about psi energy waves." Elly moved closer to the wall. "I think they're coming from the quartz."

"I'm not picking up anything except the usual." Doreen broke off, distracted. "I can hear the sled again."

Elly listened to the faint vibrating whine of the sled's motor. Frazier was still hot on their trail.

"Come on." Doreen grabbed her wrist. "We've got to at least try to find another intersection."

Elly did not take her eyes off the wall. "Look at Rose."

"What?"

"Look at her."

Rose had come to a halt directly in front of the solid quartz wall. She was standing on her hind legs facing the barrier.

Incredibly, a small hole materialized in the quartz at dust bunny height. Rose zipped through it and promptly disappeared.

The hole closed behind her, leaving Elly and Doreen gazing at the solid, glowing quartz.

Elly looked at Doreen and saw the despair on her face.

"He's closing in on us," Doreen said. "We're trapped."

Chapter 38

Cooper watched the frequency numbers waver and abruptly vanish from the screen of his personal amber-rez locator. Doreen's amber had just been fried, most likely by ghost fire. Not a good sign.

Elly's coordinates still registered strongly, though. That gave him hope. He tromped hard on the throttle, trying to coax a little more speed out of Bertha Newell's rickety old sled. There wasn't much to be had. He was already moving dangerously fast as it was. At this rate he could easily slam into an illusion trap or a ghost before he had time to steer clear.

But he had no choice. When he had arrived at Newell's private tunnel gate and discovered that Doreen and Elly hadn't made it out, he had known in his gut that things had gone wrong. That led to the chilling conclusion that Frazier was more than likely involved.

He whipped the sled around another corner and shot down a long green hallway, all of his senses open to the currents of psi power that flowed through the catacombs.

Doreen gazed, baffled, at the solid quartz wall. "It may be some form of illusion trap energy, but it's not like any I've ever worked with. I'm not sensing anything. If I hadn't seen Rose disappear through that wall just now, I'd swear it was solid quartz." She put her hand on the stone. "It even feels solid to the touch. If this were true illusion trap energy, my hand would have passed right through it, and I would have triggered the trap."

"But I can feel the energy patterns." Elly studied the wall, wonder and amazement unfurling inside her. "They're similar to the patterns I pick up from those green flowers that Rose brings me."

Doreen looked at her. "You pick up psi energy from plants?"

"It's okay, I'm not really crazy. At least, I don't think I am. The thing is, if I concentrate a little, the wavelengths in that wall become crystal clear. I can almost *see* them in a way I can't explain."

A small section of the wall shimmered. Another hole opened up. Rose poked her head through and chattered loudly. She disappeared again. The wall sealed itself.

"She wants us to follow her," Elly said.

"Maybe I can do this. Everyone in my family can de-rez psi energy waves of one kind or another. I know, theoretically, how it works."

"Go for it," Doreen urged. "Not like we've got a lot of other options here. The de-rezzing techniques are the same for ghost or illusion energy. The variables are the type of energy and the location on the spectrum. I don't know what you're working with here, but if you can sense wavelengths, the idea is to dampen them by focusing your own psi energy through your amber. I can't explain it any more clearly than that. You have to *feel* your way into the pattern."

Elly did not respond. She was too busy feeling her way into the pattern. It was easier than she had anticipated, probably because she had been attuned to plant psi energy for years, she thought.

She closed her eyes to help concentrate. She found the resonating patterns in the wall and cautiously pulsed power through her amber, sending out her own unique brand of psychic energy in a counterpoint rhythm.

She sensed instantly when the wavelengths melded and canceled each other out.

Humid warmth and a vast energy wind flowed over her, stirring all of her senses. She was enveloped in an intoxicating aura of plant psi more powerful than she had ever experienced in her entire life.

"Elly, look," Doreen whispered.

Elly opened her eyes. A large section of the wall had disappeared, revealing an impossible landscape of heavily massed foliage.

A canopy of leaves formed by trees that were at once startlingly familiar and strangely different cast a heavy veil of shadow over a world of magnificent ferns, flowers, and vines. The lush scents of a vast greenhouse filled the air.

"Jordan's Jungle," Elly said softly.

Rose appeared in the opening, still sleeked out and in full predatory mode. She rumbled a warning.

"We're coming," Elly said.

"Oh, shit," Doreen said tensely. "Maybe Frazier does have your frequency."

Elly looked back and saw the small, whirling vortex. It was coming toward them like a well-aimed spear moving in relatively slow motion.

There was no time to use the earrings to close the opening in the wall. She tugged both pieces of jewelry out of her ears and hurled them straight at the vortex.

The energy spear swerved toward the fresh bait.

"Let's go," Elly said.

Together with Doreen and Rose, she plunged into Jordan's Jungle.

Chapter 39

The frequency of Elly's amber disappeared from Cooper's personal amber-rez locator. He went cold to the bone. He did not want to think about what that might mean.

All he had now were the coordinates of Elly's last position in the catacombs. If she and Doreen moved very far from those, he would never find them.

But he was close. And Rose was with the women, he reminded himself. According to Emmett London, dust bunnies seemed to be able to navigate underground. Rose would never abandon Elly. Not if she was still alive.

He refused to contemplate the alternative.

He sent the sled skimming across a six-way intersection and shot down another glowing hallway, heading for Elly's last known location.

Elly crouched just inside the small cave, peering through the screen of ferns. Doreen knelt beside her. Rose sat on a nearby rock, fully fluffed, looking unconcerned once more. She fussed with her fur and fastidiously adjusted her necklace.

Jordan's Jungle was a surprisingly noisy place. They hadn't seen any wildlife except for a few small, very green lizards skittering over the nearby rocks, but the shrieks of unseen birds echoed through the high tree canopy.

Down below the cavern where she and Doreen hid, a large waterfall cascaded over stones, splashing into a dark pool that was covered with broad-leaved plants.

Layer upon layer of lush, thick greenery surrounded the grotto. From her vantage point, Elly could see the opening in the wall that she had created and a small section of the outside corridor.

"What's he doing?" Doreen whispered. "Can you see?"

A figure moved hesitantly through the opening and stopped almost immediately. Palmer looked around in obvious confusion and disbelief.

"He's inside," Elly said. "But he looks very nervous."

"I don't blame him." Doreen shuddered. "Who knows what's in this place? I'll bet there are all kinds of poisonous snakes and insects."

"Rose will give us a warning if something dangerous approaches."

"Fine. We get a warning. Then what? It's not like we've got anything we can use against that blue ghost light thing."

"I wonder how Palmer got my amber frequency," Elly said. "How did he even know I had one? No one except Cooper and my family know that I have some kind of psi thing going on with plants. Why would he suspect that I was wearing tuned amber?"

"I think we can worry about that later. Right now we've got other issues."

"Elly," Palmer shouted. His voice reverberated through the trees. "You are in great danger. Doreen and Cooper Boone are partners in the drug ring. Don't you get it? They're trying to set you up."

"I can't believe he's going to try a stupid line like that," Elly stated. "He must have a very low opinion of my intelligence."

"Palmer hasn't got a lot of respect for women," Doreen said. "And I'll have to admit I did my part to encourage that view."

"Don't blame yourself for not seeing through him," Elly said. "He's a very shrewd and manipulative man. He actually managed to get himself a seat on the Guild Council back home in Aurora Springs. That means he fooled my father and everyone else on the Council. No one realized just how dangerous he was until Cooper arrived on the scene. He understood right away that Palmer was a threat and took steps to remove him."

"Yeah? Too bad Cooper didn't do something a little more permanent."

"Got a hunch Cooper is thinking pretty much the same thing at this very moment."

Should have killed the bastard, or at least fried his brains when I had the chance.

Cooper brought Bertha's sled to a halt behind the one Frazier had left in the hallway. He got out and went swiftly toward the opening in the wall.

The sight of the massed greenery was stunning. *Looks like a full-blown rain forest in there.* So much for Jordan's Jungle being a myth.

He stopped at the edge of the opening, flattening his back against the wall, and inhaled the heavy scents of the jungle. The humidity was an invisible wall of heat. He could hear the cries of birds and the distant rumble of a waterfall.

Palmer Frazier's voice rang out.

"Elly, you've got to listen to me. Cooper Boone is a very dangerous man. You grew up in a Guild family. Ever heard of a blue freak? That's what he is. I can protect you from him."

Cooper listened intently. If Elly was in there, she knew enough to keep silent. As for Frazier, he wasn't too far inside the entrance.

"I know all about your ability to sense plant psi," Frazier said. "Griggs figured it out. When he visited your shop he watched you working with the herbs and realized that you could do the same thing he could do with plants. A couple of weeks ago I sent him into your shop with one of the new amber frequency readers to get a reading on your earrings. Those new gadgets are really something. All he had to do was stand a few feet away from you. He was able to get your number without you ever knowing what he was doing. It was just a safety precaution to protect you in case Boone kidnapped you and took you underground."

Cooper rezzed blue ghost light, forcing it into a vortex. Using the blue storm as a shield, he moved through the opening.

He saw motion in a heavy stand of monstrous ferns not more than twenty feet away. Frazier was sticking close to the gate in the wall, no doubt afraid to move too deeply into the unknowns of the jungle.

The storm of blue energy caught Frazier's attention.

"Boone." He pushed through a fan of giant fern fronds. "You son of a bitch freak. This is all your fault."

A blue vortex flashed across the space that separated them. It struck the shield that Cooper had constructed. When the energy masses collided there was a brilliant, intense explosion of blue light that briefly lit up the primal darkness of the underground rain forest.

Another vortex arrow followed, and then another and another, until the air was filled with violent shafts of energy. Frazier was going for an all-out assault, hoping to overwhelm and disorient his opponent.

Cooper's shield flared and pulsed in response to the hail of arrows. The strobe light flashes became so intense, so eye-dazzling, that Cooper had to close his eyes and fight with only his psi senses to guide him.

Somewhere in the vast reaches of the jungle, creatures shrieked and screamed in warning and panic. Cooper heard a wild, chaotic fluttering of heavy wings.

Rain started to fall. He heard it first because it pounded against the canopy of tree leaves, creating a dull roar of noise. Then the water began to penetrate the leafy ceiling. It descended in a steady, unyielding torrent, drenching him. When he opened his eyes, he discovered that the mist created by the deluge was so heavy he could not see more than a few feet.

If he was half-blind now, so was Frazier. The only thing giving away their positions to each other was the luminous ghost energy they used as weapons.

He stopped pulsing power through amber and moved quickly into the nearest stand of trees.

Suddenly aware that he no longer had a target, Frazier ceased the barrage of energy arrows.

"You're a dead freak, Boone," Frazier screamed. "Do you hear me? You're *dead.* When this is over, the Aurora Springs Guild is going to be my private property. And so is your handpicked woman. I'm going to screw her as often as I like, and she's going to smile at me when I do it, because if she doesn't, I'll destroy her whole damn family. Just like I'm going to destroy your family, Boone. Got to save innocent people from blue freaks like you now, don't we? It's a prime responsibility of the Guild."

Cooper watched the little sparks of blue popping and snapping a short distance away. They were the only things he could see through the steady downpour. Frazier was so out of control he didn't even realize he was summoning the stray bits of blue ghost light, didn't realize that he was giving away his position.

Cooper pulled all of the energy he could out of the atmosphere and sent it smashing into the epicenter of the dancing blue lights.

He knew he had found his target when he heard Frazier scream. The shriek of pain and rage and fear seemed to go on for an eternity.

It ended with a shattering abruptness.

Cooper walked through the driving rain to the place where he had last seen the flickers of ghost light.

Frazier was sprawled on his back, his mouth open, dead eyes wide.

Cooper crouched to check for a pulse. There wasn't any. He rose.

"Elly?"

"We're up here," she shouted from somewhere off to his right. "Be down in a minute."

Rose reached him first. He heard the dust bunny's cheerful chortle before he saw her. She tumbled toward him through the rain, her wet fur plastered to her small, sleek frame. A bracelet fashioned of green and yellow stones swung from her neck.

He reached down to pick her up. "Lookin' good, gorgeous."

Elly emerged from the trees, Doreen right behind her. Both women were soaked to the skin.

The steely tension that had been driving him for the past half hour finally began to ease. Elly was safe.

Then he got a closer look at Doreen's face.

"What the hell happened to you?" he asked.

"Long story." Doreen looked at Frazier's body. "Is he dead?"

"Yes," Cooper said.

"Excellent," Doreen said, supremely satisfied.

Elly hurled herself against him.

"I was scared to death when I saw all that blue ghost fire," she whispered. She tightened her arms around him as though she would never let him go. "Are you all right?"

"Yes. What about you?"

"I'm okay. Rose saved us by showing us the gate into this place."

"Let's save the explanations until later, okay?" Doreen urged them toward the opening in the wall. "We've got to get aboveground as fast as possible so that we can claim the most important underground discovery made since the First Generation settlers found the catacombs."

Elly pushed herself slightly away from Cooper. "You know something? You're right."

"Yep. And there's another thing here." Doreen winked one bruised eye. "At this point, as far as anyone knows, you, my friend, are the only person who can open and close that gate over there. If we play our cards right, this rain forest is going to make us all very, very rich. I suggest we hustle."

Elly laughed. "You do realize that we're going to have to share this find with Bertha Newell?"

"No problem," Doreen said, urging them toward the opening. "There will be plenty of money to go around. Elly, you'd better close up that opening in the wall after we leave. Don't want to take the chance that some other ruin rats will stumble into this jungle before we file our claim."

"All right," Elly agreed. She caught Cooper's hand.

Cooper looked at both of them. "Hate to rain on your parade, seeing that you're both already soaked and all, but we're going to have to deal with the cops before you can start in on the paperwork you'll need to file your claim on the jungle. We've got a dead body here."

Elly made a face. "And a famous detective who is sort of passed out on my kitchen floor. That will probably take a little explaining."

"No problem," Cooper said. "I'm a Guild boss, remember? I handle stuff like this."

Doreen frowned, suddenly looking distinctly wary. "That was quite a light show you put on in there. I'm guessing you probably melted amber."

"Mmm," Cooper said.

"Are you going to go out of control and turn weird on us before we get to the surface?" Doreen asked.

"Don't be silly," Elly said. Her hand tightened around Cooper's. "Guild bosses don't go out of control and turn weird."

"Not unless we're provoked," Cooper said.

Chapter 40

An hour and a half later, Detective Alice Martinez stood in Elly's kitchen watching two uniformed officers hoist a snoring Grayson DeWitt onto a stretcher.

Elly thought she detected amusement in Alice's dark eyes. There was no doubt but that the detective's mouth was twitching at the corners.

"He actually drank the tea you made for him?" Alice asked a little too neutrally.

"I didn't force him to drink it," Elly said quickly. "I made it, and I poured some for Doreen and me. He helped himself. Honest." She looked at Doreen, who was hovering nearby. "Isn't that right?"

"Absolutely," Doreen said earnestly. "Elly even warned him not to drink it."

Alice's brows climbed. "You warned him, Miss St. Clair?"

Elly cleared her throat. "I did say that if I were him, I wouldn't drink anything that had been brewed up by a person who was under suspicion for manufacturing drugs."

On the other side of the kitchen Cooper

paused in his restless pacing. Elly noticed that the intense heat of his afterburn was starting to fade from his eyes, but now he was slipping into the inevitable exhaustion.

"Sounds like full disclosure to me, Detective," he said.

"It certainly does." Alice started to smile. "And yet our ace detective, Mr. Special Task Force, went right ahead and drank the tea." She was grinning widely now. "Oh, man, this is good. This is so rich. I can't wait until they hear about this down at headquarters."

Elly watched her closely. "Does this mean that you aren't going to arrest me?"

"For what? Making a pot of tea in your own kitchen and then telling Detective DeWitt that he shouldn't drink any?" Alice chuckled. "Don't worry, Miss St. Clair, no one's going to arrest you. In fact, on behalf of the rest of the detectives of the Cadence City Police Department, allow me to extend our thanks and appreciation. You don't know what a pain in the ass DeWitt has been in the past few months."

"In fairness, he had a little help along the way." Cooper gestured toward the journal he had found in Frazier's duffel bag. "I had a chance to glance at some of the notes he made. Looks like after resigning from the

Aurora Springs Guild Council, Palmer Frazier went underground for a while and concocted a plan."

"Back home everyone believed he had moved to Frequency City," Elly explained.

"Frazier created that impression on purpose," Cooper said. "After Elly moved to Cadence, he followed, using a new identity. He did some research here in the Old Quarter and stumbled onto the very small-time drug operation that Stuart Griggs was running out of his shop."

Alice folded her arms and looked thoughtful. "Let me hazard a guess. Frazier saw the potential of the enchantment dust business and made Griggs an offer he couldn't refuse, right?"

Cooper nodded. "In his journal Frazier says he put things on a production basis and set up a small network of dealers. He wasn't giving Griggs anything resembling a fifty-fifty split, but whatever his cut was, the florist was suddenly looking at more ready cash than he had ever seen in his life. Obviously he used the windfall to buy the Jordan herbal hoping it would help him pursue his search for the jungle."

"Because that was all Stuart Griggs really cared about," Elly added quietly. "But a few nights ago, my friend, Bertha Newell, accidentally discovered his underground drug lab."

"Frazier states in the journal that Newell not only saw the lab, she also saw and recognized Stuart Griggs," Cooper said. "Griggs hit her on the head and left her lying unconscious in the tunnels while he went aboveground to call for help. By the time Frazier arrived on the scene, however, Newell had recovered enough to flee in her sled. Frazier had the sled's frequency and tracked her through the catacombs."

"Bertha can't recall the details," Elly added, "but it appears that at some point she realized that he was using the sled's locator device to follow her. She evidently abandoned the sled and hid in one of the nearby chambers. Frazier gave up searching for her and, uh, disabled the sled by attaching a ghost to it."

Actually, he'd done it with blue ghost light but she wasn't about to say that. Everyone would freak.

"When Newell tried to retrieve the sled, she must have gotten zapped," Cooper explained. "She made it as far as the nearest chamber and collapsed."

"That's where you found her?" Alice asked.

"Yes," he said.

"It's clear that Frazier was DeWitt's mysterious informant," Alice said. "What was the connection to The Road?"

"Frazier got a job there a few months ago," Cooper said. "He had planned to set Ripley up as the first major bust for DeWitt."

"Would have created a lot of media attention for DeWitt," Alice acknowledged. "But what was in it for Frazier? If he was making a fortune with the drugs, why arrange to have the operation uncovered and destroyed? And why kill Griggs?"

Cooper looked at her. "The drugs were only a stepping-stone to his real goal. When he was ready for the next step in his plan, he got rid of Griggs to cover his tracks. He didn't want to leave any loose ends."

Alice cocked a brow. "So what was Frazier's ultimate goal?"

"Getting rid of me," Cooper said quietly. "And getting his hands on Elly."

Doreen's eyes widened. "He wanted Elly that bad?"

"No," Elly said flatly. "What he wanted was to be boss of the Aurora Springs Guild. He only wanted me because I would have made him the perfect Guild boss wife."

"Marrying Elly would have cemented an alliance with her father." Cooper yawned.

451

"John St. Clair is the most powerful man on the Aurora Springs Guild Council. Frazier figured that if he controlled Elly, he could control her father. He badly underestimated the St. Clairs, of course. Knowing what I do about the clan, I think it's safe to assume that Frazier would have turned up missing shortly after he got the job he wanted so badly. But that was always one of Frazier's big problems."

"Underestimating people?" Alice asked.

Cooper smiled his dangerous smile. "The guy just didn't grasp the nuances of Guild politics."

"Wait a second," Doreen said. "I get that Frazier started dating me a couple of weeks ago so that he could keep an eye on Elly. And I understand that he forced Stuart Griggs into a partnership. But how did he know that you would come to Cadence to see Elly?"

Alice looked at Cooper. "Good question."

Cooper shrugged. "Frazier still had contacts and connections back in Aurora Springs. He had been a member of the Council, after all. Last month it was no secret that I was making arrangements to spend a couple of weeks here in Cadence courting Elly."

Elly felt her jaw unhinge. "*What?* Are you telling me that everyone back home knows you came here to try to convince me to marry you?"

He spread his hands. "You said it yourself: Aurora Springs is a small town. Every man on the Council and probably most of the members of the Guild and their families understood that I considered our wedding postponed, not called off."

Elly sagged back against the counter. "This is so embarrassing."

Doreen grinned. "I think it's incredibly romantic."

Cooper smiled at her, pleased. "Thanks. Glad someone appreciates the work involved here. As I was saying, everyone expected me to head for Cadence sooner or later. I figured six months was long enough to wait. But as the Guild chief, I couldn't just up and disappear for a couple of weeks. I had to organize matters so that Elly's dad and the Council would be able to handle Guild affairs while I was out of town."

Doreen nodded sagely. "And someone back in Aurora Springs notified Frazier of the date you planned to head for Cadence."

He yawned again. "Like I said, it was an open secret."

Alice drummed her fingers on the kitchen

counter. "You're telling me that Frazier spent months setting a trap that was supposed to end with you being arrested for dealing drugs, Boone?"

Cooper propped one shoulder and his head against the wall. He crossed his arms and half-closed his eyes. "Uh-huh. I was supposed to be DeWitt's second and biggest bust."

"Seems like a pretty elaborate sort of plan," Alice said slowly. "Why not just lie in wait in the alley out back and shoot you when it was convenient?"

"Killing a Guild boss in cold blood is sort of a big deal to the Guilds," Cooper said dryly. "Sets a bad example. Frazier didn't dare try it back in Aurora Springs because the risk was too great. Small town thing, you know? Hard to get away with a high-profile murder in a place where everyone knows you. And regardless of whether or not there was any proof, he had to be aware that he would have been suspect number one in the eyes of the Council."

Understanding lit Alice's face. "And the murder of a visiting Guild boss here in Cadence would have infuriated Mercer Wyatt. He would have turned the city upside down to find the shooter."

"Frazier had to keep himself above suspicion at all costs," Cooper agreed.

He started to slide down the wall. Alarmed, Elly hurried over to him, grabbed one arm, and slung it around her shoulder.

"You need to get to bed," she said.

Alice angled her chin at the officer in the doorway. "Give her a hand, Drayton. Boone looks like he's going to pass out. He's too heavy for Miss St. Clair."

"No problem." Drayton moved forward. "I'll handle him, Miss St. Clair. Where do you want him?"

"This way," she said.

She went down the hall to the bedroom. Drayton maneuvered Cooper as far as the bed.

"Thanks," Cooper mumbled. He fell full length onto his back on the quilt. He closed his eyes. "Are you all going to stand around this bed and watch me sleep?"

"We're leaving." Elly leaned down and kissed him gently.

Cooper smiled a little, looking content.

Elly made shooing motions at the others. They backed out of the bedroom reluctantly.

"One last thing," Doreen said from the doorway. "Why was Frazier so sure you'd come after Elly sooner or later? You didn't need her or her father's influence to become the chief of the Aurora Springs Guild. You already had the job."

"That was the one thing he got right," Cooper said without opening his eyes. "He figured I'd show up here sooner or later because he knew Elly was my weakness. Like everyone else back home, he knew that I loved her."

"He knew *what?*" Elly shrieked.

Cooper turned on his side and went to sleep.

"Typical male," Doreen said.

Chapter 41

He awoke a long time later and saw that night had fallen. The familiar emerald light of the Dead City infused the fog outside the bedroom window.

There was a small scurrying action at the foot of the bed. Rose drifted up to his chest and looked down at him with her bright blue eyes.

"Hey there, gorgeous." He smiled and patted the top of her head or at least where he thought the top of her head probably was.

Rose bounced a little. The beads of a red-and-gold bracelet necklace gleamed in the shadows.

"You're awake." Elly uncurled from the chair in the corner, put down the leather-bound journal she had been reading, and came to stand beside the bed. "Thank goodness. I was starting to get worried because you were conked out for so long. How are you feeling?"

He was vaguely surprised to see that she was dressed in a nightgown and robe, her hair loose around her shoulders. She looked beautiful, he thought. But, then, she always did, no matter what she was wearing or the time of the day. She would look beautiful fifty or sixty years from now. She would always be the most beautiful woman in the world to him. He had known that from the beginning.

"I'm fine." He raised his arm so that he could check his watch. "It's nearly midnight. How'd it get so late?"

"Time flies when you're sleeping off a bad afterburn." She sank down on the edge of the bed and rested her hand on his arm.

He wrapped his hand around hers. "What have you been up to while I was out?"

"Acting as your secretary for the most part. Taking messages."

"What messages?"

"Let's see. Bertha Newell came by. She said to tell you how grateful she was and that she'll be back in the morning to thank you in person. Emmett and Lydia London stopped in for a few minutes to make sure that we were all okay. Emmett said he'll call you tomorrow to get the details. Lydia brought Fuzz and Ginger along. Rose showed them her jewelry collection. I believe they were impressed. Lydia may have to take them shopping soon. Oh, and

458

Mercer Wyatt phoned." She paused. "I think that's everyone."

"You have been busy."

"They all made it clear that they expect an invitation to the wedding."

"Yeah?" His insides clenched, but he managed to keep his voice even. "What did you tell them?"

She leaned over and kissed him lightly on the mouth. When she raised her head again, he could see the love that lit her eyes.

"I told them that they would all get one, of course," she said.

He pulled her down on top of him. Rose scrambled out of the way with a grumpy protest, tumbled off the bed, and disappeared in the direction of the kitchen.

"I love you," Cooper said. "I fell for you the first day I met you."

She smiled. "The fall was mutual. I love you, too, Cooper. But I couldn't seem to get your attention back at the beginning."

He slipped the robe off her shoulders. "I know I didn't handle things well at the start of our relationship. There was so much going on that I didn't want you to know about."

"Like why Haggerty had dropped dead so mysteriously in the tunnels?"

"Among other things." He hesitated. "To

459

be honest, I wasn't sure how you would feel if you found out about my past. Everyone kept telling me how *sheltered* you had been."

She made a small, rude noise. "That business about my abnormal parapsych profile, I suppose. Typical hunter clan. They all assumed that just because I wasn't born to fry ghosts or untangle illusion traps, I must be fragile."

"In addition to not wanting to discuss Haggerty and my blue light work, there were a lot of problems to deal with when I first took over the Guild."

"Such as burying the news that Haggerty had been a contract killer?"

"Remember that weekend I disappeared?" he asked.

"Very clearly. You said something had come up."

"It was an emergency meeting of all of the Guild bosses to inform them about the situation with Haggerty and what had been done about it. On top of everything else, I soon discovered that Haggerty had not paid much attention to the day-to-day organizational operations of the Guild during his last year in office. The command structure was in chaos, and morale was bad. I had to fire some people and reorganize entire departments, and I had to do it quickly. Not everyone was thrilled with the changes."

"You know, I would have understood about all this if you had just *talked* to me."

"Honey, I spent years working alone or in secret with only a handful of other people who knew what I was and what I did for a living. Talking about myself and my job is not something that comes naturally to me."

"Yes, I did get that impression. Okay, you're forgiven for not opening up about your Guild problems. Tell me why, when we were dating back in Aurora Springs, you never tried to do anything more than kiss me good night at my door?"

He smiled ruefully. "I wanted you so badly, I could hardly keep my hands off you. I knew that if things got going hot and heavy between us, all of my good intentions would be doomed. I told myself you needed time to fall in love with me. The only way I could keep some distance was to focus on my work."

"You certainly did a good job of focusing. But I've got a small confession to make, myself."

"Yeah? What's that?"

"The main reason I moved to Cadence was because I secretly hoped that, given time, you might come to miss me. I mean, *really* miss me. In fact, I hoped you would miss me so much that you would eventually come after me and tell me that you loved me."

"Well, hell. You know, if you had just explained your strategy to me before you called the damned moving van, we would both have been saved a lot of trouble."

She chuckled. "Now do you see the value of communication? But in the end, it was all for the best. If I hadn't moved here, I would never have found my calling."

"The herbal tonic business?"

"I may keep that as a sideline, but I do believe my real future is in the exciting new field of alien botanical research. I was born to work with the plants in that rain forest, Cooper."

"I understand."

"Who knows what we'll find there? In the short time Doreen and I were hiding in that grotto cave, I sensed literally dozens of different species. All of them felt familiar and yet somehow different."

"Like Rose's flowers?"

"Yes. I think we're going to find out that the plants in that jungle are all native to this planet but mutated by the artificial environment in which they've been growing for heaven only knows how many centuries.

The possibilities are endless."

"The commute back and forth between Aurora Springs and Cadence is going to be a pain, but we'll make it work," he promised.

"Forget the commute. Oh, sure, we'll be coming back here a lot, because Doreen is my best friend in the entire world, and she and I are part of the consortium that is claiming discovery rights on the rain forest. Also, Rose will probably want to visit with Fuzz and Ginger, and I'd like to see Lydia again. But I don't want a commuting marriage."

He cocked a brow. "You've got a plan?"

"As it happens, I do. I did a lot of thinking while you were out like a light. I'm going to establish the first Alien Botanical Research Lab. The headquarters will be in Aurora Springs. I do believe it will put our hometown on the map."

"How can you have the headquarters for the lab there when the jungle is under Cadence?" he asked.

"Over the years there had been others besides Mary Tyler Jordan who claimed to have stumbled into a mysterious underground jungle."

"So?"

"Not all of those references were in the Cadence area." She nodded toward the book she had been reading. "That's one of the private diaries that Griggs tracked down. It belonged to a prospector from the Aurora Springs area. Forty years ago he evidently walked through a quartz wall in our neck of the woods and found himself in a jungle. When he got out, he was never able to find the entrance again, and everyone wrote him off as crazy."

"You think you can find another jungle under Aurora Springs?"

"I wouldn't be surprised if there are jungles beneath *all* of the ancient ruin sites. In fact, an underground rain forest may well connect every site."

"What do you mean?"

"Think about it. The aliens were obviously not at home aboveground on Harmony. They seemed to have lived beneath the surface in their catacombs or confined within the walls of their cities. I suspect that there was something about this world that was toxic to them. The psi energy of the quartz was probably an antidote of some sort."

"Interesting theory."

"But it is highly unlikely that they survived on psi energy alone. Like other living creatures, they needed a viable ecosystem. The one aboveground didn't work for them, so they engineered a modified version of it underground. I'll bet the rain forests provided the source of the oxygen, plant life, and everything else they required to keep their civilization going here."

"I think I see where you're going with this."

"There's another thing," she continued.

"What?"

"My guess is that the ability to resonate with plant psi isn't unique, no more unique than the ability to work blue ghost light. Sounds like Stuart Griggs had the talent, for example. But folks with abnormal parapsych profiles tend to keep quiet about it for fear of being labeled weird."

"Plant psi para-rezzes will probably start coming out of the woodwork once the news about Jordan's Jungle hits the media," Cooper observed.

"Probably."

"Hmm," Cooper said.

"Hmm, what? You've got that Guild boss look. What are you thinking?"

"I'm thinking that every botanist in every city-state on the planet and everyone who thinks he or she can work plant psi is going to want to head underground very soon."

"Wouldn't be surprised."

"Everyone knows you can't send a bunch

of researchers and academics into the cata-combs without hunters to protect them," Cooper said. "And that rain forest will very likely contain a lot of brand-new dangers. Can't have people running around in it without bodyguards."

She smiled. "I think I see where you're headed here."

"Any way you slice it, there's going to be a lot more work for the Guilds in the near future. We need to make plans to handle the situation. I'll make some calls to the other bosses first thing in the morning."

"Oh, my."

"Something else. The fact that the Aurora Springs Guild was involved in the discovery of Jordan's Jungle will be a major media bo-nanza for all the Guilds. We need to get the public relations departments of both the Cadence Guild and Aurora Springs going on this immediately."

"Spoken like a true Guild boss." She col-lapsed, laughing, onto the pillows. "We started out discussing our marriage and making plans for a life together, and sud-denly we're talking about broadening the Guild's business opportunities. No wonder they gave you the job, Boone."

He pulled her into his arms. "I wouldn't give a damn about the future of the Guilds or anything else if I didn't have you."

She stopped laughing. "You really mean that?"

"You make everything worthwhile, Elly. Especially the future. I realized that the day you gave my ring back to me."

She kissed him on the mouth. "Works both ways, Boone. I've been waiting for you for six very long months."

"Yeah?" His eyes gleamed with love. "If I'd known that, I would have come here a lot sooner. But I thought I had it all figured out, see? I had a plan."

"I was wondering what took you so long. Now I know it was just a Guild boss thing."

About the Author

Jayne Castle, the author of *After Glow, After Dark,* and *Harmony,* is a pseudonym for Jayne Ann Krentz, the *New York Times* bestselling author of *All Night Long, Falling Awake, Truth or Dare, Light in Shadow, Smoke in Mirrors, Lost and Found, Summer in Eclipse Bay, Dawn in Eclipse Bay, Eclipse Bay,* and other novels. She has been featured in such publications as *People* and *Entertainment Weekly,* and is also known for her books written under the name Amanda Quick. A former librarian with a degree in history, she is also the editor of an award-winning essay collection, *Dangerous Men and Adventurous Women: Romance Writers on the Appeal of the Romance.* You can find her online at www.jayneannkrentz.com.

The employees of Thorndike Press hope you have enjoyed this Large Print book. All our Thorndike and Wheeler Large Print titles are designed for easy reading, and all our books are made to last. Other Thorndike Press Large Print books are available at your library, through selected bookstores, or directly from us.

For information about titles, please call:

(800) 223-1244

or visit our Web site at:

www.thomson.com/thorndike
www.thomson.com/wheeler

To share your comments, please write:

Publisher
Thorndike Press
295 Kennedy Memorial Drive
Waterville, ME   04901